The

GOOD MAN'S DAUGHTER

Roger Stokes

Matador
5 Weir Road
Kibworth Beauchamp
Leicester LE8 0LQ, UK
Tel: (+44) 116 279 2299
Fax: (+44) 116 279 2277
Email: books@troubador.co.uk
Web: www.troubador.co.uk/matador

ISBN 978 1848766 662

British Library Cataloguing in Publication Data.
A catalogue record for this book is available from the British Library.

Typeset in 11pt StempelGaramondRoman by Troubador Publishing Ltd, Leicester, UK

Matador is an imprint of Troubador Publishing Ltd

Printed and bound in the UK by TJ International, Padstow, Cornwall

For Amber and Laura;
And Bridget, for her belief and encouragement.

PROLOGUE

In the dark feudal days of the 12th century there was a part of France where the light of *renaissance* shone like a beacon.

The Counts of Toulouse held sway over a vast territory that was rich in soil and culture. Into this land new ideas fell like seeds onto fertile minds. Amongst these notions was a revolutionary movement calling itself Cathar (from the Greek *Katharos*, meaning Pure). More spiritual than ecclesiastical it challenged the doctrine of the established Roman church and spread rapidly to every corner of the region.

For nearly a century the new religion of the Cathars flourished in the enlightened environment of the Languedoc. Noble and peasant alike took comfort from preachers, the Good Men, who spoke to them in their own language; of a benevolent God who forgave all sins and offered the promise of reincarnation and a place in Heaven.

By the beginning of the 13th century the Pope had become frustrated by this challenge to his authority and the affront to Catholic dogma.

In 1209 he ordered a Crusade to eliminate 'these unholy heretics'.

His army descended on the region slaughtering thousands of believers and sending many of the Good Men to be burnt at the stake.

Within a generation only a few hundred of the Cathar faithful remained, living in relative peace amongst the deep valleys and forests of the Pyrenean foothills.

But their lives were soon to be threatened again as the inquisitive tentacles of the Catholic Church began to reach into their domain. Amongst them were a Good Man and his daughter – a young woman, full of life, who would soon have to decide whether survival was reason enough for living.

PART ONE

LANGUEDOC: 8TH JUNE 1243

'Come on, Michel!' teased the girl, shielding her eyes from the sun, 'Don't be such a baby, it'll be good for you.'

'No thanks, Lou-Lou' he shouted back, shaking his head, 'this is quite far enough. If my feet are cool my head stays cool too.' With that he extended his legs slowly until his toes touched the cool, shallow water flowing over the stones. Enjoying the sensation, he leant back on his elbows, content to watch the girl as she dived under the water.

On the other side of the river another pair of eyes watched the girl. A young man on horseback, hidden by the dense forest that covered the riverbank. He leant forward and gently stroked the animal's neck to keep it quiet. He savoured this idyllic scene, even though he knew he was intruding.

By now the girl had reached a shallower part of the river and slowly stood up. As she rose from the water her cotton shift clung to her body, exposing every intimate curve of her body. Her hands swept up to smooth the water from her face and with one backward flick of her head her long, dark hair described a perfect circle in the air, a thousand droplets arcing above her, flashing and glittering in the sun.

She moved with complete innocence yet the sight of her aroused different emotions in the minds of the three men watching.

The girl's father, wading further upstream, saw again his young wife before she became a mother. His eyes filled with tears and his throat tightened as he remembered both her beauty and the pain of her death. Michel saw that the tomboy he had known for most of her eighteen years had suddenly become a young woman. And the young man on horseback knew he was looking at the most beautiful girl he had ever seen.

The tranquil scene was shattered by the arrival of the young man's hunting companion.

'Now there, Cousin, is a prey worth chasing! Wouldn't you like to shove your cock between those thighs?' He laughed loudly and slapped his cousin on the back.

At the sound of the man's voice a look of fear clouded the girl's face and she dropped swiftly beneath the surface. Under the water she could hear her father calling her, as if from a distance.

'Elouise, come out now, come and dry yourself, child. We still have a long way to walk.'

The girl made her way slowly to the safety of the riverbank. Michel helped her out with one hand, passing her cloak to her with the other. With the minimum of delay Elouise, her father and Michel were soon on their way again.

But the young horseman didn't move. He watched them as they moved into the forest, his thoughts racing.

CHAPTER ONE

Elouise walked along the wooded path that followed the river, arm in arm with her father. Michel walked a little way in front, enjoying the sun as it streamed through the trees, but keeping alert for any sound he didn't recognise.

'When do you think we'll get to St. Julien?' Elouise asked her father. They had been walking since leaving Puilaurens earlier that morning, only stopping to rest by the river where she had bathed.

'Well if we continue at this pace I think we should be there by late afternoon,' he replied. 'Michel knows the way and I think he would like to find the Borrel family before it gets dark.'

'Do you know these people, Papa?'

'No,' he answered 'but Michel has met them before many times.'

Elouise hesitated before speaking again. 'And do you think they can be trusted?'

'Well, my child, Michel tells me they are a family of *croyants*. We must put our faith in Michel and the Good Lord. If He wants us to be safe then He will make it so.' He smiled as he looked at his daughter and gave her arm a reassuring squeeze.

Up ahead Michel turned round and waved as the trio continued along the path which now began to climb steeply, leaving the river flowing some way below them. The trees were dense, mainly oak, elm and ash, and as the noise of the river faded, the sounds of the forest became more distinct. Birdsong began to fill the air as blackbird, thrush and wood pigeon called to their mates. Now and then there was a rustle of leaves as a squirrel scratched around for roots and nuts, before leaping in an instant onto the nearest branch at their approach. Occasionally a slight movement could be detected out of the corner of an eye and a deer would be revealed, feeding nervously, always alert.

But soon a new sound could be heard. A sound that made the deer vanish into the trees, sensitive to the slightest hint of danger. It was not a natural sound of the forest but the noise of hooves on the dry mud path behind them. A pair of horsemen appeared around the bend, travelling at a confident trot as if their task had been completed successfully. In the time it took the two riders to reach Elouise and her father, Michel had retraced his steps. Now he stood in the space between the two horsemen, and the father and daughter.

The two riders were dressed and armed for hunting. Their jerkins were made of soft goat skin and their leather boots shone in the afternoon sun. Bows and arrows were slung across their chest and a freshly-killed deer was draped across the saddle of the younger man. It had been a good hunt and the riders were in a relaxed mood.

'Good day,' the young man said in a warm friendly tone. 'It's a fine afternoon to be walking. Have you come far?'

'Good day to you too, Sir' replied Michel politely. 'We left Puilaurens this morning'.

'Some distance indeed,' observed the young rider, 'and where are you heading to?'

'We hope to reach St. Julien today,'answered Michel.

'Well in that case you should be there before nightfall.'

'We hope so too,'said Michel.

During this exchange Elouise kept her gaze to the ground and her father stood motionless by her side, content to let his travelling companion talk to the strangers. But now the young rider turned his attention towards the older man.

'And you Sir, do you have friends in St. Julien?' he asked.

Jean pushed back the hood of his cloak, as was the polite custom, and for the first time looked directly at the young man on horseback. He saw a handsome face, between youth and manhood, with clean-shaven cheeks and thick, auburn hair that parted in the centre and reached to his jaw.

'Indeed I do,' he replied, 'I like to think I have many friends there.'

The horseman pulled gently on the reins to keep his horse still and spoke again, this time more seriously.

'And may I ask the purpose of your journey?'

Jean fixed his eyes directly onto those of the young man and held his gaze for several moments.

'And may I know who is asking?' he enquired, calmly.

The young horseman looked across at his companion and laughed. 'Forgive my bad manners! Allow me to introduce ourselves. My name is Guillaume de Quillan and this is my cousin, Bruno. We are loyal knights of my father, the Comte de Quillan, and as you can see we have been enjoying the hunt.'

Cousin Bruno, who had been mentally undressing Elouise during this exchange of conversation, decided to join in.

'Is this not the young maiden who bathed so beautifully in the river?' he asked with mock surprise. 'It's been a long time since I've enjoyed...' he paused, relishing the memory, '... such sheer pleasure.'

At such a remark many girls of her age would have blushed with deep embarrassment but Elouise chose this moment to lift her gaze and look directly at Bruno. She noticed the strong family resemblance between the two cousins, yet while the younger man's face was handsome and gentle, Bruno's darker features and unshaven cheeks gave him a brooding, predatory look. This man is cruel and probably dangerous, she thought, but she wasn't afraid.

'At least I can say I'm clean in both body and mind,' she threw back at Bruno and continued to stare fiercely at him until he looked away. Michel clenched his fist slowly and took a step forward towards the horseman.

'Please excuse my cousin's rudeness, young lady,' said Guillaume, sensing that there was a need to calm the tension. 'He is angry because he wasn't successful at hunting today. Isn't that so Bruno?' He glanced over towards his cousin and gave him a playful dig in the ribs. Bruno brushed the hand away and gave Guillaume a scowl that indicated he didn't appreciate the joke. Guillaume looked back towards Elouise and for the first time their eyes met. The determined look on her face only seemed to increase the beauty that he had seen at the riverbank. They continued to hold each other's gaze intently, neither breaking away, until Elouise eventually spoke.

'Apology accepted,' she said in a quiet voice, giving Guillaume a slight nod of her head to confirm her acceptance.

Guillaume turned his attention back to Elouise's father, keeping his voice pleasant.

'So now you know who we are Sir, may we know the names of our fellow travellers?'

Jean had registered de Quillan's name. He realised he must be the son of Sybille de Quillan, the Count's wife and good friend of the Cathars; a woman he had met before. He decided to keep this information to himself for the time being.

'Indeed you may, young man. I am Jean de Rhedones, this is my daughter Elouise and this is our travelling companion and good friend Michel Benet.'

Guillaume considered this information for a moment before continuing.

'And tell me, Jean de Rhedones, you seem to wear the cloak of a *Parfait*,' his voice took a more serious tone, 'are you one of the Good Men?'

4

It was true that Jean wore a dark cloak, one of the symbols of the *Bons Hommes*, although he chose to wear dark blue instead of the more traditional black.

'I try to see good in all men,' he replied with an enigmatic smile, 'but if you wish to know why I am travelling to St. Julien then I can say with all truthfulness that I go there to pursue my skills.'

'And what skills might those be?' asked Guillaume, smiling in return.

'You see before you a tailor, Sir,' Jean replied. 'In fact I made the cloak that you so kindly noticed.'

'A tailor indeed! That is good news,' exclaimed Guillaume. 'I'm sure we all could make good use of your talents. My father always tells me that a good tailor is hard to find.'

'And are you the tailor's assistant?' Bruno asked, addressing Michel with more than a hint of sarcasm.

'No Sir,' Michel replied, forcing a smile 'I am a simple shepherd and entertainer; a herder of sheep and a singer of songs.' And with this he gave Bruno an elaborate bow, as if to conclude a performance. This movement seemed to release the tension and by the time Michel stood up straight again everyone was smiling, with the exception of Bruno who kept his aggressive stance.

Guillaume pulled again on his horse's reins and turned to face the path ahead.

'Well we shouldn't delay you good people any longer, you still have a way to go. It's been a pleasure to meet you.' He looked again at Elouise and noticed for the first time the increase in his heartbeat. 'I hope we meet again,' was all he could say, his voice coming out slightly strangled as if his throat was being constricted.

Elouise returned his look with a smile that offered friendliness, but said nothing.

'Adieu,' said Jean. 'Go in peace.' And with that the two horsemen continued along the woodland path and soon disappeared around the next bend.

As they rode along Guillaume thought about the conversation with the travellers. He hadn't been fooled by Jean's explanation, even though he believed he was telling the truth when he said he was a tailor. He'd seen other similar men at the Chateau talking to his mother many times. He knew she was a *croyante*, a Cathar believer, and she had often offered sanctuary to the Good Men, usually with the tacit, if unspoken, support of her husband. Guillaume and his sister, Helene, had been raised by their mother to follow the teachings of the Cathars, although their father always insisted they attend mass as well.

Meanwhile Bruno was having his own thoughts, which mainly revolved around what he would like to do to Elouise. 'We should have killed the men and taken it in turns to mount the girl', he thought to himself, 'that would have wiped the smile off her face.' And for the first time since they'd caught up with the travellers his thin lips spread into a crude smile.

CHAPTER TWO

Jean de Rhedones had lived most of his life in the Sabarthes region, with its rugged mountains and rivers that raged with the melting snows. He had been born in the autumn of 1198 in the town of Foix, where his father was a successful weaver and tailor. Jean's father passed on to his son all his tailoring skills but he also wanted him to have an education. Once a week, from the time he was ten years old, Jean would spend the day with the priests at the Abbey learning to read and write. Many of his impressions of the church and its priesthood were formed during these years of study. As his education progressed, so he also learnt about the lax behaviour of the priests, many of whom were lazy, open to bribes and indulged in the pleasure of having a mistress.

When Jean was sixteen his father died, falling victim to the fever that had followed a cut from a blade. Yet Jean's tailoring skills had developed so well that he was able to run the family business with the help of his mother. Over the next ten years the workshop flourished and he and his mother lived comfortably. The only thing missing in his life was a wife, but this was soon to change. One day a young woman came to his premises with a dress that needed altering. It only took one look for Jean to know that he had found his true love, and so he spoke.

'Good Day to you Miss, is this your dress?' It was the only thing he could think of saying.

The girl laughed and said 'Indeed not, Sir. If you're the tailor you would know that this dress is far too big for me,' she teased. 'It belongs to my mistress and she has gained some weight these past few months so she needs you to alter it.'

Jean blushed and told the girl the dress would be ready in one week's time. By the time she had said goodbye and the door closed behind her Jean had decided what he was going to do.

When the girl returned a week later, Jean had the alteration ready for her inspection. As she ran her fingers over the stitching on her mistress's dress Jean slid another package across the counter.

'This is for you,' he said.

The girl looked at the package with surprise, but encouraged by the look on Jean's face she slowly undid the wrapping. Inside was a dress, the most beautiful dress she had ever seen. Jean had chosen a blue material that he knew would match precisely the blue of her eyes, the memory of which he had kept since he first saw her. And with his tailor's eye he knew the dress would fit. Now it was the girl's turn to blush.

'I don't know what to say, it's beautiful,' she murmured.

Then Jean spoke the boldest words he had ever said in his life. 'Just say you will marry me.'

The girl looked at Jean unable to speak. 'But you don't even know my name,' she said eventually.

'Then tell me your name,' asked Jean.

'Blanche,' the girl replied, her hand still resting on the blue dress, 'Blanche Maury.'

'Well, Blanche Maury, when does your mistress let you have some free time that we may meet and get to know each other better?'

Blanche thought for a moment, her mind still racing at the directness of Jean's proposal.

'My mistress goes to Mass on Sunday, but I choose not to.'

They agreed to meet the following Sunday outside the house

of Blanche's employer. With the two packages firmly tucked under her arm Blanche left the tailor's shop, still bewildered but excited too.

As soon as the door closed Jean leapt up the stairs to find his mother. She was seated at a table by the window, a garment spread out in front of her, needle in hand.

'My dearest son, you look very pleased with yourself, what brings you bounding up the stairs two at a time?' Jean couldn't contain his happiness, 'Mother,' he announced, a broad grin upon his face 'I have found the girl I am going to marry!' His mother smiled but stopped herself from asking any questions. She knew that her son could be a very determined young man, so she decided to wait and see how events might unfold.

The next Sunday morning found Jean waiting outside Madame Lauze's house, as arranged. Blanche had debated with herself endlessly about whether to wear the dress Jean had made for her.She'd already tried it on and much to her delight it fitted her perfectly, just as he had imagined. In the end she decided she would wear it, even if it was a little too grand to wear for a stroll. 'After all,' she reasoned to herself 'it's not every day a girl gets given a beautiful new dress'.

From the expression on Jean's face when he saw her she knew she'd made the right decision. His broad smile and look of undisguised delight calmed her nerves and she walked up to him with a confidence borne of the effect she was having on him.

From her earlier indication that she didn't go to Mass, Jean had guessed, correctly as it turned out, that she was one of the Cathar believers.

'I thought we might go and listen to one of the Good Men preaching today,' he suggested as they walked side by side in the sunshine. Blanche looked up at Jean and nodded, but didn't speak. Now that she was close to him again she realised how much she had been looking forward to seeing him and some of her nervousness returned, her senses heightened. They made their way to a small field on the outskirts of town where a crowd had already gathered. Moving quietly they found a place to sit down on the warm grass and listened to the *Parfait*. He spoke in gentle tones and told again the story they all liked to hear. How there were two Gods, one good, the other evil, and how those who were pure in spirit would take their place besides the Good God in Heaven, and how the Evil God had created the Earth as hell where everyone lived, trapped in their human form. The *Parfait* preached that there was no truth in the concept of going to Hell if you committed a sin, as commanded by the Catholics, as Hell was already here on earth, therefore the notion of salvation was not relevant. 'God alone can absolve sin,' he said 'we have no need of confession'. He reminded those present that the Good God was always in their hearts and took upon Himself any sins they might commit as ordinary mortals, and forgave them unconditionally. Finally he urged them to live their lives as purely as possible so that they might sooner enter the kingdom of Heaven, otherwise they would have to be re-borne many times before they might be admitted.

Despite his gentle tones the Good Man delivered a powerful message and when he had finished the crowd knelt before him and waited for his blessing, a slight touch upon their bowed heads. When the simple ceremony was over a happy mood quickly spread through the crowd as blankets and baskets were produced and laid on the ground and everyone began eating and talking.

Jean and Blanche sat close together, neither of them hungry for food but both thirsty for more knowledge about each other. Jean told her about his childhood and how he had learnt to be a tailor and taken over the business when his father died. Blanche looked sad when he asked her how long she had been with Madame Lauze. 'Since my mother died of the coughing sickness three winters ago. Madame Lauze is a distant cousin of my father's and she offered me a home in return for working as her maid.'

'And what happened to your father?' Jean asked gently, aware that Blanche seemed close to tears. 'My father was killed at the siege of Lavaur. He had gone there to help defend the town of his birth from the Pope's soldiers. When he was captured they called him a Cathar heretic and threw him down a well.' A large tear rolled down her cheek and landed on Jean's hand as he reached out to take hers. Nothing was said for a while, then Blanche looked up and gave Jean a brilliant smile. 'I'm fine now, really. And happy too.'

Jean looked relieved. 'Does that mean you have an answer for me?'

'Yes, I do,' she laughed. 'And yes, I will marry you!'

Jean lifted her hands to his lips and, kissing them gently, looked into her eyes, the same deep blue as the dress he had made. 'We are going to be so happy, I promise you.'

It was as simple as that. Within two months all the arrangements had been made and Jean and his new wife were living in the family home above the tailor's shop.

Jean and Blanche worked together, laughed together and loved each other with a joy and passion that brought immense happiness not only to themselves but to their friends and family as well. It came as no surprise when Blanche announced to Jean one morning that she was pregnant. They felt blessed and began to watch with excitement as Blanche's belly began to swell with each week that passed.

He and Blanche felt sure they would have a baby girl and Jean was working on the intricate stitching of another fine smock when his mother called out to say the baby was on its way. He rushed up the stairs to be with Blanche while his mother went to fetch the local midwife.

Jean refused to leave when the woman arrived. 'But it is most irregular,' she complained, 'this is women's work and no place for a man.' But Jean would not be moved and insisted on staying with Blanche, holding her hand and wiping the perspiration from her brow as the strength of her labour pains increased. After what seemed like hours the midwife announced that she could see the baby's head and urged Blanche to give one more push. Blanche strained until the veins stood out on her neck and clung to Jean's hand with all her strength. Suddenly she gave birth and the baby slipped from her womb and into the midwife's safe hands.

'You have a girl! You have a beautiful baby girl,' exclaimed the midwife, as she expertly cleaned the baby and wrapped it in the swaddling cloths that were already prepared. Blanche slumped back exhausted but still managed to give a weak smile of achievement to Jean. Soon their baby daughter, their Elouise, for that was the name they had chosen, was in her arms and she and Jean gazed in wonder at this small miracle.

But something was not right. The midwife had a worried look on her face and had begun to tear up strips of cloth.

'What's wrong?' asked Jean, 'What's the matter?'

'Your wife is losing blood, too much blood, and I need to stop it,' she whispered.

'I don't understand,' said Jean 'We have our Elouise now. Surely that's a good sign?' but he was beginning to feel anxious as he looked at Blanche's pale face and listened to her shallow breathing.

Jean's mother had watched all this from the doorway and now a shadow of fear entered her mind too. Quietly she slipped out of the house and hurried to where she knew she would find her *Parfait*. She and her husband had always been firm believers in the Cathar approach to salvation and she knew what her duty was now. By the time she arrived back at the house with the

Good Man and they had climbed the stairs her worst fears were confirmed. Jean was cradling Blanche in his arms and begging her with whispered words to open her eyes and speak to him. Jean's mother looked over to the midwife and her unspoken question was answered by the midwife's slow shake of the head as her hands indicated the bloodied pile of cloths on the floor. When Jean saw the Good Man his first reaction was to tell him he wasn't needed, to go away, but he looked again at his wife and his heart told him that she needed the blessing that only the *Parfait* could give her.

'Have courage, my son,' said the Good Man as he knelt down besides Blanche. He began to recite the *Consolamentum*, the Cathar sacrament that would allow Blanche's sins to be forgiven and her spirit released to be reborn into the soul of another new child. Whilst the *Parfait* conducted the simple ceremony Jean held his wife and Elouise together in his arms until he had finished. Jean's mother and the midwife left the room and the Good Man gently touched the top of Blanche's head with the book of St. John's Gospel before he too backed away quietly.

Jean clung to his wife and daughter, torn between the love for his dying wife and his tender feelings for the child that now slept through the first sad moment of her new life. The three of them lay together and time seemed to stand still as Jean stroked his wife's hair and held his daughter's tiny hand. Suddenly Blanche's eyes fluttered open and she turned her head slowly towards Jean. She managed to smile as she looked down at their sleeping daughter then looked back into her husband's distraught face.

'I love you, Jean,' she whispered, 'Look after our beautiful Elouise. I'll see you both again in heaven.'

They were the last words she spoke and the only sound Elouise would ever hear from her mother.

CHAPTER THREE

Michel continued to lead Jean and Elouise through the woods towards the village. By now the warmth of the afternoon sun was beginning to fade and he knew they would soon be arriving at St.Julien. They had seen no one else on the path since their encounter with Guillaume and Bruno, but he knew there would be villagers working in the fields who would be curious about the arrival of three strangers. Soon, instead of seeing dense leaves and branches, Michel detected a change in the level of brightness and began to make out the greens, yellows and browns of the fields ahead. He waited for Jean and Elouise to catch up with him.

'It's better if you wait here for a while. I'll go ahead and make sure the Borrel family can take us in. I'll be back soon.'

Jean and Elouise did as they were told, finding a fallen tree trunk to sit down on and, trusting Michel completely, continued their discussion on the different healing properties of plants.

It only took a short while for Michel to emerge from the wood. In front of him he could see the cultivated fields surrounding the village, rising in slopes to follow the shape of the hill on top of which sat the village of St. Julien de Roc. The village houses encircled the crown of the hill, each one joined to its neighbour as much for support as for defence. Michel could make out the bell tower of the church and, looking further upwards, he marvelled once again at the massive structure of the fortified chateau perched on top of the steep Roc, looming above the village, its dark stone contrasting with the pale walls and wooden shingles of the dwellings.

Within moments two men digging turnips had noticed Michel and they stopped their work, straightening their backs to look at him.

Michel fixed a friendly smile on his face and took confident strides towards them.

'Good afternoon, Gentlemen,' he began, 'and how is the turnip crop this year?'

The two men said nothing in reply but their features relaxed visibly as they felt no threat in Michel's warm greeting.

'It's been a while since I visited your charming village,' continued Michel 'Does the Borrel family still live here?'

The two men looked at each other then one of them spoke.

'If you mean Claude Borrel's family, indeed they do. I should know, I'm married to one of his daughters!'

And with this he broke into a broad grin, which then spread to his companion and soon the three men were laughing together. At this outbreak of laughter other villagers stopped their work to see what was happening. As Michel and the two men began to make their way towards the village they were soon joined by other men, women and children who had decided that any excuse to stop work for the day was a good enough reason. By the time they reached the stone gateway that formed the entrance to the village there were a dozen or more people following Michel, each one keen to tell his family and neighbour about the new arrival.

Raymond, Claude Borrel's turnip-digging son-in-law, led the way to the Borrel home. It was typical of the other village dwellings, built on a single level in the local limestone with a shingle roof that began at shoulder height and sloped upwards at a shallow angle. Stepping into the small yard Michel smelt the familiar odour of animals and manure mingled with the wood smoke rising slowly from a hole in the centre of the roof. Michel could easily have lifted one of the roof tiles to see inside the dwelling, as was the local custom, but he decided it would be more polite to knock on the thick wooden door. The door was opened by a boy of about ten years old.

'Good day, young man,' said Michel in his politest voice 'Is your mother or father at home?'

The boy stared at Michel but didn't say a word.

'I recognise that voice' came a woman's reply from inside the room.' Is that you, Michel? Come and show yourself.'

He stepped inside past the boy and allowed his eyes to adjust to the gloomy interior. The woman stood up and approached him, wiping her hands on her apron.

'Michel, come here. What a wonderful surprise.' She embraced him with a strong hug and kissed him on both cheeks.

'Hullo, Jacotte, you look as well as ever,' replied Michel returning her warm welcome. She held him at arms length and inspected him as if to find any changes since she'd last seen him.

'Still as handsome of face as of voice,' she teased, taking in the blue eyes and blond curls that surrounded an almost too pretty face. 'What are you doing here? What brings you to St. Julien?'

Michel knew he could trust Jacotte Borrel so he came straight to the point.

'I have two friends who need shelter,' he replied. 'A man, one of the Good Men, and his daughter.'

'A *Parfait* with a daughter, now that is unusual,' remarked Jacotte, raising her eyebrows.

'Do you have room for them? They're waiting in the wood,' continued Michel.

'As long as they don't mind sleeping in the barn with the animals,' Jacotte replied. 'Go and fetch them before it gets dark. Claude has taken some sheep up to the chateau but he'll be back soon. Go on, hurry!'

And with that she turned him round and pushed him gently towards the door. As Michel stepped back into the yard two thoughts sprung immediately into Jacotte's head. Why had this Good Man and his daughter come to St. Julien? And what on earth was she going to give them for supper?

By the time he arrived back at the Borrel home with Jean and Elouise the entire family was assembled. Claude had returned from his business at the chateau, Jacotte was stirring a pot over the fire, their eldest daughter, Claudette-the one married to Raymond-was peeling vegetables, Bernardette, the younger daughter was helping her sister, and Jacques, the young boy, was trying to keep out of everyone's way and wondering why they were all looking so serious.

When Jean stepped into the house all the family, including young Jacques, stopped what they were doing and knelt in front of him, their heads bowed. They had been brought up to observe the *amelioration*, a simple rite that acknowledged the presence of a Good Man and allowed him to give them his blessing. Jean moved between the family and blessed each one with a simple touch on the head then lifted them gently by the chin so that he could see their face and they could look into his. When this small, intimate ceremony was over everyone seemed to relax. Jean addressed the family, speaking in his slow, clear voice.

'Michel has told me all about you on the way here and it is most kind of you to allow us to stay in your home. These are difficult times for people who hold our faith but you must put your trust in God, for He knows you and He loves you.'

Jacotte acknowledged Jean's words with a warm smile.

'Come,' she said, taking over proceedings 'you and your daughter must be hungry. Sit down with us and share our meal.'

Everyone in the family knew this was not a case of sharing a simple family meal. Ever since Michel had left the house to fetch his companions they had been running around to assemble the ingredients for a meal suitable to offer their guests. The biggest problem had been finding fish. Jacotte knew that the Good Men did not eat meat but they would eat fish.

Luckily she remembered that her neighbour two doors away had been fishing that morning so she despatched her eldest daughter to see if she could exchange a piece of bacon for some fish. Claudette had returned with a look of success and held up a fat trout for her mother's inspection.

'I think that will be perfect for a *Parfait*,' said Jacotte, with a satisfied smile on her face. 'Now give your sister a hand with those vegetables. And Jacques,' she instructed her young son, her voice rising to the challenge of organising the meal, 'make sure there's plenty of wood for the fire, and get some fresh water and a jug of wine too!'

There was not space at the table for everyone in the crowded room. Jean, Elouise and Michel sat down with Claude and Jacotte, whilst Raymond and Claudette shared a bench against the wall and Jacques and Bernadette sat in front of the fireplace. Jacotte produced a loaf of bread and placed it on the table in front of Jean. He proceeded to bless the bread, making small circular motions with his hand over the loaf, which he then broke into several pieces. Each person then took a piece of the blessed bread for themselves and the meal began.

Everyone was hungry and they tucked into the food without much conversation. Jean complimented Jacotte on the delicious trout she had cooked and she and her daughter exchanged a secret smile. But as the meal came to an end and the crumbs were swept from the table and the mugs refilled with wine, Claude could not wait any longer to ask Michel about what news did he bring from his travels. Michel kept the mood light and entertained the Borrel's with all the gossip from other towns and villages, told in as much detail as he could remember. They smiled and laughed or sat open mouthed in amazement as he recounted his tales of births, deaths and marriages, and of fights, debts and mistresses. When he had exhausted his fund of news and information there was a short silence. Claude took this as his cue to ask the question that had been on his mind since the visitors had arrived.

'So tell us, Michel,' asked Claude 'why have you brought this Good Man and his daughter to our home?'

Before Michel could answer, Jean gestured with a motion of his hand that he would reply to Claude's question.

'You have every right to ask and we have every reason to be grateful for your hospitality' began Jean. 'I have been travelling for many years across our region preaching and comforting the faithful like yourselves. Although we are a people that no longer have to fear those who would take away our lands, we still have to endure those who would take away our religion. The Pope's inquisitors are on a mission to arrest all men and women such as myself and accuse us of being heretics. Now they are putting pressure on every town and village to give up its believers and restore the power of their Roman church. Many *croyants* have doubts and it is my duty to talk to them and try and help them if they are confused. Even in villages such as yours the enemies of our faith will set family against family, brother against brother, friend against friend.' He paused for a moment to let his words sink in. 'I know your hospitality comes from your heart and your friendship with Michel, and for that we will always be grateful, but you must also realise the danger you may be putting yourselves in. So, if you wish us to leave I will understand.' Jean's words hung in the air like the smoke rising from the open fire and no one said a word. Then Claude slammed his fist down onto the table and everyone jumped.

'Nobody tells my family who we can and can't invite into our home,' he shouted 'and I say you are welcome to stay as long as you like,' he added, as if to give extra emphasis to his words.

The mood in the room quickly returned to the relaxed atmosphere that had been there during the meal and now it was Jacotte's turn to speak.

'I think it's time we all went to bed. Claudette, fetch that bedding for our guests and Raymond please get a lamp and show them to the barn.' She turned towards Jean with a look of apology and a shrug.

'I hope you will be comfortable in the barn' she said quietly.

'Dear lady,' replied Jean, 'we have slept in far less agreeable surroundings. You will hear no complaints from us. God bless you all.' And so, gradually, the extended Borrel household retired to bed, although for Jacotte and her husband sleep came later as they reflected on Jean's words.

CHAPTER FOUR

After Blanche died Jean went to pieces. He couldn't eat or sleep and showed no enthusiasm for the tailoring business. He would sit at his bench and hold the blue dress to his cheek and weep, until it was soaked. The magnitude of his love for Blanche turned to anger that she had been taken from him. At times he was angry with Elouise for being the cause of his wife's death, then he would feel guilty for even thinking he could put any blame on such an innocent child.

Most nights he would lie awake, struggling with a conflict of emotions that tested the strength of his love for Blanche and the conviction of his faith and beliefs. And as much as he loved his child, and talked to her and held her, he was incapable of looking after Elouise whilst he grieved for his young wife.

It was left to his mother to take on the practical care of the baby girl. She had no difficulty finding a wet nurse, a young woman who had lost her own child at birth, and she soon settled into the routine of raising a child again, just as she had done with her own son.

The only consolation for Jean in his sorrow was his faith and the belief that Blanche's spirit would now have entered a new borne child and that it would bring to that baby's soul all her goodness. The more he thought about his feelings the more he came to realise that he needed to do something better with his life. His early education at the Abbey had left him with a strong distaste for the Catholic priesthood and the church it represented.

And since the Cathar faithful were under increasing pressure to recant and return to Rome's embrace he began to realise what his path must be. He would dedicate himself to his faith and give up his life to his religion.

Within two months he had spoken to all his customers and found another tailor. He negotiated a good price for the business, which allowed his mother to keep her home, and there was sufficient money for her to live comfortably and get help with looking after baby Elouise.

The day he left Foix was a day for heavy hearts and many tears. His mother understood the turmoil he was in and could not stand in his way, yet it was difficult to stifle the concerns she held for her son. Poor little Elouise didn't understand what was happening at all but decided to join in the mood and shed her own tears. She wasn't to know it would be two years before she saw her father again.

Jean left the town on foot with his belongings in one small bag. He was heading for the Champagne region to the north, a journey that would take him at least thirty days. There he would find the teachers who would train him in the breadth and depth of the Cathar religion and where he would finally receive the sacrament of the *Consolamentum*, that would rule his life and his destiny. From that moment on he would have to lead a life of purity; to renounce all his worldly goods, to give up eating all meat save for fish, to abstain from sex, to work with his hands in return for food and accommodation, to wear his dark robe and to preach in the language of the people and give comfort to those in need. Only then could he become one of the Good Men.

It took two years of training and study before Jean was ready to receive his baptism into the Cathar faith. During the long months of instruction he had little news from home, but from the occasional words he did receive from people passing through he knew that Elouise was alive and well. He promised himself that as soon as his studies were complete he would return to Foix to see her.

And so it was that Jean set off again, this time in the company of a fellow initiate as they travelled southwards towards the land of his birth. As each step was taken and each day passed Jean tried to imagine what his daughter would look like and how she would react to him. He knew he was in a difficult position. It was almost unheard of for a *Parfait* to have a child, as sex was forbidden to them. In its purest interpretation the Cathar faith forbade *Parfaits* from even touching a woman, a rule that seemed at odds with their belief in equality of the sexes and where many women had became *Parfaits*. But the faith was nothing if not forgiving, its entire belief being based on the act of forgiveness. God forgave your sins and there was no need for them to be confessed as long as you kept God in your heart. Thus Jean knew that having a child, a normal result of loving his wife, and his natural desire to see and hold his child might be considered a sin, he also believed that God would know this and would have forgiven him already.

When he arrived at the house in Foix his first thought was that nothing had changed. The street, the houses, even the smells in the air seemed exactly the same as when he had left two years before. But when the door opened nothing could prepare him for the reception he received. His mother, bless her, looked exactly as he remembered, not a day older. Which was more than could be said for the shock she received when she saw her son.

'Oh my God, Jean. Look at you, you're so thin,' she gasped, and it was true that a combination of a meagre diet for two years and walking for four weeks had caused him to lose a lot of the weight from his once sturdy frame, 'and your hair, when did it turn grey?'

'I'm fine, mother, don't worry about me, I've never been so

fit,' was his reassuring reply, his hand brushing across the top of his cropped hair. 'Now where is she? Where's my Elouise?'

His mother stepped to one side and Jean saw a small figure standing nervously at the end of the hallway. His heart did a somersault as the little girl began to walk towards him. Jean knelt on one knee and opened his arms to receive her.

'Is that you, Elouise?' he asked gently, his voice breaking with emotion.

'Papa!' the little girl cried and began to run towards him. This time Jean's heart melted. He swept her up into his arms and hugged her tightly and covered her with kisses.

'Look at you, look at you.' He held Elouise at arms length and whirled her around. She was the image of Blanche and for a moment he could only see his child with eyes that were blurred with tears.

'Come, Elouise,' said Jean's mother, 'let's show Papa to his room and then we can all sit down to eat.'

Jean let Elouise slide gently to the floor. She took his hand and led him towards his old bedroom.

'This is my bed,' said Elouise in a serious voice as they entered the room pointing to a small bed next to a low table.

'And that's Papa's bed.' She pointed towards the wall and the bed that Jean remembered from the time before he was married.

'And what are all these things?' said Jean looking down at the bedside table. It was covered in an assortment of small stones, tiny strips of material, dried flowers and even a few odd buttons and buckles.

'These are for you,' said Elouise in a small, shy voice.

'She collects something nearly every day,' explained his mother, standing in the doorway. 'I told her you'd be back to see her one day and she wanted to give you a present, only we didn't know when you would return so we've got rather a lot of presents for Papa now, haven't we Lou Lou?' They all laughed and Jean gave his daughter an extra hug and thanked her profusely for all her gifts.

Later that evening, after they had eaten and Jean had been given the privilege of putting Elouise to bed, Jean kept his mother up for half the night with questions about his daughter. He wanted to know every detail about her health, her habits, her temperament, until his mother said she was exhausted and she wouldn't answer any more questions until the morning when, she informed him with a hint of mock pleasure, it would be his turn to get up and make Elouise her breakfast.

Jean stayed at the house for the next two months, making up for lost time with Elouise. But he knew that it couldn't last for ever as he had made a promise to serve God. And so began a phase in their lives where Jean would be away for several months, visiting the towns and villages throughout the region, from Foix to Quillan and from Ax-les-Thermes to Mirapoix. At each place Jean would talk and preach to any group of people that wished to hear his words, answering their questions and soothing their concerns, for they had all heard rumours about the questioning methods of the bishops and their enforcers from the Dominican brotherhood. Jean's tailoring skills came in useful too and more often than not he returned a family's hospitality by extending the life of many an item of clothing.

At the end of each journey Jean would travel back to Foix and spend a few more weeks with Elouise and his mother before heading off again.

This to-ing and fro-ing continued until Elouise was nearly six years old and then the inevitable happened. Jean's mother, by now well into her fifth decade, caught a winter chill that soon turned into pneumonia. She bravely managed to keep herself going until Jean returned from his latest journey. But she was weak and could not fight the infection and died within days of his return. At least he was able to bestow on his own mother the salvation of the *Consolamentum*.

As well as the sorrow that befell Jean, his mother's death was a major shock to Elouise. Her grandmother had been the closest Elouise would ever have to a real mother and the two of them had become extremely close to one another as they waited for Jean to return from his preaching missions.

Jean told his daughter she must try to be brave and to imagine her *meme* in heaven, meeting Blanche and telling her all about Elouise and what a good girl she was. Elouise seemed content with this explanation. It was an image she would carry in her head for many years about the two most important women in her life.

After Jean had buried his mother and put her affairs in order he was faced with the dilemma of what to do with his young daughter. He knew many families he felt sure would love her and raise her as one of their own. But he couldn't deny his own love or his daughter's right to the love and care of a parent. After much anguish he came to a decision, one that would shape their lives in the future. He decided that Elouise would travel with him. He reasoned that, although she was still very young, she was intelligent and healthy and would probably benefit more from the experiences they would share on the road than from the more predictable life in a village. He would be her tutor, teaching her to read and write as well as passing on to her the more practical skills of cutting cloth and making clothes. He also had to admit to his own instincts to protect her and of being there to watch her grow. He knew that these circumstances were not strictly in accordance with his own tuition as a *Parfait*, where he might have been expected to put his duty to God before his duty as a parent. But he reasoned that he shouldn't have to make the choice between being a good parent and a Good Man; that somehow God would understand and forgive him.

And so, one bright morning, they set off on their travels together.

Jean made Elouise a small satchel to carry a selection of her precious items. Her buttons and buckles, some shiny stones and pressed flowers, and a lock of her grandmother's hair to go with the small curl from her own mother. Jean carried the rest of their belongings; their clothes, his tailor's tools, his copy of St. John's Gospel and, wrapped carefully at the bottom of his bag, the blue dress he had made for Blanche when they first met. He knew he would give this dress to Elouise one day and when she wore it she would look as beautiful as her mother.

CHAPTER FIVE

Michel woke up in the barn as the first light filtered in under the eaves. He looked across at Jean and Elouise as they slept on the straw and a smile spread over his face. 'For one who can look so beautiful even when you're sleeping you certainly can snore,' he thought as he looked at Elouise, stifling a giggle. He resisted the temptation to give her a nudge and make her move.

He lay back on the straw and let his mind wander. He began thinking about the first time he had met Jean; he must have been nearly fourteen years old. He had been a shepherd boy since he was eleven when it became clear that there was not enough work in his family's fields for himself and his three brothers. Being the youngest, he was hired out to a neighbour who needed someone to help him with his sheep. For the next two years he followed the neighbour, and his flock, as they criss-crossed the region moving between pastures. He soon learnt to memorise the routes they took as they travelled from valley to valley, using the high passes to cross the ranges between the mountain peaks. The neighbour was a kind soul whose marriage had been blessed with three daughters, so he looked upon Michel as the son he never had. As well as showing him how to tend to the sheep and make sure none of them got lost, he taught him many of the skills that a good shepherd needed. How to read the sky to tell if a storm was brewing; how to find his way in the mist when the clouds descended; how to set traps and hunt for food; how to make cheese from the sheep's milk, and how to shear the wool or deliver a newborn lamb. Much of the time they spent out in the pastures, sleeping at night in one of the many shepherds huts that dotted the region, but occasionally they would enter one of the villages along the way to allow the neighbour to negotiate the sale or purchase of a few sheep. Although he loved the sense of freedom and the stillness of the high pastures Michel always looked forward to these visits to a village. He would listen intently as the adults conducted their business and exchanged their news and, most importantly, their gossip.

It was during such a visit that he first met Jean, although he didn't take much notice of him at the time. Jean was talking with a group of men in the village square but Michel wasn't listening to what they were saying. He was more interested in following the lurid account being told by one woman to another of a man who had returned home early from a hunting trip only to find his wife in bed with his brother. The women leant their heads together and nudged each other in the ribs, whilst the thought crossed Michel's mind that the woman telling the story might indeed be the woman in the story. It was only later that day that the neighbour told Michel they would be having the company of a Good Man, as he referred to Jean, on the next stage of their journey. It seemed the *Bon Homme* needed to get back to his home in Foix and the neighbour had told him they were headed that way and they could show him a quicker route.

After those first two years Michel's neighbour realised that the boy had a natural aptitude as a shepherd. He was good with the flock, he didn't panic if the weather changed or if a sheep got lost, and he only needed to travel a route once before he had memorised the way there and back. So he decided it would make good business sense if he invested in some more sheep to make up another flock for Michel to look after by himself.

From then on Michel would spend the months between spring and the first snowfall of winter moving his flock across the high pastures that formed the backdrop to most of the region. Although a typical day would find him with no one to talk to except his sheep it wasn't unusual for him to meet other people on his travels. Sometimes it would be another shepherd driving his sheep along the same route and they would stop and share their food and exchange any news and gossip. Other times it might be a villager driving his mule to the nearest local market to exchange his produce for household goods such as cloth or lamp oil.

Given that they both had their respective flocks to care for it was no surprise that Michel would see the Good Man Jean from time to time as their travels took them across the same region. He soon came to recognise the tall figure in the hooded cloak walking along slowly but steadily with his stick in one hand and his small bag of belongings slung over one shoulder, and he began to look forward to their encounters. Jean would always give Michel his blessing whenever he approached and afterwards they would sit and talk and share whatever food they had between them. Sometimes, if nightfall was approaching, Michel would lead the way to the nearest hut where he would light a fire and prepare a meal. In return Jean might put a repair in Michel's clothes whilst they waited for the food to be ready. Often there would be other shepherds in the hut and they would all sit and listen as Jean talked to them whilst they ate their supper. Because of their meanderings throughout the region Jean knew that the shepherds had a broader perspective of current affairs than their more isolated cousins in the villages. So he was just as likely to talk to them about the merits of the various local markets for wool, as he was the points of difference between the Catholic and the Cathar doctrines. These discussions would often turn into lively debates as the shepherds, after many days in solitude, would love to exercise their voices. And it wasn't just spoken words that were aired. As the evening wore on it was quite likely that one of the shepherds would start to sing. Often the songs would be renditions of well known tales about local heroes and tragic events, of broken hearts and brave deeds, stories that were handed down from generation to generation. But sometimes someone would start to sing a song they had made up, usually to occupy themselves as they looked after their sheep. These songs would be much more topical and could be as humorous and ribald as they could be loving and gentle. They would be listened to intently and the words and tune remembered so that they might be sung again at another gathering.

It was on one such occasion that Michel asked a fellow shepherd if he could try the lute-like instrument he had been playing to accompany his songs. The shepherd showed Michel how to hold the instrument and where to put his fingers to make a chord. After a few fumbling attempts at strumming Michel handed the instrument back with an embarrassed smile. But the shepherd told him he could keep it until the next time they met as he had business to conduct in the village and the instrument would only get in his way. It was to be a significant moment for Michel, although he didn't realise it at the time, as it would be music that eventually determined the rest of his life and not a flock of sheep.

From that day on Michel would spend every spare waking moment learning to play the instrument. His solitary life gave him the ideal environment to practice. There were only sheep and wild birds to hear the dire sounds he produced as his hands and fingers fumbled around the chords and strings. He may have been able to hold a tune in his head but it was many months before the sound from his instrument began to resemble the music he had in mind.

He was pleased with his progress and would practice every day as soon as he had moved his flock to a new pasture and the sheep were grazing contentedly. Soon the sheep seemed to recognise his strumming as much as his whistled commands and it amused him to see them lifting their heads and stop chewing when he played a particular sequence of chords.

As he persevered with learning to play the lute Michel began to make up his own verses to sing along with the tunes he had learnt. He felt quite self-conscious to begin with as he allowed his singing voice to emerge. Only the sheep had to listen to his warbling and they seemed to be the perfect audience, appreciative yet uncritical.

Many months later when he had met up with some fellow shepherds and they were sitting around in the evening after sharing a meal, one of them saw the lute and asked him to play a song. At first he refused, claiming he didn't have enough experience, but they all joined in teasing him and eventually persuaded him to sing.

He began rather nervously but the shepherds stopped talking and began to listen as he strummed and sang in what had turned out to be a strong, clear voice. When he had finished there was silence for a while from his audience but then they all started to clap and cheer their encouragement and shouted out for another song. It was the first time he had experienced such approval and he began to feel embarrassed at such attention directed at him. But soon he was noticing different feelings – the excitement and satisfaction that seemed to follow his performance. It was a heady moment, like the first time he had drunk too much wine, and soon he was starting another song, then another one until he had exhausted his limited repertoire. His fellow shepherds continued to applaud until someone suggested they needed to sleep before the dawn began to seep into the eastern sky.

Lying on his straw bed that night Michel reflected on this new, powerful skill that had the power to make men silent one moment and cheering the next. He felt a warm glow of satisfaction and smiled to himself in the darkness as he thought about the evening's performance. Before he fell asleep his mind raced ahead thinking about new words and tunes that seemed to fall over each other to emerge. He couldn't know that this would be the beginning of the end of his life as just a shepherd and the start of his life as a travelling entertainer, like the troubadours of a hundred years earlier.

As Michel lay in the Borrel's barn remembering his days as a young shepherd he looked over towards Elouise, still asleep. He watched as the small patch of sunlight resting on her folded arm travelled up towards her cheek and he knew that the warmth from that early morning sunbeam would be enough to wake her.

He had first seen Elouise at the time when Jean decided to take his daughter with him on his travels. Elouise was six years old when she left her childhood home after the death of her grandmother. Carrying her most precious belongings in a small bag on her back and with a determined look on her face she tried to match her father's long stride with two or three shorter ones of her own. She always looked as if she was skipping along.

It was a late afternoon in May and Michel was with his flock on the higher pasture on the northern slopes of the hills above Montaillou, making the most of the new season's grass. As usual he had spent most of the day practicing a new tune but now it was time to gather the flock together and head towards the nearest shelter for the evening, for the nights were still cold at this altitude. Michel had just stood up and was scanning the pasture to make sure none of the flock had wandered too far when he detected a movement on the skyline. By now the sun was lower in the sky and Michel had to shield his eyes to see if he could recognise who might be travelling on this lonely path. Soon a cloaked, hooded figure with a long staff in one hand came into view and he knew from the height of the man and his lengthy stride that it was his friend, Jean. But this time something was different. Attached to Jean's free hand was a smaller figure, hopping and jumping over the stones on the path that the tall man took easily in his stride.

Michel waved until the Good Man saw him and then continued to assemble his flock, slowly making his way down the pasture to meet Jean and his small companion. When they were within a few paces of each other Michel knelt on one knee so that he might receive the *Parfait's* blessing. Jean smiled down at the shepherd and gently placed his hand on Michel's bowed head. When this short, intimate ceremony was over Michel stood up and looked first at the Good Man and then at the child. His look must have implied a question and so it was Jean who spoke first.

'May I introduce you to my daughter, Elouise'. He raised an arm towards Michel. 'Elouise this is my good friend the shepherd Michel. I hope in time he will become a good friend of yours too.' Michel looked down at the child unsure of what to say or do, but before he could think of anything Elouise had extended her small hand towards him, looked him straight in the eye and said in a small solemn voice 'God be with you, Michel.' Her father had to suppress a smile at the effect this serious greeting had on Michel for he had seen the same look of surprise on the faces of other travellers they had met when receiving the same salutation from his daughter.

Eventually Michel blurted out 'And the same to you,' and then composed himself to add the words 'young lady'. This had the effect of not only making Jean smile again but also caused a blush to colour the girl's cheeks.

Michel guessed that this was not the time to ask Jean what he was doing walking in the high pastures miles from the nearest village with his young child, so decided to keep to practical matters.

'I was just about to round up the sheep for today and head for the nearest shelter, so perhaps you should come with me and rest there for the evening too.'

'Indeed we will,' replied Jean. 'Its been a long day for us too. I've told Elouise all about my many evenings in the company of the shepherds, so don't be surprised if she asks you to sing one of your songs.'

'It would be an honour to sing for such a polite young lady,' said Michel with mock seriousness, bowing slightly towards Elouise, which of course made her blush again and bury her shy face in her father's cloak.

The odd trio and the flock of sheep made their way slowly across the meadows towards the hut that would be their shelter for the evening. There was still some distance to travel and it wasn't long before Michel could see that Elouise was tired from walking. He offered to carry her on his back and within moments she had fallen asleep with her head resting on his shoulder. It was like this that the Good Man and the shepherd and the Good Man's daughter arrived at the door of the hut.

From that day on the paths of Michel, Jean and Elouise would cross and re-cross many times as they tended their respective flocks. Meeting each other amongst the mountain pastures and deep valleys between Foix and Ax les Thermes, or the thick woods and hill top villages that spread between Fanjeaux and Quillan.

CHAPTER SIX

'What are you looking at?' enquired Elouise through half-closed, sleepy eyes. She focused on Michel, who had been waiting for the warmth from the sunbeam to reach her cheek and awaken her, just as he had predicted.

'Good Morning, young maiden' replied Michel. 'No need to ask if you slept well, judging by the noises you make. I don't know how you'll ever find a husband who'll put up with such a good impression of a truffle-hunting boar.'

'Don't tease me, its not polite,' replied Elouise as she stirred slowly and began to pluck pieces of straw from her hair. 'Besides, who said I was looking for a husband? But if I did have one surely he would love me enough to put up with a few tiny sounds of a contented night's sleep.'

'Don't bet on it,' said Michel. He smiled and stood up, raising a miniature dust storm that danced through the rays of the sun that had begun to illuminate the barn. 'And give your father a shake as well, its time we were moving.' He slid down from the hayloft onto the barn floor.

But Jean didn't need to be woken. He had been awake for some time turning events over in his mind and contemplating the day ahead. Besides, he liked to listen to the playful banter between his daughter and Michel. 'Just like two fox cubs falling over themselves' he thought to himself as he gathered his cloak around him and followed the two young people out of the barn.

Jacotte Borrel and the rest of the family were already up and gathered round the table that was now set with bread and cold ham, together with jugs of fresh water and wine. A small dish of fish left over from the previous evening had been saved for Jean. As he entered the room the family fell into a respectful silence until Jean had blessed them and their food. Jacotte made sure that her guests helped themselves first before allowing the rest of her family to tuck into breakfast with their usual gusto.

It was Claude who broke the silence first with a question directed at Jean.

'So, Jean de Rhedones, now that you are here what are your plans and how can we help you?' he gestured around the room with a sweeping motion of his arm to take in all his family.

Jean smiled at Claude. 'You have already done enough for us with your kindness and your hospitality. We couldn't ask for more nor do we expect it. Today, as you well know, is the feast day of your village, St. Julien, and we shall take this opportunity to continue our work in the village.'

'But you cannot preach salvation in the village today,' replied Claude, with a rising sense of alarm, 'There will be too many people and you cannot trust that everyone believes as we do. The Dominicans have eyes and ears everywhere-it will not be safe for you.' He glanced nervously across the table at Jacotte as if to underline the concern he felt for his family as well as their guests.

'Do not worry,Claude,' replied Jean. 'I shall not set out to save souls today nor would I take risks with your family's safety. My daughter and I have other work to do. There are always clothes to mend and alterations to make, so I expect we will keep our hands busy even if our minds are not occupied with higher matters.' And with that he smiled and everyone in the room relaxed visibly, which was the effect Elouise knew that he had intended.

By the time they had finished eating and gathered up their belongings the bells of the village church were already chiming the seventh hour of the day. The warmth from the June sun could already be felt as Jean, Elouise and Michel made their way along the narrow paths between the houses and barns towards the centre of the village. Everyone loved a Feast Day and already there was a steady stream of people moving in the same direction in anticipation of a good time, not least because it was a wonderful excuse not to be working; like villagers everywhere they would much prefer to rest and play than to work.

Dogs barked, chickens squawked and sheep and goats just got in the way as people bade each other good day and children skipped and ran, playing tag and pulling faces at each other.

The centre of the village formed a square roughly seventy-five paces across. On its north-western edge a wider path, wide enough for a cart and two oxen, led to the upper gateway of the village. From there the path zigzagged up the hillside towards the chateau that straddled the granite outcrop and gazed down at the village and onto the river a thousand paces below. The upper ox path was matched by another that exited from the south-eastern side of the square, leading down to the lower gate, where it emerged to meander through the fields and down to the river that it forded before disappearing into the woods on the far hillside where Michel had emerged the day before.

The church of Saint Julien, from whom the village took its name and whose feast day was being celebrated on this ninth day of June, occupied a site on the southern edge of the square. Built from the local limestone and roofed with wooden tiles it was not a large structure but it did possess an impressive circular bell tower, tall enough that no house in the village could escape from view, something the priest, Bernard Villac, took advantage of as he watched his parishioners moving about their business.

Opposite the church stood an old building that housed the village tavern. Owned and run by the fearsome, and fearless, Emilie Fouet, whose husband had died long ago leaving her in sole possession of the establishment, she served wine to the men of the village and had been known to dispense rough justice to anyone who got too familiar with her or her daughters.

Next to the tavern a magnificent chestnut tree with thick branches and broad leaves provided a welcome natural shade during the summer heat. It was a popular place for groups of men to sit and discuss important matters of the day, like complaining about the latest tax levy from the bishop, which united them, or the best way to trap a squirrel, which would usually divide them. Their discussions could often carry on for hours, fortified by jugs of wine brought to them by one of Emilie's daughters, whose buxom figure would be guaranteed to start another lively debate.

On the northern side of the square stood a raised stone trough, fed with fresh water from an underground spring. Here the women of the village would gather daily to fill their pots. As they waited their turn they would take the opportunity for a few moments of rest and indulge in one of their favourite pastimes, the important business of exchanging gossip, before balancing the pot on a small cushion on their head and making their way home, trying not to spill any of the precious contents.

A steady flow of surplus water ran from the trough and down into a channel gouged out of the ox path that divided the village in half, so that a stream of water constantly flowed through the village and out of the lower gate, carrying with it some of the debris and detritus that littered its path.

Opposite the water trough stood another opportunity for the womenfolk to meet and exchange their daily news. The communal oven, owned by the Count and supervised by one of his vassals, was where the women would gather to bring their dough and leave it to be baked into loaves. In return they paid a small annual fee, usually a few chickens, or a goose, sent up to the chateau with the regular supply of eggs.

By the time the trio arrived at the heart of the village it was already alive with activity. People were setting up stalls and awnings, jostling and joking with each other as they sorted out which position they wanted, judging where the shadiest positions would be according to the presentation of their wares. Those with perishable items like olives, wine, herbs, salt and spices preferred to be in the shade while those with tools and pots chose the sunnier spots to allow their wares to sparkle.

St. Julien was not a large village, certainly not big enough to need a market. Most daily food items were either home grown or bartered between neighbours, exchanging food and produce in return for help in the fields or the loan of a tool. But on a Saint's Day like today the village became a destination for the travelling merchants who circulated throughout the region, bringing their goods for sale to those who rarely or never visited a town. Rope makers brought ropes and cords of all strengths and sizes; cloth merchants displayed lengths of white cotton and fine wool in a range of colours to tempt any villager needing a garment for a special occasion, perhaps a wedding or a christening. Other stalls belonged to the leather merchants who would be selling straps and harnesses, belts and buckles, and maybe even a fine pair of soft leather boots for the few who could afford them or for the majority just to wish for and dream about.

In amongst the more organised stalls of the merchants other one-man ventures were getting themselves ready. A feast day always attracted its share of story tellers, fortune tellers, menders and repairers, sellers of potions to cure any ailment of the body and soul, even a man willing to pull out a tooth or straighten a broken finger for those brave enough to submit themselves to his evil looking implements.

Weaving their way in and out of this throng of activity, like a colourful ribbon tying everything together, were the entertainers. Perhaps a musician strumming a sad tune alone, others in small clusters providing the music for a happy group of dancers, jugglers tossing and catching with ease any item their audience chose to throw at them, acrobats tumbling and turning somersaults to applause. There was even a performer who would follow behind an unsuspecting villager, mimicking his walk and making fun of his appearance, much to the amusement of the other folk watching. If the unlucky victim turned around the mime would strike a pose of complete innocence, increasing the amusement of his audience as he pretended to look round to see what was the source of all their laughter.

By the time the church bells had struck the ninth hour of the day the activities in the village square were in full swing. Jean and Elouise had found themselves a comfortable spot in the shade of the chestnut tree and were already turning their skills to the tasks in hand. Jean spent some time discussing with one young woman how to turn the length of cloth she had brought to him into a new winter cloak. He had already taken careful measurements of her size and height and soon his practiced hands were guiding the scissors through the cloth, creating the body panels, the sleeves and the hood that he would pass to Elouise to sew together. She in turn had accumulated a growing pile of tunics, chemises and children's clothes, with requests to lengthen, shorten, patch and mend or simply to try and salvage another winter's wear. During their years of travel together her father had taught her all his tailoring skills and he would have had to admit with a degree of pride (if his soul would have allowed him such an emotion) that with her young eyes and swift hands she was already a better tailor that he had ever been.

From time to time Elouise glanced up from her work and caught sight of Michel. He had positioned himself, quite intentionally, not far from the doorway of Emilie Fouet's tavern. She smiled to herself as she watched him begin to go through his repertoire of songs and respond to the requests from the tavern's customers. Michel enjoyed the pleasure he found from playing to an audience and he delighted in the way he could entertain the crowd. One moment drawing a hushed silence as he sang of battles won and lost, next raising loud guffaws of laughter and much nudging of ribs as he strummed his way through a ribald tale of love and lust. Someone always called out a request for their favourite song and Michel would tease his audience by pretending he hadn't heard and playing a few notes of his own before starting the familiar tune, knowing that he would probably have to play the same song again before the day was done.

Michel returned Elouise's glance with a wave between songs and wiped his brow in mock exhaustion. She laughed but the loss of concentration made her prick herself and she looked at him crossly as she put the thumb to her mouth. He grinned and slapped his thigh at her misfortune, just as any big brother would have done, and continued to play for his enthusiastic audience.

Having climbed the stone steps inside the church tower the priest Villac looked down on the colourful scene spread out below. He had been born and raised in St. Julien and as his gaze wandered around he ticked off in his mind the names of the people he recognised. His eyes travelled from stall to stall looking to see what people were buying and filing the information away for future reference. He calculated that if any of his congregation showed they had money to spend then they might also be prompted, with a little religious persuasion, to make a donation the to church. And God knows, he thought, he needed the extra income to pay for some of the luxuries he had developed a taste for lately.

The priest continued his perusal of the scene below, his eyes flicking from face to face until suddenly they backtracked and rested on a face he didn't recognise. He was looking at Jean and with increasing interest too.

He could see that Jean was skilled with cloth and scissors and also had the help of an assistant, whose fresh beauty, even from this distance, was enough to stir his robe. Rising above that carnal thought what really interested Villac was the behaviour of some of the tailor's customers. They seemed to dip a knee and lower their head as if trying to kneel in front of him before handing over their cloth or garment. The priest watched as Jean tried to avoid this mark of respect, encouraging the customer to stand up with an upward motion of his hand. But not everyone would rise until Jean had placed his hand on their head, leaning forward to whisper a few words.

'Well well, Mon Dieu, look what we've got here,' the priest thought to himself, as his inquisitive eyes took in the dark, hooded cloak that Jean was wearing. 'Seems to me we have one of the heretics in our midst.' He lifted his eyes and gazed beyond the village walls as he mulled over the threat, and the opportunity, that this new discovery presented and how he might use the information to his advantage.

From his position in the bell tower Villac had a circular view of the whole village. His thoughts were interrupted by a movement on the steep track that led down to the north-western gate. Turning his head he could make out five people on horseback descending slowly from the chateau. 'Time to prepare myself for the procession,' he concluded, turning away from his viewpoint and descending the worn steps to his chamber below.

In the body of the church an eager group of parishioners waited for the priest to emerge from his robing room. They had already lifted the statue of St. Julien from its usual resting place behind the alter and placed it on the processional bier, ready for its annual tour of the village.

The statue was housed inside an intricately carved heavy wooden casket, open at the front to allow the image of the saint to be seen. The feet of the statue rested on a dull gold box said to contain a relic of St. Julien, an early martyr beheaded by the

Romans for converting centurions to Christianity during the occupation of Gaul.

Villac emerged from the vestry wearing his best white linen surplice and with a heavy gold cross resting on his chest. He motioned to the processional group to kneel while he delivered a short prayer, asking for the strength and fortitude to help them carry the blessed saint on this very special day. As he finished speaking, the noise of people cheering and the sound of hooves clattering on stone steps filtered through the open doors of the church. The sounds were soon followed by the arrival in the church of the mounted group that he had seen descending from the chateau.

The Most Reverend Bishop of Pamiers stood outlined in the doorway, resplendent in purple robes and golden bishop's mitre, holding a staff inlaid with mother of pearl and topped by a solid silver cross. He had been escorted to the church by the knight Guillaume and his cousin Bruno, who now stood either side of him in the doorway. Behind them stood Guillaume's sister, Helene. She had decided to accompany her brother on this visit to the village, not so much for religious reasons but because she needed to escape the confines of the chateau and enjoy the excitement of the Saint's day celebrations. Once the religious proceedings were over she was determined to mingle with the crowds and soak up the festive atmosphere. At the age of eighteen and with a husband yet to be chosen she needed some relief from the boredom of life within the chateau's walls.

Villac stepped forward to greet the Bishop. 'Good day to you my lord Bishop, welcome to my humble church. We are honoured by your presence on this special day for our village.' The priest knelt and kissed the ring on the Bishop's outstretched hand.

'Arise, my son,' replied the Bishop. 'We always try to visit the villages within our fold. You are a good servant of the church and I am pleased to be able to celebrate your Saint's day with you.' In truth the Bishop's visit to St. Julien had less to do with a Saint's anniversary and more to do with his discussions at the chateau with the Count. But he was not about to spoil Villac's obvious pleasure at having a Bishop in his church. Besides, the man had been feeding him some good information of late, information that he had been happy to pass on to the Dominicans.

'Come, Villac. Let us get this procession under way and afterwards, if I may, I will say a mass in your church to honour your Saint.'

The priest could not prevent himself from rubbing his hands with pleasure at this perceived request from the Bishop for his permission to pray in his church.

'Of course, my lord' he gushed, 'you would be doing us a great honour if you were to speak to my flock in our humble church. It would be a memory we would carry to our graves.'

And so the procession commenced, stepping out from the church into the hot June sunshine led by two altar boys wafting their bowls of incense as the bells signalled the start of the parade.

The crowd of people on either side of the processional route fell silent and began to kneel before the Bishop as he blessed them with the sign of the cross. As the Bishop and the priest continued on their way the people stood again, cheering and crossing themselves as the statue of St. Julien passed by, held aloft by the bearers who struggled and sweated to keep the heavy wooden bier above their shoulders.

Guillaume and Bruno decided the Bishop no longer needed the protection of their escort and began to stroll in the direction of the tavern. Helene, meanwhile, had already detached herself from her brother and cousin and had disappeared into the maze of stalls determined to find something to buy, maybe a silk scarf or a silver clasp to fix to her new dress.

As Guillaume covered the ground between church and tavern he noticed the tailor and his daughter busy at work by the chestnut tree. He felt his heart begin to thump in his chest and his throat start to dry.

'You carry on,' he said to Bruno, pressing his cousin on the shoulder and steering him towards the tavern, 'I'll catch up with you later.' Bruno didn't need any further encouragement. He was desperate to get his hand round a drink and, ideally, the other hand around one of Emilie's daughters. He strode into the tavern, noticing as he crossed the doorway the young musician playing to a rapt audience and wondered briefly where he'd seen his face before. He left this thought at the door and concentrated instead on the serious business of getting drunk. After a few mugs of wine he even found himself singing along to the tunes that drifted through the open door, penetrating the dark corners of the tavern's interior.

Elouise's concentration was broken by the shadow that fell across her. With a degree of annoyance she lifted her head and put one hand up to shield her eyes from the bright sky and see who had caused this interruption to her sewing.

She found herself looking up into the blue, serious eyes of Guillaume. Within a moment, to her surprise, she also felt a blush begin to reach her cheeks.

'Good day to you, Mademoiselle. Forgive me for interrupting your work, I didn't mean to disturb you. I didn't expect to see you again so soon.' His few words gave Elouise enough time to compose herself.

'Good day to you too, Sir' she replied 'Nor I, either.'

They continued to look at each other without speaking for several moments until Elouise glanced back to the work in her lap and pretended to pick at a stitch.

'Do you have something that needs mending?' Elouise asked, regretting immediately what a silly question this must sound to a man who probably had his own personal seamstress.

'Thank you, no,' replied Guillaume, trying to keep his voice sounding normal, whilst his eyes couldn't help taking in again the breathtaking beauty of the young woman in front of him.

'Actually, now that I've found you I'd like to speak to your father.'

Elouise couldn't resist the chance to tease this earnest young knight.

'Well I didn't realise we were lost,' she replied, 'But by all means talk to my father' and with that she called over to Jean.

'Papa, there's a young man here who seems intent on having a word with you.' She gestured with her hand to indicate Guillaume as she kept her head turned towards her father.

Guillaume took this to be the end of his conversation with Elouise and moved forward a few paces until he was standing in front of the seated *Parfait*. Jean looked up at the tall young man and smiled.

'God be with you, my son. I'm glad you're on foot this time and not on horseback so I don't have to strain my neck to see you.'

A smile spread across Guillaume's face at this warm greeting. It was a smile that softened his earnest knight's features and one that Elouise noticed spread to his eyes as well as his mouth.

'Good day to you, Jean de Rhedones. I was just saying to your daughter how pleased I was to see you both again,' began Guillaume. 'In fact it's saved me time in trying to find you.'

'And why would you want to find us?' enquired Jean in a softer voice that didn't convey suspicion but still indicated that he might be proceeding with caution.

'Nothing serious, I promise you' replied Guillaume trying to get a sense of reassurance into his voice. 'I told my father I'd met a tailor on my travels and he instructed me to find you. Seems my parents have been needing the services of a good man like yourself for some time and they would like to invite you and your daughter to come and be our guests at the chateau.' Guillaume hoped he'd put enough emphasis on 'good' to convey to Jean that he'd also told his father he'd met one of the *Bons Hommes*.

'Well, my son, it would be impolite of us to turn down such a kind invitation. I'm sure my daughter and I would be delighted to accept,' said Jean, wondering to himself what the real purpose of this invitation might be.

'That's excellent,' continued Guillaume, with relief. 'My parents will be pleased to meet you. And please bring your musical companion too; my father says we could all do with some cheerful entertainment.'

Guillaume was about to start explaining what arrangements he was going to suggest when he felt his sleeve being tugged firmly.

'Guillaume, Guillaume come with me quickly, there's something I want you to see.' He felt himself begin to lose his balance as his arm was pulled further away.

'Ah, little sister, I suppose you've found something to amuse you,' he said, as he resisted her tugging and restored his balance. 'Come and meet these good people. This is Jean de Rhedones and his daughter Elouise. Allow me to introduce my sister, Helene'

Helene nodded vaguely in the direction of Jean and Elouise, wondering why her brother was so interested in these two trades people.

'I've just invited them up to the chateau,' continued Guillaume. This only seemed to add to her confusion, but Helene was too polite to allow her puzzlement to show.

'Well I'm sure that will be very interesting for all of us,' she managed to say, without really conveying much interest at all. 'Now come with me Guillaume, you must see these wonderful boots I've found.'

This time Guillaume did not resist her pull and allowed himself to be led away.

'I'll come back to fetch you when the feast is under way.' He said this over his shoulder as he disappeared into the crowd, but not before taking another long look at Elouise who, frustratingly for him, chose that precise moment to concentrate on her sewing and not return his gaze.

The procession of St. Julien had reached the north-western gate and was making its way around the eastern perimeter of the village towards the gate in the south-east. All along the route people knelt and crossed themselves as the Bishop went by, giving them his blessing in return. The crowd stood and cheered as the saint's statue continued its passage through the village. The bier swayed alarmingly as the men struggled to maintain their footing on the uneven pathways. Several times they had to stop to adjust their grip, taking advantage of these rests to drink from the flagons that were offered by the sympathetic onlookers.

When the procession reached the south-east portal it was traditional for the gateway itself to be blessed to keep the village safe for another year. Even the untended fields beyond the gate seemed to be enjoying a welcome day off from the business of growing crops.

The parade turned back towards the church, following the main cart track that led through the middle of the village. It was steep enough to test the diminishing strength of the men carrying the statue but at least, as the church tower came back into view, they knew that not only would they earn some grateful prayers from the Bishop for themselves and their families, but also they had done their turn and wouldn't be asked to repeat the task next year.

As the bells struck the midday hour the procession finally re-entered the church and the Saint's statue was returned to its place of honour above the altar to watch over the congregation for another year. Behind the procession a stream of villagers crowded from the hot sunshine into the cool interior of the church until there was no room left to stand or sit. They waited patiently for the celebratory mass to begin. In other years their own priest would have conducted this but today the congregation anticipated with pride the holy words from the Bishop, honouring this memorable moment for their village.

Not everyone was in church to celebrate Saint Julian's day.

The smoke from several fires began to drift through the village, carrying with it the appetising smell of meat cooking over hot embers and mingling with the aroma of stacks of fresh bread. People began to move towards the tempting smells, hungry from their activities of the morning. Tasty, finger-sized portions of chicken, rabbit and pork were soon disappearing rapidly from the stalls and being devoured with pleasure by the throng of people as they continued wandering through the stalls or rested in small groups in whatever shade they could find. Children ate quickly and continued their games as their families sat and watched, knowing that the combination of food and warm sun would soon give them a rest from so much energy.

Not surprisingly, Jean and Elouise were absent from church. Their beliefs would not allow them to enter such an edifice built to celebrate God, for their own church needed no such premises. Fortunately their tailoring work provided a good excuse for their absence and they continued to cut and sew and mend the large pile of garments that had been left with them. On another day Jean might have taken the opportunity to speak to those believers who sought his guidance, but this was not the right day. But it did not prevent a steady stream of villagers finding themselves in front of Jean so that he could give his surreptitious blessing to their food before it was eaten.

Over by the tavern Michel was taking his own welcome

break from entertaining the crowd, although he was not left entirely on his own. Sitting on the ground in front of him, watching him eat, were several keen admirers, mainly young girls, who could not disguise their attraction to his potent combination of talent, youth and good looks. They ate very little themselves but feasted on the smiles and words he directed towards each one in response to their shy questions. Really he would have preferred to have been left alone to enjoy a few moments of peace, but he was experienced enough to know that an entertainer could not disappoint his audience.

Inside the tavern Bruno had at last given up trying to persuade Emilie's daughter to sit on his lap, much to her relief. She was used to the drunken groping of her regular clientele but there was something about Bruno that made her flesh creep. His head rested on the table and he drifted off to sleep in a haze of alcohol, his empty wine pot and a half-finished platter of food beside him. Only the tavern's cat kept him company, padding across the table and reaching out a paw to steal a scrap from his plate.

Outside in the afternoon sun a quietness descended on the feast day scene. Many of the villagers began to make their way back to their homes. There would be more singing and dancing to look forward to later on, together with the highlight of the evening, two enormous wild boar that were already roasting on spits. But for now it was time to attend to the mundane chores of fetching water and feeding animals, then they could take advantage of this annual rest day to enjoy a welcome nap before the activities began again.

In the vestry attached to the small church, which also served as study and bedroom, the priest had been doing his best to entertain the Bishop after the celebration of mass. Lilianne, the young girl who cooked and washed for the priest and now acted as his serving maid, had put flowers in a wine jug on the table. She'd even found a linen napkin for the Bishop and set a proper place for him. The Bishop had thanked her for her kindness and blessed her, which prompted the poor girl to prostrate herself at his feet until he told her to stand up. What the Bishop didn't realise was that this was a position she often adopted in front of Villac, except on those occasions she would most likely be found with hips raised and her skirt pulled over her waist.

When the meal was over and Lilianne had cleared the table the Bishop lowered his chin onto his steepled fingers and addressed Villac.

'You have been most hospitable, my son. I'm glad that I had this opportunity to visit you on this special day. It does me good to see for myself how respectful the people are to our faith. It does you great credit.'

Villac said nothing but felt a warm glow of pride spread through his body at these words of praise from his Lord Bishop.

'You have been most diligent in collecting our taxes and sending us your information,' continued the Bishop, 'Do you have any other sinners you wish to draw to our attention?'

The question hung in the air for a few moments before the priest replied.

'I try to keep my flock on the one true path, my lord,' he began 'but it is always the weak ones who fall by the wayside and become easy prey for the heretics. I am keeping a watch on certain families who I believe have continued to turn away from the church. Of course they still come to mass on Sundays but I know that's just to maintain appearances. Sooner or later they'll give themselves away, either in public or in front of one of their neighbours. There are those who are willing to point the finger of suspicion and when they do you shall know about it.'

The Bishop looked at his priest and suppressed a feeling of distaste for this man who seemed so eager to please by betraying the very people he had grown up with. He wondered what secrets the priest might have himself that would allow him to break the trust of his congregation, even from the sanctity of the confessional.

'You do well, my son. And it does not go unnoticed. We may have to find a larger canvas for your talents,' replied the Bishop with a smile, knowing that his words of encouragement would have to be enough to satisfy this priest for the foreseeable future.

Villac responded to the praise from his master as any pet would, eager to please again.

'Well I did see someone this morning who might be of interest to us,' he began, attempting to put himself at the same level as the Bishop. 'A man with all the appearance of one of the heretic preachers, one they call a 'Good Man'.'

At this mention of a *Parfait* the Bishop's interest in what Villac had to say was suddenly sharpened.

'Go on.'

'Yes, my Lord. I saw him near the tavern. He's not local, I think he must have come with the other travellers and merchants. He was working as a tailor but I saw enough to make me suspicious.'

'And what exactly did you see?' enquired the Bishop impatiently.

'Well, there were three things I noticed my Lord. Firstly he was wearing a dark, hooded cloak, secondly he seemed to be in deep discussion with some of his customers and lastly, I saw some people kneeling in front of him.'

'Hardly enough to send a man to the stake,' the Bishop thought to himself.

'Well you'd better keep an eye on him whoever he is,' he instructed, 'and when you have some more solid foundations for your suspicions then you must let me know. Now leave me in peace. I wish to rest before I return to the chateau.' And with that the Bishop dismissed Villac with a wave of his hand and promptly settled himself down on the priest's rather uncomfortable bed, unaware that he would soon have the opportunity to meet this mysterious *Parfait* himself.

At the same time that the Bishop was settling down, Bruno was beginning to wake up. The alcohol, which earlier had softened his mood, now made him thirsty and his head throbbed. He looked around the tavern and saw that most of the patrons, including the two serving girls, had either left or were asleep themselves. He cursed and shook his head and decided he needed some fresh air. Clutching the door frame for a few moments Bruno blinked and rubbed his eyes as he accustomed himself to the bright sunshine outside. Still swaying slightly he made his way out of the tavern and thought vaguely about finding Guillaume. As he began to move off in the direction of the water trough he noticed Michel who was now in the shade of the chestnut tree having a humorous conversation with another young man. A sudden instance of recognition filtered to the front of Bruno's fuddled brain. 'Now I know who you are, you little bastard,' thought Bruno.'You're that clever little pisser we met in the woods,' and with that thought in his head Bruno redirected his legs towards Michel. The young man was listening intently to his friend Andre, one of the shepherds in the village for the sheep sale, and catching up on all the news. They didn't notice Bruno approaching until he was standing next to them.

'Well, look who we've got here,' exclaimed Bruno as if delighted to find an outlet for his bad mood. 'If it isn't the brave defender of the fair maiden. And who's this with you? One of your arse loving friends?'

He mouthed an exaggerated kiss in the direction of Andre.

Andre was about to take a step towards Bruno when he felt Michel's arm across his chest.

'Don't,' Michel advised his friend. 'This man's been looking for a fight since yesterday.' He turned towards the drunken knight. 'Still no luck with the hunt Bruno, or has some other quarry turned you down?' taunted Michel.

Bruno turned his attention towards Michel and rested his hand on the hilt of his sword.

'I could cut you in half right now, you piece of pig shit,' Bruno threatened, drawing a few inches of blade from its sheath.

'And if you did that how would I be able to play for your master, the Comte de Quillan?' replied Michel without a trace of fear in voice.

Bruno's face clouded whilst he absorbed this information.

'What are you talking about?' he demanded.

'Well, while you seem to have been drinking the day away I and my travelling companions have been invited to the chateau to meet the Count. I don't think he'd be at all pleased if the entertainment failed show up, so I suggest you put that away before you do yourself some damage.' Michel waved his hand in the direction of Bruno's sword.

Bruno continued to stare at Michel. 'This isn't finished yet. You'd better watch yourself,' he warned, 'one of these days that sharp tongue of yours might get itself cut out.' And with a final glare at the two young friends he turned and continued on his way to look for Guillaume.

Michel gave him a mock wave to send him on his way.

'See you soon!' he teased. But inside he knew that next time he saw Bruno he'd have to be extra careful. If he was to continue to protect Jean and Elouise he didn't need an enemy like Bruno.

As the sun began its slow descent over the hills that shielded St. Julien de Roc from the southwesterly weather, Jean and Elouise began to pack up their scissors, threads and needles. It had been a long day and their eyes and hands ached from hours of work. They'd lost count of the patches they'd sewn, the alterations made and the lengths of cloth turned into new clothes.

Elouise looked across at her father. She could see that he was tired and, not for the first time, she wondered if his beliefs and vocation were beginning to weigh him down. Since the spread of the Dominican purge Jean was, to all intents and purposes, a wanted man. There were few *Parfaits* left these days and those that did survive had been pushed back into the hills and mountains that separated the Languedoc from the lands of Aragon.

'Do you really think this is good idea, us going up to the chateau? I mean what do we know of lords and ladies? What if it's some kind of trap?'

Jean could see the concern on his daughter's face and tried to calm her fears.

'Don't be such a worry puss, Lou Lou,' he said, making an effort to put a cheerful note in his voice. 'Where else could we be safer than inside the walls of a chateau? Besides, we'll have that handsome young knight to look after us. I think he's taken quite a shine to you.' He knew he was teasing his daughter and sure enough he saw a blush rise to her cheeks.

'You don't know what you're talking about,' protested Elouise, but she was aware of the sudden increase in her heartbeat at this mention of Guillaume. 'Anyway, I wasn't thinking about him,' she continued, trying to erase her blush. 'I was referring to the Comte de Quillan. What do you know about him exactly?'

'The truth is, my child, I know very little about this man but I did meet his older brother. He was a brave man who gave his life defending his land from the northern invaders. In fact he saved this village from destruction.'

'What happened?' asked Elouise quietly.

'Simon de Montfort sent an armed force to lay siege to the chateau. In those days they were interested in taking over the whole region but they used the persecution of our faith as the justification for their deeds. The captain of the army threatened to kill every person in the village and burn it to the ground unless every *croyant* surrendered to him. The captain knew that the Count was sympathetic to our beliefs and had supported the Cathar bishops in their quest for a peaceful solution to the conflict. He gave the Count two days to make up his mind.' Jean paused as the memories came back to him.

'Go on,' prompted Elouise.

'The Count wanted to avoid a repeat of the dreadful massacre at Beziers and so he offered to give himself up as a hostage in return for the safety of the village. The captain agreed to this and ordered his soldiers to withdraw. The capture of a nobleman was a feather in his cap and he liked the idea of taking over the chateau himself without having to reduce it to ruins.'

'What happened to the Count?' Elouise asked, in a quiet voice.

'As soon as he surrendered they severed his head from his body and stuck it on a pole at the gates of the village. It was a warning to his family and a message to any one else who dared to defy de Montfort.'

Elouise flinched at the thought of this savage reprisal and a shiver ran through her body as she looked around at the village still bathed in warm sunshine.

'Why do they still hate us so much?' she asked her father.

'It's not that they hate us, my child,' Jean replied, 'they don't understand us, and so we've become their enemy. They think we're a threat to their power over the people. Strange isn't it, when we both believe in God?' Jean finished putting away his tools into his workbag and, with a deep sigh, stretched his arms above his head.

'Come and rub my shoulders for me, Lou-Lou while we wait for Michel' he said at last, 'You know how good you are at making me feel better.'

Elouise smiled and stood behind her father and began to

massage his neck and shoulders. As she eased his aching limbs and listened to her father's contented sighs her worried thoughts subsided.

As the village began to stir from its afternoon slumbers Elouise and Jean sat and waited for Michel who had gone to the Borrel's to fetch the rest of their belongings. People were beginning to make their way back to the centre of the village where the spit-roasted boars would soon be served. Such meat would not usually be part of their diet as hunting wild boar was the preserve of the land owner. But tonight, to honour the Saint's day, the Count had ensured that his family's custom of providing the food for the feast was maintained. Lit torches and flares began to appear around the village as dusk descended. The heavy wooden gates were closed and guards began their nightly circuit of the boundaries. Saint's day or not, there was always a need to be vigilant against the bandits and mercenaries who roamed the countryside looking for any easy opportunity to rob and steal.

'Where have you been? We've been waiting for ages,' complained Elouise when she saw Michel finally appear around the corner, unable to disguise her impatience.

'I bumped into Andre and he wanted my advice about some sheep and so we went over to the sheep pens and then I've been to collect our things and the Borrel's insisted I have a drink with them, and here I am, O Impatient One,' teased Michel all in one breath.

'I expect you're both hungry. Why don't I go and get us all something to eat while we wait for your knight?' he continued.

'That would be nice,' said Elouise, now calming down 'and he's not my knight. Why does everyone keep saying that?' but she was smiling now and Jean and Michel exchanged a shrug and a raise of the eyebrows.

Michel walked off in the direction of the communal oven, guided by the tempting aroma of another batch of fresh bread.

Father and daughter sat and waited in silence, content to watch the steady stream of people passing by on their way to the feast, their eager faces illuminated by the flames from the torches they shared to light their way.

From time to time the pair would nod and give a wave to a face they recognised, perhaps a customer from earlier in the day or someone Jean had blessed.

It wasn't long before Michel returned. 'Dinner is served,' he announced with a flourish as he set down a large wooden platter covered in roast meat and fresh bread. 'Look, I've even found some fish for you Jean so you won't go hungry.'

'You're a good boy, Michel,' replied Jean, thanking him 'I don't know what we'd do without you. I shall bless you, as always.'

Michel felt a small wave of embarrassment tinged with pride at these kind words from the Good Man. To cover his feelings Michel made another announcement.

'And here's something for us to drink,' and with a magician's flourish he pulled out a flask of wine that he had hidden in the folds of his tunic.

'And there's more!' he continued, and proceeded to produce from his other sleeve a dish of blackcurrants and gooseberries.

Jean and Elouise laughed and clapped at his performance. Soon they were eating and talking at their own al fresco feast looking, to any passer by, like a happy family on a day away from their usual labours.

Guillaume appeared out of the throng of people and strode up to his father's guests just as they were finishing their meal.

'Are you ready?' he enquired politely. 'I've arranged some transport for you. It's waiting at the village gate with the others.' He offered his hand first to Elouise and then helped Jean to stand. 'Let me help you with your baggage,' and he began to gather up their various belongings.

The group moved off through the crowd that now filled the village square. They followed Guillaume as he walked along the track that led to the north-western gate. He chattered away to cover the nervousness he felt at being so close to Elouise, but she seemed to be lost in her own thoughts and held on to her father's hand, as if needing his reassurance as they took these steps towards an unfamiliar world.

Bruno was waiting on horseback at the gates and held onto the reins of Guillaume's mount.

'I see you've rounded up your strays,' he sneered at his cousin, looking down with disdain at Jean and Elouise.

'That's enough,' warned Guillaume. 'These people are guests of my father. You would do well to remember that.'

One of the Count's servants had already been despatched to the village with a bullock cart in which Helene now sat next to the figure of a man.

'Allow me to introduce the Bishop of Pamiers,' said Guillaume. He spoke slowly, hoping his tone would deliver a warning to Jean.

'He is also a guest of my father's. Bishop this is Jean de Rhedones and his daughter Elouise.'

The Bishop turned and looked down at father and daughter, unable to mask the disdain in his eyes. No pleasantries were exchanged between the two men beyond a slight nod of the head, but an immediate tension was evident in the space that separated them.

'Please,' offered Guillaume to Jean and Elouise, indicating that they should ride in the cart with the other two. Out of politeness Jean and Elouise climbed into the cart and sat down, but an air of discomfort seemed to descend upon the four passengers. Michel lifted their bags into the cart.

'I'll walk,' he announced, and proceeded to move alongside the servant who was attempting to hold the rope to lead the bullock in one hand and a torch to light the way in the other.

'Here, let me take that,' said Michel and took the flare from the servant's hand. The wheels of the cart creaked as the party moved off on the short journey up the path that zig zagged its way to the gates of the chateau.

In the darkness that swiftly enveloped them Elouise again sought out the security of her father's hand. This time she felt a strong reassuring squeeze in return.

CHAPTER SEVEN

Villac lay on his bed and reflected on the day. All in all he considered it to have been a great success, although he was peeved that the Bishop had not invited him to go with him to the chateau. This minor disappointment apart, he hoped that the information he'd been able to pass on would serve to get him promoted to a wealthier parish, perhaps even a move back to the abbey itself.

Now approaching thirty-five years of age Villac felt he had spent too long in this shabby village of his birth. His path to becoming a priest had been an accident, literally. Until his fourteenth year he'd been happy as one of the village youths, helping his father in the family's fields. Then one day his world changed. He and his brothers were felling a dead tree for firewood when a branch split and fell on him, breaking his leg in two places. The limb had been bandaged and a splint attached, but it never healed properly and he was left with a painful limp. He was of no further use in the fields and could not earn his keep, so the family had taken up an offer from the their priest to send Bernard to the nearby abbey to be trained for the priesthood. It had been ten years of hardship but he learnt quickly and soon began to see the advantages of being a priest, despite the beatings and abuse he received at the hands of some of the monks. His ability to observe the behaviour of his tutors and fellow students whilst hiding his own feelings eventually brought him to the notice of the Abbot, who recognised in Villac the emerging credentials of a loyal informer. By the time he was ordained at the age of twenty-five he had already proved his usefulness and was looking forward to advancing his career under the patronage of the Abbot. But fate took a hand when the Abbot was struck down by sickness and died soon afterwards. His successor took the view that the young priest needed more practical experience and promptly despatched him to St. Julien to take over the recently vacated position. Thus the new priest found himself back amongst his own people, but this time as the guardian of their souls. His position created awkwardness for his former friends and neighbours and a separation was soon established between himself and the rest of the village. Villac began to use this distance to his advantage, allowing him to manipulate those parishioners that could usefully serve his needs. After a while the relationship between priest and parish became pragmatic. The village required a priest to look after the serious matters of life and death and it was better to have one of their own than a stranger. But they didn't really like Villac and many people, in the privacy of their own homes, would admit that they didn't trust him either.

A knock on the door roused him from his thoughts. Lilianne entered the room with a candle and a request.

'Will you be needing me for anything else, Father, or can I go home?' The priest raised himself up and turned to look at the young girl who hovered in the doorway. She had been looking after him ever since her mother, who previously held the position, had fallen ill, and with a father who had disappeared before she was born Lilianne was the sole provider of food and comfort to her mother.

'Come over here, my child,' Villac said softly and motioned her to approach. Lilianne moved towards him but kept her eyes on the floor.

'You have been a very good girl today, Lillianne. The Bishop told me how much he had enjoyed the food you prepared.'

The girl's face lit up with this praise and her simple mind searched for something else to please her priest.

'Would you like to be inside me?' she finally asked, knowing that this was one way she could satisfy him.

The thought of entering Lilianne caused his penis to stiffen and Villac took pleasure in a few moments of heightened anticipation before replying.

'Kneel down,' he instructed, his voice hoarsening with the arousal.

The girl knew what was required and slowly sank to her knees.

Villac swiftly released his penis from the restraints of his shift and slid his hips forwards towards Lilianne's face. The girl carefully encircled the rigid member with the fingers of her left hand and guided the tip between her lips.

The priest groaned at this instant pleasure and tried to maintain the position but he couldn't control the urge that coursed through his groin. He grasped the back of the girl's head with his outstretched hand and pulled her forward, thrusting himself into her mouth. Lilianne choked for a moment as his stiff flesh filled her mouth and touched her throat but she was helpless to move. She managed to relax her breathing and waited for him to finish. She didn't have long to wait, his quickening groans warning her of what was to come. With a few final thrusts he ejaculated into her mouth, still keeping a firm grip on her head. Then she felt him relax and the swollen thing in her mouth began to shrink. The priest fell back onto his bed, lost for a while between the sensation of spent pleasure and the first stirrings of guilt.

Lilianne stayed on her knees and waited for the priest to speak.

Eventually he lifted his head and looked at the girl in the

candle light. Her face betrayed nothing of the act. 'I shall say a special prayer for you and your mother,' he managed to say in his most pious voice. 'You shall both be rewarded in heaven. You may go now,' and he made the sign of the cross over the girl.

Lilianne stood and turned towards the door. Closing it quietly and making sure she was out of earshot she spat out the priest's semen she'd been holding in her mouth. She took a drink of water and wiped the back of her hand across her face. Then she helped herself to the remains of the food that had been left over from the Bishop's lunch.

'This will be a much better reward for us than your prayers,' she thought as she slipped out of the door, making her way home amongst the feast day revellers.

CHAPTER EIGHT

Elouise woke from a deep sleep and for a few moments was disoriented by the unfamiliar surroundings. Her eyes took in the heavy wooden door, the chest of drawers set against the curved wall and the thick rugs on the floor. A shaft of sunlight spread across the foot of the bed, beaming down from the high, narrow window set into the solid limestone wall.

The events of the previous evening began to come back to her. Their late arrival at the chateau, a brief introduction to Guillaume's father who welcomed them warmly, then Elouise and her father being shown to their separate rooms whilst Michel was taken to the servants' quarters.

Elouise got out of the bed, shivering in the cold air as she tiptoed over to the window. She wanted to get a good view of the chateau in daylight but the window was set too high so the only sight she had was of blue sky and passing clouds. She scampered back to the warmth and comfort of the bed and lay there thinking.

One thing was for sure; she had never spent a night in a chateau before. She was more used to the simple accommodation she had shared with her father on their travels. Often it was a shepherds hut, like the one Michel had taken them to the first time she had met him. Sometimes it was in a village in the home of friendly believers, like the Borrel's, but more than once she and her father had been happy to settle down on a warm summer's night in a dry hollow with nothing but a million stars for a roof.

Since the day her grandmother had died and Jean had taken her on his journey they had hardly ever been separated. She remembered when she was little how she walked with her father, sometimes in front of him, sometimes behind, but usually side-by-side holding his hand. She didn't say much but took everything in with her serious blue eyes. She would listen while he told her all about the sights and places they visited and then tried to answer the flood of questions she asked every day. He was amazed at her inquisitiveness and smiled with encouragement as she struggled to express her increasing thirst for knowledge. She was like a sponge, soaking up every scrap of information. 'Papa' she would say, 'Why is that sheep white and that one black?' Or, 'Where does the rain come from?' and Jean would try to find a simple way to explain to an eight year old the concept of parental inheritance or the idea of evaporation.

At first Elouise had no idea why they were wandering throughout the region. But she remembered clearly the long months she had spent waiting for her father's infrequent visits home, so she was perfectly content to be spending each day by his side now.

She knew that her father spent a lot of his time talking to people and she could sense that these people seemed to feel secure listening to his calming voice. To begin with she didn't understand what he was telling them but she knew that the words 'god', 'heaven', and 'salvation' seemed to be spoken just as much as 'pure' 'kind' and 'good'. The people her father spoke to were often surprised he had a young child with him but they soon got used to her being there and, when they happened to meet the same people again, they would make a fuss of her, treating her like one of their own, like a special daughter. The fact that he had a young child to care for seemed, if anything, to enhance Jean's standing with those who sought his advice.

By the time Elouise reached her tenth birthday she had a

clearer idea of her father's vocation. He hadn't attempted to explain to her the differences between his Cathar beliefs and those of the Church of Rome but she understood enough to know that there were people who needed his guidance when it concerned their spirit and soul. She began to realise that his was an alternative religion, one that spoke to its followers in their own language and which seemed to have a more relevant place in their everyday lives. She absorbed what he had to say to those who sought him out, probably more than he realised, and saw with her own eyes the simple gratitude with which they received his words of encouragement. Above all she saw the respect in which he was held and the humble way in which he accepted their respect. If she had needed to put it into words she would have said that people loved her father, but in a different way to her own love for him.

Jean himself was sometimes concerned at the seriousness of his young daughter and he was always pleased, even relieved, to see that she could also laugh and play. Usually this happened when they were in the company of the shepherds. From the day her father had introduced her to Michel, Elouise had loved the times she spent with him and the other shepherds. Many of them were barely older than her and became like brothers to her. They taught her many things. How to read the clouds and the wind, how to find her way in a mountain mist, how to recognise the berries that she could eat, how to help a ewe give birth, how to whistle and how to spit. In return she would teach them how to mend a tear in their clothes, how to clean and bandage a wound and how to say a simple prayer to keep them safe. She loved it when they spent nights in the huts out in the hills. The shepherds, men and boys, had an unswerving devotion to Jean and they would always kneel and ask for his blessing before they shared their food, the evenings drifting on into gentle songs, soft laughter and quiet memories.

Just before her fourteenth birthday Jean told Elouise that he needed to travel north. His former tutors required his presence and he couldn't be certain how long he'd be away. He explained gently that he couldn't take her with him this time but he had arranged for her to stay with one of the women *croyantes* they knew, Madame Cassignol in the village of Belcaire. Elouise knew Clementine Cassignol very well, she had seen her in the market square selling her potions and remedies and had asked endless questions about her craft. She also knew she had a daughter, Eugenie, about her own age, so she was not unduly worried when Jean said his goodbyes, although she knew she was going to miss him; it would be the first time they had been apart in nine years.

As it turned out it was a fortunate time for Elouise to be in the company of another girl. One morning, not long after Jean had departed, Elouise woke up to find a trickle of blood between her legs. At first worried, then embarrassed, it was Eugenie, taking the role of older sister, who told Elouise that this was normal for all young women and that she could expect it to happen every month from now on. There was a natural understanding that from the moment a girl began her monthly flow she was also capable of bearing a child. Eugenie informed Elouise that this was all part of the process of becoming a young woman, along with her budding breasts and rounder hips. They both agreed it was unfair that boys didn't have to go through this part of growing up, but they giggled when they realised they would never have to spend time shaving either.

During the time she stayed in the Cassignol home Elouise spent many days following Clementine as she collected her supply of roots and leaves. 'See these,' said Clementine, pointing to a bunch of juniper and rosemary, 'If you mix them with some nettles you can make a potion to overcome fatigue. And this one,' she said, holding up a root of bindweed 'if you press this into a wound it will stop bleeding.'

'And what about these?' asked Elouise one day as she watched Clementine boiling up some peach leaves.

'They'll be good for overcoming morning sickness if you're with child.' She continued the lesson, showing Elouise the peel of an orange and lemon. 'If we mix these with a little dried mint and some rosewater it will make a lovely sweet perfume. We'll make some together if you like.' Elouise became a most willing helper and before long was able to make potions of her own to sell alongside Clementine's in the market place. She was very proud of her new skills and couldn't wait to surprise her father.

As it turned out it would be another nine months before they saw each other again. Elouise had missed Jean every day he was away, but she was always grateful for the time she had spent with Eugenie and her mother and when the time came to leave she promised, amongst many tears, to visit them as often as possible.

Watching the sunlight making its way across the bedroom Elouise's mind settled on the day of her sixteenth birthday. Her father had decided to give her the silver necklace that had once graced the throat of his beloved Blanche. As she pulled her hair up and he fastened the necklace around his daughter's neck Jean hadn't been to able prevent a tear falling onto her bare shoulder. She'd felt the wetness on her skin and asked quietly 'Why are you crying Papa, are you thinking of her?'

'Forgive me, Elouise', he'd replied. 'I shouldn't be shedding tears on your birthday.' Elouise had turned and given her father a big hug. 'It's beautiful, thank you,' she said, stroking the heart shaped pendant. As he looked at his daughter Jean couldn't help but be amazed at the resemblance to her mother. The dark hair, her blue, almost purple eyes, the clear softness of her skin, even the shape of her body, all served to remind him of the woman he had lost. He'd held his daughter tightly and closed his eyes, and for a few moments felt as if he was back with Blanche in the short life they had shared together in Foix.

Elouise folded her arms behind her head and let her gaze drift up to the wooden beams in the ceiling. Here she was at eighteen years of age, a young woman with her life ahead of her. She began to tick off in her mind the things she thought she could offer the world. To begin with, thanks to her father, she could read and write. This in itself made her unusual, for very few young women were given this opportunity unless they were of noble birth or destined for a life in the confines of an abbey. Added to this she had a quick, intelligent mind that she had used to understand not just how practical things worked but also how people behaved. She learnt quickly and had a mine of information filed away in her head. During their countless visits to dozens of villages she had often wandered from her father and found herself listening to the conversation of other people, usually groups of women.

Once they began to recognise her they included her in their discussions and shared their gossip with her. It was in this way that Elouise learnt about the myths and superstitions that ruled the lives of so many people. With her rational mind she would try to interpret the real reasons behind these beliefs but they were usually too deeply ingrained for people to change their minds. But she had learnt a lot about remedies and recipes too. She knew now which plants might help cure ailments of the body and the mind, as well as being shown how to cook the crispiest roast potatoes and the tastiest rabbit pie. She had grown to love and respect these women whose lives might seem to be full of gossip and old wives tales but who were often the strongest member of their families.

As she grew older and her body began to change Elouise had

to put up with a lot of teasing from her friends amongst the village women. They always wanted to know when was she going to get married and have children, and were forever putting forward the names of suitable candidates who might make a good husband or, much to her embarrassment and their laughter, a rampant lover. The truth was that this was one area of her life where Elouise had little experience. She knew of course where babies came from. She'd seen plenty of lambs being borne and heard enough tales of child birth to know about the physical role that women had to play in the bearing of children. But as far as the act of sex itself was concerned she was quite innocent. She was aware of the looks she received from some of the men in the market, but for the most part she was considered to be more of a tomboy, something her rough clothes did little to disguise.

Until now there had only ever been two men in her life. Her father, who had been her guide and mentor and whom she loved as a daughter, and Michel, her childhood friend and companion whom she loved as a brother. Now Guillaume had come into her life and she was confused. Of course he was handsome, any girl could see that, but it was the expression in his eyes when he looked at her and the sound of his voice when he spoke to her that caused these different feelings to emerge, feelings that she hadn't experienced before. She realised she knew nothing about him, which should have put her on her guard, but she couldn't deny the tingle of excitement she felt at the anticipation of seeing him again.

A knock at the door prevented her thoughts about Guillaume from wandering further. A second knock was followed by the door slowly opening. A young woman, not much older than Elouise, entered carrying a bowl and pitcher of water with a large cloth folded over her arm.

'Good morning, Miss' the girl said and placed the bowl and the water on top of the chest of drawers.

'Good morning to you,' replied Elouise 'and you don't have to call me Miss, my name is Elouise. What's yours?'

'Annie,' the girl replied 'Annie Bouichet. I was told to come and wake you.'

'And what do you do here, Annie?' asked Elouise.

'I make the beds and help Lady Helene to get dressed, Miss' replied the girl, struggling to call Elouise by her name.

'Well you certainly won't need to help me get dressed, Annie,' laughed Elouise. 'The clothes I arrived in are just about the only ones I possess,' and she saw a smile start to form on Annie's serious face.

'Will you be coming down for breakfast?' continued the girl.

'Do you think I should, Annie'?

'Well everyone will be there so perhaps you should,' replied Annie, who wasn't used to being asked all these questions, being more accustomed to being told what to do.

'Well in that case I'd better do as you suggest,' agreed Elouise and swung her legs out of the bed.

'Would you like me to dry you after your wash?' asked Annie, now desperately trying to avoid saying 'Miss' or 'Elouise.'

'No, I think I can manage that for myself thank you, Annie. What else do you have to do?'

'Well I'd better go and see if my Lady needs any help,' replied the girl, and for the first time she looked directly at Elouise and they both exchanged a knowing smile.

Annie closed the door behind her and Elouise quickly finished getting washed and dressed before stepping through the doorway herself.

She found her way along a stone corridor then came to an open stairway that descended into a large hall with curved walls. As she took the first steps down she stopped to take in the scene below. A large wooden table at which a number of people were already breakfasting dominated the room. She recognised the

Count seated next to a woman, whom she took to be his wife. She saw her father, looking a little uncomfortable and next to him was Guillaume. Across the table she noted the Bishop and Bruno and then two or three other people she didn't know. At one end of the room a fire blazed in a large hearth, the wide chimney disappearing into the ceiling above. The walls of the room were hung with various tapestries and three heavy iron candelabras hung from the ceiling. Two large, black hunting dogs padded round the room, occasionally nudging up to someone's lap hoping for a morsel of food.

Elouise took another two steps down until the movement of her entrance was noticed. The sound of talking stopped and heads turned in her direction. There was a moment's awkward silence before the Count stood up from the table.

'Come my dear, come and join us,' he motioned with his arm, 'you must be hungry. Come and sit next to your father.' The other men in the room stood up as Elouise descended the remaining steps and crossed the floor. The Count sat down and continued his discussion with the man seated to his left whilst the Countess turned and gave Elouise a warm, friendly smile. Elouise was grateful to be close to her father and sought out his hand for comfort and reassurance.

'Did you sleep well?' asked Jean, squeezing her hand as she had hoped for.

'It was strange not to be near you Papa but, yes, I did sleep well. After the day we had yesterday I was really tired. Who are all these people?' A servant placing a dish in front of her that held an assortment of cold meats and a large chunk of fresh bread interrupted her question. 'Thank you,' said Elouise politely. She'd noticed a large bowl of fruit in front of her and picked out an apricot instead.

'Well you've met the Count and you already know Guillaume and his cousin and the Bishop of course. The lady sitting next to the Count is his wife, the Countess Sybille, and the man on his left is one of his neighbours, Henri de Peyrolles. The man sitting opposite is the Count's steward, Pierre Biscaye'. Elouise took a bite on her fruit and looked around the room as she absorbed this information. Her eyes travelled to Guillaume who was sitting next to his mother and she noticed how his speech seemed to dry up in mid sentence as he saw her looking at him. He returned her look with a broad smile and mouthed a 'good morning' to her before returning his attention to his mother.

Elouise tugged at her father's sleeve. 'I hope Michel is alright. I didn't like the way we were separated last night.'

'Don't you worry about him, Lou-Lou,' replied Jean. 'If I know Michel he'll have charmed the kitchen into serving him a breakfast fit for a king this morning. That boy only has to play a tune and people are like soft dough in his hands. I only wish I had half his talents!' They both smiled at this image of Michel. Elouise decided she was hungry after all and began to tuck into the plate of food in front of her. Jean had managed to avoid the cold meats and instead had satisfied his modest appetite with some fruit and goat's cheese.

Servants came and went, bringing more food and carrying away empty plates while the two dogs continued their circuit of the table, seeking out tid-bits and any crumb that dropped to the floor.

The Count looked around the table. 'Guillaume,' he began, 'Your mother needs to discuss her requirements with the good tailor Jean and I need to talk to the Bishop with Pierre and Henri. Why don't you give this young lady a tour of the castle? I'm sure she'd find that interesting'.

'Am I too late for breakfast?' The enquiring voice came from the top of the stairs.

'Ah, daughter of mine,' sighed the Count as he looked up at Helene. 'You look lovely as always, but yes our meal is over.

Perhaps you should try eating first and getting ready for the day afterwards.'

Helene's perfect face flushed with annoyance at being teased in front of people she hardly knew, but she continued her graceful descent into the room. 'Perhaps if Annie had woken me sooner I wouldn't be so late,' she retaliated, sending a fierce glance in the direction of Elouise.

The Count stepped in to smooth this unladylike display of temper from his daughter. 'Look,' he said, revealing a plate behind him, 'I've saved you something to eat. I know what a late riser you are. Come here and give your father a good morning kiss.' Helene did as she was instructed, a faint smile of victory on her lips, and sat down to eat, taking a few mouthfuls herself then feeding large helpings to the dogs who rapidly devoured the unexpected bonus.

'So, which part of the chateau would you like to see first?' said Guillaume as he approached Elouise. He gave her a warm, open smile and looked genuinely pleased to have this opportunity to show her his home. 'We could start at the top and work our way down if you like.'

'That sounds fine,' replied Elouise 'but first I must speak to my father.'

'Of course,' said Guillaume, 'I'll wait by the door.' Elouise walked across the room to where her father stood waiting for the Countess to finish talking to one of the maids.

'Will you be alright, father? Do you need me to help you? I won't go if you need me.'

'Don't you worry about me, Lou-Lou' replied Jean, smiling at his daughter. 'I'm sure I can still manage to cut and sew by myself. Look, I've got my scissors and needles with me already,' and he patted the leather bag at his side. 'I want you to enjoy your tour of the chateau with Guillaume. Go on, he's waiting for you.' Jean gave his daughter a kiss on each cheek then gently turned her shoulders and gave her the slightest push in the direction of Guillaume, like sending a toy boat across a pond. Elouise smiled and almost ran across the room to where Guillaume held the door open and they stepped out into the sunshine together.

'They look well together, your daughter and my son. She's a very beautiful girl.' The Countess had turned to speak to Jean. 'Now that I've seen her for myself I can understand why he seems to have been in a trance these past few days.'

Jean stopped rummaging through his bag and looked directly into the eyes of the Countess. 'Thank you, my Lady. She looks exactly like her mother.' It was all he needed to say.

A moment or two passed before the Countess spoke again. 'Come Jean, there's a lot of work to do and we have much to talk about.' She placed her hand under the Good Man's elbow and gently steered him in the direction of her own chambers.

Guillaume led Elouise towards the base of one of the circular towers set at intervals around the walls of the chateau. Inside the tower they climbed steep steps that spiralled upwards until they emerged into the daylight through a small doorway that led out onto the ramparts. From here Elouise could look down at all the buildings that were enclosed within the chateau's walls. People and animals mingled together within the vast courtyard and smoke rose from several chimneys. The whole area was a hive of activity; it was if a complete village existed within the walls unknown to the outside world.

'I didn't realise there'd be so many people,' she exclaimed 'What do they all do? Do they all live here?'

Guillaume stood just behind Elouise so that his outstretched arm followed her line of vision. He pointed to his far left to a row of low buildings, 'Over there are the stables for our horses, and next to the stables are the hay barns, then there is the armoury and next to that is the blacksmith. See where the smoke from his fire is?' Elouise nodded but didn't speak. Guillaume continued, moving his arm in front of her. 'Over by the far wall is the vegetable garden and next to that are the sheep and pig pens, and the barn next to them is for the cattle.' Pointing again, he continued. 'That's where the kitchen and ovens are and then there are rooms for the workers who live at the chateau. The other people come up from the village every day. Now along this side,' he moved his arm to the right, 'are the knights' quarters. There are usually about twelve of us in there.'

'Is that where you sleep?' asked Elouise, staring down at the roof. 'Sometimes. And sometimes I sleep in my room in the Keep. It's next to the one you slept in last night.' Elouise's eyes had been following Guillaume's arm as he described an arc around the chateau so that now her face was turned towards him. They looked at each other without speaking, the wind blowing over the castle walls spreading Elouise's hair across her face so that her eyes appeared and disappeared.

Guillaume bent his head towards her, concentrating on the exact place on her lips he wanted to kiss. Elouise kept looking into his eyes as his mouth came closer then, just as she felt his breath on the bridge of her nose, she turned her head and pushed him away. She took a few steps along the rampart and stood with her back to him. Guillaume paused for a moment before moving towards her. He put his hand up to touch her shoulder then stopped before he could complete the gesture. 'I'm sorry,' he began, 'I didn't mean to offend you. I just wanted...' His voice trailed off.

'You didn't offend me,' replied Elouise, still facing away from him 'I'm just not used to that sort of thing.' A silence hung between them but then she slowly turned to face him and he was relieved to see a warm smile that said she wasn't angry. 'So, what about the rest of this chateau of yours? What's that down there?'

Elouise pointed to a low stone structure with a domed roof that adjoined the wall of the keep.

'Apart from these thick walls that is one of the most vital buildings of the entire chateau,' he replied.

'What is it?'

'It's the cistern. It's where we keep our water. We're too high up on the Roc to sink a well so we have to rely on the rainwater we collect from the roofs; that and any supplies we can haul up from the village. See that wagon?' He pointed to a large cart that had just entered through the main gates, two oxen straining under the heavy load of large barrels. 'We have to send that down to the village every day during the summer months. We try to keep enough water in the cistern to last three weeks, maybe longer if we're careful.' The seriousness in his voice indicated to Elouise what a precious commodity water must be to the occupants of the chateau.

'Come on,' said Guillaume, as if to lighten the mood 'We make all our visitors walk around the ramparts at least once during their stay. It's the best way to appreciate the view.' He laughed and led her gently by the arm as they began a circuit of the great stone walls that seemed to rise out of the solid rock below. They passed the narrow slits set at intervals into the wall, just wide enough to allow two bowmen to shoot at opposite angles. Elouise peered out as the landscape unfolded. It was easy to see why the chateau had been built on this particular rocky outcrop. It would be impossible to approach the chateau from any direction without being seen from a considerable distance. To the north and east the land spread out beneath the high Roc, exposing chunks of bare white rock that perforated the sparse grazing land. To the west the eye could follow the length of the valley as it meandered into the distance in the direction of Quillan. To the south three ranges of heavily wooded hills folded upwards, each one higher than the one in front, providing a natural protection from both enemy and weather. And in the far distance, as she shielded her eyes from the bright sunlight, Elouise could make out the snow capped peaks of the massive Pyrenean range that seemed to stretch from one end of the horizon to the other.

As they made their way along the ramparts, stepping through each of the six towers that stood guard over the entire length of the wall, Elouise allowed Guillaume to take her hand as he continued to talk.

'The chateau was built on the ruins of a Visigoth castle and centuries before that a Roman fort stood on the Roc. We were under the protection of the lords of Carcassonne so my family prospered in the peaceful times but we shared in their battles too.' Guillaume stared at the floor and tightened his grip on her hand. Some of this recent history Elouise had learnt from her father but she let him continue without interrupting. 'When my uncle was murdered by de Montfort's men my father was forced to hide in the hills. He waited until the invaders had retreated and a kind of nervous peace returned to the region. Then the de Quillan family went back to the chateau. Now we are obliged to perform a balancing act; trying to preserve the freedom of the people who look to us for protection whilst living with the restrictions of the treaties we have been forced to sign with the Roman church and a distant king.' He shrugged, 'it's for those reasons that my father is obliged to entertain the Bishop.'

The serious way in which Guillaume explained the past and the present impressed Elouise deeply. Up till now she'd thought of him as an attractive young man without too many worries, but now she saw a more determined side and it gave her a stronger sense of wanting to be with him.

They had completed their circuit of the wall and now stood side by side on the ramparts looking out at the village below, where daily life was slowly returning to normal after the excitement of the feast day. They stayed silent for several moments, sharing the same view but pondering their own thoughts. Guillaume was first to break the silence.

'Right, that's enough history for one day,' he said, recapturing his happier self. 'Now I'm going to take you riding in the forest. We'll find a quiet spot and you can tell me all about yourself.'

Elouise thought he said all this with such conviction she decided this would not be the moment to tell him she was completely terrified at the idea of getting on a horse.

CHAPTER NINE

Jean and Sybille sat together in her dressing chamber surrounded by cloth of various lengths and colour. They had already decided on the material for a dress and now they were choosing the best cloth to make a new riding cloak. Jean selected a heavy wool that would keep her warm and give some protection from the wind and rain.

'I think this would be best for you,' Jean began 'It's good quality and should last you well.'

'Does it have to be so dull, Jean? said Sybille, disappointment in her voice.

Jean thought for a while.' Well, I could embroider a design onto it. Or perhaps there's a favourite bird or an animal you would like?'

Sybille smiled. 'I don't think I want any animals on my cloak, thank you. Maybe you could design a shape for me, something symbolic, or perhaps a flower. I'll leave it to your good judgement.'

He continued with his measurements and began to mark out where he needed to cut the cloth.

'So tell me, Jean, what news do you bring from your travels?' asked Sybille. 'What prospects do those of us with our faith have of being allowed to pray and worship as we choose?'

Jean paused and looked across at the Countess. 'Ah, Sybille,' he began, he knew he could address her as a friend in the privacy of her own chamber, 'these are difficult times for us *croyants*.

Our number has already diminished in the towns. The Dominicans are finding it easy to pursue their quarry and there are always those ready to save their own skin by accusing someone else. Some believers have gone back to their families in their villages but even there they are not always safe from the local priest. We are being pushed further back into the hills; at least here we will be harder to find.'

'Are you afraid, Jean?'

'For myself, no. I'm not afraid to die. I look forward to the day I can leave this earthly Hell and let my spirit rise to Heaven. But there are still those who seek salvation and I shall continue to help them wherever I can.'

'And what about your daughter?' continued Sybille, gently.

Jean's face softened. 'As a father my natural wish is for her to be happy with her life. As her *Parfait* I will continue to guide her on our path,' he replied. 'Elouise is a strong young woman with her own mind. I'm sure she will make the right choices as and when the time comes.'

They both remained silent for a while.

'And what about you and the Count?' asked Jean, resuming his measuring. Sybille thought for a while before replying.

'We live from day to day, we do not have great ambitions. In private we try and lead a simple life and set a good example to our children and the people who live here in the chateau.'

'And in public?' asked Jean.

Sybille smoothed out the material spread across her lap, a resigned look on her face.

'We compromise,' she replied. 'Armand must keep the peace with those who rule our borders so that people can sleep safely. And then we must pay certain taxes to the Bishop so that those of us who are not impressed with the teachings of Rome might be left alone. But it's not easy, Jean. Already I see evidence of the effect of the Dominicans in the village. People are beginning to look with suspicion at their neighbours. I've already seen some poor souls wearing the yellow cross of repentance. It won't be long before the authorities decide to make an example of someone.'

Jean didn't say anything but continued with his task, aware that the Countess had more to say. After a few moments she continued.

'You must be careful yourself, Jean. The Bishop has already been asking questions about you, and it won't be long before that fornicating lapdog of a village priest gives him the answers he's looking for.'

Her bluntness didn't surprise him. 'Then in that case, my Lady,' said Jean, standing up and looking directly at her, 'it is you and the Count who should be careful, not I.'

Sybille looked into his eyes and then, on an impulse, knelt in front of Jean. 'Bless me, please,' she said quietly 'It's been such a long time since we have had a *Parfait* at the chateau.' Jean placed his right hand gently on top of her head. 'I bless your soul, Sybille, and the souls of all your family. May you live in peaceful times.'

Sybille stood again, a contented look on her face.

'Come,' she said, 'It's a beautiful day. Let's go for a walk, I'll show you my herb garden. You can tell me if you think my plants are doing well.' She smiled at Jean and led him towards the doorway of her chamber.

CHAPTER TEN

The horse was tethered loosely to a branch and grazed on a patch of fresh grass, occasionally lifting a foot and swishing its tail to keep the insects at bay. Earlier at the stables Elouise had to confess to her fear of horses. To his credit Guillaume hadn't laughed as she thought he might. Instead he had been most concerned and apologised for his assumption that she could ride. He had suggested they go for a walk instead but she didn't want to spoil his idea so he had asked if she would be prepared to ride behind him, an offer she was grateful to accept.

After they had found a quiet place amongst the trees Elouise spent a long time answering all of Guillaume's questions about her life with her father and Michel. Now the pair sat silently together in the shade of a willow tree on the riverbank, listening to the sounds of the forest all around them. Guillaume tossed a small piece of bark into the river and watched it float away on the current.

'What will you do now? Where will you go next?' he asked, leaning back on his elbows and turning his head so that he could see her profile.

Elouise kept looking ahead and it was a while before she answered.

'I don't know,' she said eventually. 'I suppose I'll stay with my father. He's not getting any younger; I think he needs me now. Besides he's taught me so much. I've been following in his footsteps all my life.' She paused, as if she was coming to a decision. 'Maybe it's time I followed the same path too.'

'You mean you'd become a *Parfait*?' Guillaume made it sound as if this would be a dangerous step to take. Now it was Elouise's turn to face him.

'Maybe,' she said. 'I have the same beliefs, I've seen how people turn to him for comfort and strength. I've travelled enough to know there are still many people who trust him with their souls.'

'Wouldn't that require a lot of courage, especially for a woman?'

Elouise allowed a smile to lighten her serious face. 'Despite my lack of courage when it comes to horses I'm not afraid to die for what I believe in. When my soul leaves this body it doesn't matter to God whether I'm a man or a woman. We are equal spirits in his eyes.'

Elouise could see that this discussion was giving him some cause for concern so she decided to change the subject.

'Anyway, what about you? What's in your future? Isn't it about time you were married?' She turned her head away from him and lay on her back and waited for his reply, watching the sun sparkling between the leaves above her head. Guillaume gathered his thoughts for a while, relieved that she hadn't seen him blush at her last question.

'Well,' he began, 'I expect I'll stay at the chateau. I've been trained to fight as a knight but I hope we'll have peace for long enough for me to take over the estate from my father when the time comes. But if we are threatened again I'll go and fight, of course.'

'So you not afraid to die for what you believe in either?'

Guillaume paused, his thoughts drifting off to a time a year ago when he was with his father and four other knights travelling south to cross the mountains into Catalonia. They'd been ambushed one morning by a gang of drunken thugs, anxious for weapons and gold. The fight had been short but brutal. Only three of the gang survived to escape back into the hills, but two of the knights had given their lives too. Guillaume had witnessed combat at close quarters and knew there was nothing gallant in death, only pain and suffering. He looked up, clearing his mind of the image.

'No, I'm not afraid to die, although I'm not sure if it would be for a belief or out of a sense of duty.'

'That's a good answer,' replied Elouise, admiring his honesty.

'And what about the marrying part?' she knew she was teasing him a little. 'You must be a very eligible young man, what with your title and your lands.'

Guillaume laughed. 'I think my sister is likely to attract a better suitor than me. Our lands are much diminished now; we are not a wealthy family, but I'm sure my parents would be delighted if I was to get married and raise a family.'

'So what's stopping you?'

This time he answered without laughing. 'Maybe I'm not ready yet; or perhaps I haven't found the right girl.' His answer floated in the air between them and neither of them spoke. He glanced across at her lying on the grass and again was overwhelmed by her beauty. He wanted to kiss her but was afraid to make the same mistake he'd made earlier in the day.

'Come on' he said, and began to stand up 'We should be getting back.'

'Yes, of course,' said Elouise, sounding a little sorry. She'd been wondering whether he would try and kiss her again and thinking that maybe this time she would let him.

Guillaume mounted the horse and held out his hand to lift her up behind him. 'Comfortable? Not nervous this time?' he asked his passenger. Elouise didn't reply but instead of gripping Guillaume's tunic as she had done on their ride to the forest, she gently slid her arms around his body and lent against his back, her head resting on his shoulder. As he steered the horse at a gentle pace back to the chateau Guillaume smiled as an image of himself as her protector formed in his mind.

CHAPTER ELEVEN

They found Jean in the herb garden. 'There you are,' he said, standing up and wiping his brow with the back of his hand. 'What have you two been up to?' Like typical young people when asked the same question they looked at each other then both replied in unison,

'Nothing.'

Jean smiled at the pair of them and noticed, not for the first time, how happy his young daughter seemed to be in the company of Guillaume.

'What are you doing here anyway?' asked Elouise, trying to divert the attention away from herself. 'Don't we have a lot of clothes to make? Have you seen Michel?' she added.

'Well, this young man's mother wanted to show me her herb garden and then she asked me for some advice about the plants. So I've spent a very pleasant afternoon just pottering about. It's been very peaceful, very relaxing'. Jean slowly brushed the soil from his hands.'But you're right, we do have a lot of work to do so I hope you're going to help me. As for Michel, I saw him a little while ago. He asked after you and said he was trying to compose something new.'

Guillaume turned to Elouise.

'I should go and find my father, I'll see you both tonight at dinner.' He smiled at her and then bowed in the direction of Jean. They watched him as he strode off towards the Keep, then Jean took his daughter's hand. He knew it was forbidden for a

Parfait to touch a woman but he felt that on this occasion God would forgive him for a gesture that would have come naturally to any father.

'Come on,' he said, as led her out of the garden towards the Countess's chamber, 'I hope your fingers are feeling nimble. We've got a lot of stitching to do.'

Jean and Elouise surveyed the lengths of fabric that were still spread out on the floor and across the chair. 'How long do you think we'll be here?' asked Elouise, as she tried to estimate how much work there was to be done. Jean began to gather up the pieces of cloth he had already cut for the cloak.

'Well, let me see. We have at least one dress and one cloak to make. That's before we start on anything for the Count, or his daughter if it comes to that. I'd say we'd be here for ten or twelve days at least. It will make a change for us not to be travelling all the time.'

Elouise mulled over this information for a while. 'Do you think we'll be safe here, Papa?'

'I can't think of anywhere safer,' replied Jean. 'You've seen the thickness of the chateau's walls; and Guillaume looks like he has some strong arms too. I think we'll both be very well protected.'

Elouise knew when her father was teasing her and smiled. 'Very well,' she said, picking up the folded roll of needles, 'where would you like me to start?'

On their second evening at the chateau Jean and Elouise were invited to eat with the Count and his wife. Also seated at the heavy oak table was their daughter Helene, Pierre Biscaye, the Count's steward and the Bishop. Elouise already knew that Guillaume would not be there. He'd told her earlier that he would be dining in the Knight's quarters. Although it was still early in the evening very little light penetrated the small windows. The room was lit by the flickering flames of the flares that sat in metal sconces fixed around the walls, sending shadows that leapt erratically around the great room. A low fire burnt in the fireplace, in front of which the Count's two hounds now slumbered, their black chins resting on the hearth. When the servants had finished bringing in the dishes of food and flagons of wine the polite conversation petered out and the Bishop stood up.

'Perhaps you will allow me to bless this meal?' he addressed the head of the table.

'By all means' replied the Count, motioning with his hand and rising to his feet, 'we are honoured to have you with us.'

The others at the table followed suit and stood up. Elouise began to feel nervous, never having been this close to a Bishop's blessing before, but she sensed her father standing calmly beside her. Everyone lowered their head as the Bishop closed his eyes and began to intone in Latin an unnecessarily elaborate prayer, but one that he felt was appropriate to his rank in front of this, to his mind, rather rural audience. Jean blocked out the drone of the Bishop's voice by reciting to himself the only prayer he ever spoke, the Lord's Prayer. By the time he got to the end it coincided with the end of the Bishop's offering and they both mouthed 'Amen' in unison. If the Bishop had opened his eyes whilst he was making his sign of the cross over the table he would have noticed that neither Jean, Elouise nor the Countess had crossed themselves, unlike the others who made the gesture out of politeness.

Everyone began to help themselves from the generous array of dishes while one of the servants circulated the table with a flagon of wine.

Elouise found herself making conversation with Helene. Her first impressions of Guillaume's sister had led her to think she was rather stuck up but as their conversation progressed she began to realise that Helene's aloofness was really a disguise for her shyness. Although they were similar in age Elouise could see that, despite her privileged position, Helene had very little experience of the real world. She found herself pressed for information about life in other villages and towns and soon began to feel a little sorry for this cloistered young woman whose destiny seemed to lie between entry into a suitably convenient marriage or admission to an appropriate convent. For her part Helene began to realise there was a lot more to Elouise than being the daughter of a rather unusual tailor. Although Helene was close to her mother, perhaps here was a young woman with whom she could share her hopes and fears, and maybe some of her secrets too. Soon they were laughing together as they compared experiences, Elouise promising to bring some new ideas to Helene's wardrobe in return for Helene's help in overcoming her fear of horses.

Meanwhile Sybille and Jean had been in deep conversation. She always found it a comfort to talk to him, his measured tone and thoughtful responses to her questions a welcome contrast to the bluff and bluster she had grown used to from the menfolk around her. Armand, she knew, in his most tender moments could still make her feel loved and desired, but in the main she suffered like most women the blight of being talked at rather than talked to. From time to time she glanced over Jean's shoulder and was amused to see her daughter and Elouise in such animated conversation. 'It seems to me this young lady is having an interesting effect on both my children,' she thought to herself and smiled.

'Why the smile?' asked Jean 'Did I say something to amuse you?'

'No, Jean, I'm sorry. I was just thinking that first of all your daughter seems to have captivated my son and now she seems to be having a similar effect on my daughter. You do seem to have raised a remarkable young woman.'

Jean looked around at Elouise and Helene, their heads tilted towards each other as their conversation increased in speed and their hands waved in the air to emphasise their words.

He turned back to Sybille. 'She's a very special girl; it does me good to see her making friends with someone her own age. Goodness knows she spends enough time with her old father.'

'Nonsense, Jean,' replied Sybille 'she loves you, that's easy to see. But look at her, she's a woman now, with strong opinions of her own, I'm sure. One day she's going to want make choices for herself.'

Jean looked at Sybille and for a moment a look of sadness entered his eyes. 'I know, dear Lady,' he said softly. 'I'm absolutely certain of that.'

Sybille said nothing but gave Jean's arm a gentle squeeze to reassure him that she understood his concern.

Across the table Pierre and the Bishop had been in discussion with the Count. Jean hadn't been paying much attention to them but from the few words he'd heard he could tell they were chewing over some familiar topics, such as land and tithes. As usual there had been conjecture about what was happening in Toulouse and Paris and the Bishop had taken it upon himself to interpret what he understood to be the latest news from Rome, a place he had only ever been invited to once.

A lull in the conversation allowed the Bishop to steer his next remarks towards Jean. He wiped the grease from his chin with a napkin; it was the first time he had addressed Jean directly.

'So, Jean de Rhedones, you seem to be a very well thought of tailor. Do you have any other nobles amongst your customers?' He said this with a slight smirk on his face as he manoeuvred a toothpick into his mouth and began to poke at his teeth.

'I have many people who need me,' replied Jean. 'Noble or peasant, the work is very similar.'

'And do you travel far?' continued the Bishop, dislodging a fibre of meat and sucking it off his toothpick.

'In my work I have to go wherever people gather. I could not afford to wait for people to come to me.' Jean kept his voice at a pleasant level, realising that the Bishop must have his suspicions about him and could be trying to lay a trap. Whilst he would have welcomed the opportunity to embark on a theological debate he had no desire to do so whilst they both shared the hospitality of the Count. That would not only be impolite it would have put the Count in the impossible position of being an adjudicator.

'Have you ever been to Pamiers?' asked the Bishop, making it sound as if a visit to the seat of his bishopric was the equal of a visit to Rome.

'Only once,' replied Jean. 'I was born in Foix; I know my father took me there but I don't remember much about it, I was quite young at the time.'

'Well I've heard there's a shortage of tailors in the town now. Why do you suppose that is?' Now the Bishop's gaze was completely focussed on Jean, his voice conveying a hint of a challenge.

'Perhaps there's no longer enough work to go around. A good man can only ply his trade if there are enough people willing to trust him.' Jean tried to keep a lightness in his voice but he wanted to let the Bishop know he wasn't afraid to stand up to him or his rank. 'Maybe I should come to Pamiers again to see for myself?'

'The sooner the better for all of us,' answered the Bishop, a trace of menace in his voice as he brought the discussion to an end.

While Jean and the Bishop had been talking the conversation around the table had dwindled to a halt. The Count was quick to appreciate that the two men were in danger of locking horns and swiftly moved to change the subject.

'My dear lord Bishop, my dear tailor, everyone. You must

try some of this wonderful summer berry pudding,' he motioned to the large dish that had just been placed on the table. 'It's my cook's speciality and I can assure you it is delicious. Bishop, can I tempt you?' he said this with a friendly smile knowing that the man found it hard to resist food of any kind.

'Temptation is a sin, your Lordship, as you well know. But I believe on this occasion I can forgive myself. Besides,' said the Bishop, attempting to say something witty, 'it would be rude of me to turn down the fruits of your cook's labours.' The others laughed politely at his weak attempt at humour, except Elouise who turned to her father and pretended to vomit.

The remainder of the evening finished pleasantly enough. The flares on the wall grew dimmer, the servants gathered up the dishes and drinking vessels, and the two dogs began their circuit of the table looking for scraps. The Count cleared his throat and addressed the Bishop, although this time more formally.

'My lord Bishop, it has been an honour for us to have you staying here at the chateau. I know you are keen to get back to your abbey at Pamiers so I have arranged for one of my knights to escort you in the morning. Bruno will see to it that you arrive at your destination safely.'

The Bishop rose to his feet. 'I thank the Comte de Quillan and the Countess for their most gracious hospitality and for the offer of an escort. It has been a most interesting visit. May the Lord be with you all.' He made a loose sign of the cross in the vague direction of the table, lifted the hem of his robe then turned to leave the great hall.

CHAPTER TWELVE

Days at the chateau continued to pass peacefully. Jean and Elouise had already completed the new dress and cloak for the Countess and had made a start on the Count's wardrobe, making repairs to several tunics and his formal robes, most of which had seen better days.

Some mornings Elouise would rise early and explore on her own. She was still surprised at the self sufficiency of the enclosed community. She visited the kitchens and the bakery and showed a real interest in the people who worked there, her questions being answered and rewarded with bowls of soup and chunks of bread. She wandered through the animal pens stroking the sheep and pigs and cows, giving each one a few words of greeting. On one occasion she took the opportunity to step inside the coolness of the cistern and watched as buckets of the precious liquid were drawn and despatched around the chateau. When she approached the stables her footsteps quickened in pace, her fear of horses still evident, but recognising Guillaume's horse she was brave enough to stop and stroke its nose. Since their ride in the woods she hadn't seen so much of him as he had returned to the knight's quarters. She resisted the impulse to look for him and hurried by, her head bowed as if deep in thought.

One morning she got up very early to pick some of the wild flowers she'd seen growing against the chateau walls. She wanted to have a bouquet ready by the time the Countess was having breakfast. It was to be a token of her thanks for the kind hospitality given to her and her father. As Elouise bent over to pick a bunch of the wild valerian that grew in clumps of white and purple she was aware of a shadow falling across her shoulder and sensed that someone was standing behind her.

'Well, that is certainly the loveliest site my eyes have seen for many a day.' Elouise recognised the voice and slowly started to stand up. She turned and found herself looking into the ugly face of Bruno. She tried to look into his dull brown eyes but he had the advantage of height over her. As he looked her up and down she had the unpleasant feeling that he was imagining her naked. The thought of it made her shudder.

'What do you want?' she tried to keep the loathing out of her voice.

'Now that's no way to talk to your boyfriend's cousin, I'm sure. Can't we be friends?' He leant a little closer to her face until she could smell the stale garlic on his breath and see the open pores on his sunburnt nose.

'I have no wish to be unfriendly, Bruno,' she said, taking a small step backwards. She clutched the bunch of flowers tightly in front of her.

'Good' said Bruno, 'because I thought you might be able to do a small job for me. I hear you're very talented with your needle and thread.'

'And what job would that be?' she said, keeping her voice steady.

'Well I seem to have a tear in my leggings, just here.' Bruno raised the hem of his tunic with one hand while the other one travelled towards his groin and he began to finger a small hole in the material. Elouise glanced down to where his hand was now beginning to rub himself in front of her. She felt the blood rise to her cheeks, not the colour of a blush but the fierce redness of anger.

'Well if you want me to do something about that you'll have

to take them off,' she said, a look of defiance on her face.

Bruno made a move as if to loosen his belt but realised quickly how stupid he would look with his leggings around his ankles. Someone could pass by at any moment; besides, he'd only wanted to frighten her.

'You think you're so clever,' he said, bringing his face even closer to hers so that now she could see the spittle on his teeth. 'You want to be careful, you and that heretic father of yours. I've got my eye on both of you. Next time maybe I won't be so friendly.' He continued to stare at her, expecting her to look down out of fear but she held his gaze steadily even though her heart was racing. Bruno grunted like a hungry pig then strode off in the direction of the barracks, leaving Elouise still clutching her flowers and feeling sick in the stomach.

After a while, when her heart beat had slowed to normal, she returned to the wild flowers, slowly selecting the best stems until she was satisfied with the bunch she had gathered. The rhythm of the task calmed her down and she decided to keep the whole unpleasant episode to herself.

The next day, when Jean and Elouise were in the Countess's chamber working their way through what seemed to be a growing pile of clothes that needed mending, there was a knock on the door. 'Come in,' they called out together. It wasn't the first interruption they'd had to contend with that morning.

'So this is where you've been hiding.' Michel's head appeared around the doorway.

'Come in, come in, my boy,' said Jean as Elouise jumped up and threw her arms around Michel's neck as he entered the room. 'Where have you been?' she demanded 'I haven't seen you for days!'

'Ah well, Miss,' replied Michel, putting on a heavy peasant accent and pretending to tug his forelock, 'I've been living with the servants, you see? I know my place. In fact I shouldn't really be here at all. If the Count finds out he'll probably have me thrown over the wall!'

'Don't be such a silly boy!' chided Elouise, pulling him across the room. 'Come and sit down and tell us what you've been up to. I want to know everything.' For the rest of the morning they chatted amongst themselves, Jean listening to most of their conversation whilst he carried on sewing, fascinated at how much the two of them had to say to each about so little. It was true that Michel had spent most of his time at the chateau with the staff. He now knew all their names, who did what job, who lived with who and which maids were having problems with their men folk. He made Jean and Elouise laugh with his impersonation of some of the Count's elderly retainers and they nodded in understanding when he told them how loyal the people who lived in the chateau were towards the Count and his family. 'I haven't heard a bad word said about him,' concluded Michel 'I think these people really do love him.'

'So what else have you been doing?' asked Elouise, wanting more news from her friend.

'You mean apart from casting my expert eye over the Count's sheep and giving advice about how to make the best cheese?'

'Yes,' she demanded.

'Well in that case I'll show you.' Michel drew towards him the instrument that was never far from his side and began to strum. As he concentrated on playing Jean and Elouise stopped what they were doing and let themselves surrender to the music. When he had finished there was a brief silence before Elouise spoke, her voice quiet in admiration. 'That was really beautiful Michel. What is it?'

'Just something I made up myself,' he replied bashfully.

'Does it have any words?' asked Elouise.

'No, not yet' he said, 'I'm working on those.'

'Well promise me I'll be the first to hear them' she urged, wanting to give him as much praise as possible.

'You have a real gift, Michel,' said Jean, offering his own words of encouragement. 'I'm very proud of you.' Michel couldn't stop himself blushing, he wasn't used to receiving such praise.

'I'm hungry,' he announced, his confidence returning. 'Why don't you come with me and I'll see if I can persuade that nice cook to let us have some of her excellent soup.' Jean and Elousie smiled, put away their scissors and needles then followed him out of the door. They knew, with certainty, that if anyone could charm a cook it would be Michel.

Life at the chateau began to acquire a rhythm. Jean and Elouise would work together in the mornings then go their separate ways after midday. Elouise to continue exploring the chateau and Jean to spend time looking after the Countess's garden, something he found increasingly enjoyable.

Sometimes Michel would see Elouise walking by and he would catch up with her and they'd spend the afternoon exploring together. They'd chat away just as they'd always done, completely at ease in each other's company.

'How long do you think we'll be here, Lou-Lou?' asked Michel. They were sitting with their backs against the warm stone of the walls, looking down the valley of the river that eventually flowed into the Aude at Quillan to the west.

'I really don't know.' She let out a long contented breath, closing her eyelids and feeling the sun's rays warm her skin. 'This is the longest I've ever stayed in one place. I think we'll finish our work in the next few days so I expect we'll be moving on soon after.'

'Would you like to stay here?' he asked.

'What, here at the chateau?'

'No, that would be too grand! But maybe down in the village; I can't imagine a better place to live.'

'I don't know, Michel'. Elouise paused and thought about it. 'Everyone has been really kind to us but I think my father will want to carry on travelling, and where he goes I go too.'

'And what about Guillaume?' he asked gently.

'What about him?'

'Oh come on, Lou Lou, you can't fool me. I've never seen you quite so distracted before. Don't tell me you don't find him attractive.'

Elouise conjured up an image of Guillaume's earnest face and smiled.

'I don't know what I feel really, it's all so new. I feel happy, more relaxed, when I'm with him, but it makes me feel a little guilty too. I want to keep the faith with my father and he needs me as well.'

'You shouldn't worry so much about your father, he's quite capable of looking after himself. Besides, he has his own journey. As for you and your faith, you'll always have that. It's what you do with it that you have to think about.'

Elouise said nothing, absorbing what Michel had just said. After a while she asked, in a quiet voice 'What do you think I should do, Michel?'

He turned his head slowly towards his beautiful friend and smiled.

'Pray' he said, 'pray that you'll have the right answer when the time comes.'

Elouise mulled over his advice. 'I hope you're right,' she said eventually.

They sat for a while, each lost in their own thoughts about the future.

'Come on, it's too hot for me up here.' He held out his hand, 'Let's go and find a cold drink.' They both stood, stretching their arms and legs, then descended the stone steps in the direction of the kitchen.

That night, as she lay in the cool bed with the blanket pulled up to her chin, Elouise turned over in her mind the conversation with Michel. It was true that she expected to be moving on with her father as soon as their work was finished, but she had to admit that she was enjoying their extended stay at the chateau. Of course this was a way of life she'd never experienced before, but it was more than the luxury of her own room or the trappings of privilege. She decided that the feeling she was getting was of a sense of security; that the chateau, with its strong walls, provided a safe haven that did not permit the problems of the outside world to enter.

She thought about Guillaume and his family. They seemed so close and loving towards each other, it made her realise what she had missed in her own life. She wasn't jealous, far from it, she would never exchange her life with her father and Michel. But she couldn't help imagining what it might have been like to grow up with a mother and a sister. Elouise turned on her side and allowed her thoughts to drift towards Guillaume. What exactly was it that made her feel so attracted to him? Certainly he was good looking, but that in itself was not the reason. Words like 'kind', 'polite', 'caring,'came into her mind. All these were true, but still not the answer. She thought harder. He seemed confident in his own world but she detected a vulnerabilty in him as well, maybe that was the appeal. And a sense of humour too; he had made her laugh several times. Not teasing like other boys, but funny things that made her relax and laugh with him. With her eyes closed and a smile on her face she thought about their time at the river and how she had hoped he might try again to kiss her. Just before she fell asleep the notion entered her mind that perhaps she would give him another opportunity.

CHAPTER THIRTEEN

'Are you very busy?' Elouise caught up with Guillaume as he came out of the stables into the sunshine.

'No, not really. I need to check on the traps in the wood, that's all. Why do you ask?'

'It's such a lovely day I thought we could spend some time together.'

She had a look on her face he hadn't seen before. Her smile was in its normal place but her eyes were sending him a more intense message.

His face lit up with an idea. 'Why don't you come with me?'

Elouise hesitated for a moment, 'You mean on your horse again?'

He laughed,' I promise I won't let you fall off, you just have to hold on tight. I'll go and get my horse ready and meet you by the gate.'

Elouise hurried off in the direction of the kitchen. She'd decided that some food and wine should be part of their day. By the time she'd made her way back to the gate she found Guillaume and his horse already waiting for her. He reached down and took her hand and pulled her up behind him.

'Ready?' he said. She tied the basket to the saddle and put her arms around his waist and leant against his back. 'Yes, I'm ready,' she replied.

They spent the morning meandering through the wood, checking the traps as they went. Guillaume swiftly despatched rabbit and squirrel into his sack and reset the traps whilst Elouise wandered along the path, collecting leaves and herbs to make potions later. By the time the sun was high in the sky they had reached the riverbank and Guillaume's sack was full.

'Let's stop and eat here,' suggested Elouise, 'it's so beautiful.'

Guillaume made sure the horse was tethered securely, then untied the basket of food and took his cloak from the saddle. He took Elouise's hand as she guided him to the dappled shade of an oak tree that hung over the river.

'Come on,' she said 'let's cool off .' She sat on the grass and pulled off her boots then stepped down into the cold water until she was up to her knees. She cupped her hands, dipping them into the sparkling water and splashed her face. It took Guillaume a little longer to remove his boots but then he jumped in beside her, creating a splash that soaked them both.

They held hands as they negotiated the slippery pebbles on the river bed and paddled upstream, feeling the current push against their legs. Turning back, refreshed, they made their way to the bank, climbed out of the water and lay down together on the cloak, still holding hands.

They lay like that for a while, without speaking, letting the warmth of the sun dry their wet skin. Elouise was the first to stir.

'Hungry?' she asked, looking across to Guillaume. He nodded, his eyes closed against the sunlight that sparkled through the canopy of leaves.

Elouise leant across him to reach the basket and found herself looking down into his face. At that exact moment Guillaume opened his eyes and looked directly into hers. Without hesitating he raised his head until their lips brushed together and they kissed for the first time. For a moment Elouise thought she couldn't breathe and pulled away, then she saw him smiling and closed her eyes and lowered her lips onto his again. This time there was more passion in their embrace. Guillaume raised himself on one elbow and gently pushed Elouise onto her back. Their lips were locked together and as their arms wrapped around each other their bodies began to press together urgently. Elouise could feel the hardness of his penis and knew that she had reached the point of no return. As if reading her mind Guillaume stopped kissing her.

'Are you sure this is what you want?'

She looked up into his eyes and gave him her answer with a nod and a smile. 'Yes, please,' she whispered. Quickly they removed their clothes and lay together side by side on the cloak. It was the first time either of them had seen the opposite sex naked and they were both shy and a little nervous.

'Kiss me again.' It was the encouragement Guillaume needed. He leant forward and gently placed his lips on hers. Soon their kissing became more passionate and their hands caressed each others body. Guillaume raised himself and tried to enter her but he was not an experienced lover. Elouise, instinctively, found his erect penis and gently guided him to the right place. She felt a stab of pain and gasped as he entered her. Guillaume stopped moving as he heard her stifled cry but she raised her hips up to him to encourage him to continue. Soon they were moving in unison, lost in the new sensations that were taking over their bodies. Guillaume thrust himself deeper and deeper inside her until he groaned and shuddered and his hips slowly stopped moving. Elouise held him tightly as she felt his semen flow into her. She was amazed at this feeling of oneness, of being connected to this man. As he rested his head, now damp with perspiration, on her shoulder, Elouise felt the warmth of the sun on her face and listened to the sounds of birds and insects close by. She closed her eyes to lock the memory of the moment into her mind.

Guillaume opened his eyes to look at her.

'That was truly amazing,' was all he could think of saying.

Elouise smiled at him and kissed his forehead, then the tip of his nose and then his lips.

'My pleasure, kind Sir,' she replied, feeling slightly embarrassed, and snuggled her face into his neck.

They lay like that for a long while before Elouise lifted her head to speak.

'I seem to remember asking if you were hungry.' Guillaume opened his eyes to look at her. 'Actually I'm starving,' he grinned broadly.

Whilst Guillaume, still naked, fetched the food Elouise found her shift and pulled it over her head to retain a degree of modesty. She moved to a new patch of warm grass and pulled the cloak over her legs. Guillaume joined her under the cover and spread the food on their laps. They ate the bread and cheese and passed the flask of wine between them, not talking but listening to the sounds in the trees above them and the river flowing by at their feet. Having satisfied their hunger it seemed only natural to lay back and fall asleep.

Guillaume awoke first. He didn't know how long they'd been sleeping but as the sun was still quite high in the sky he estimated it must be mid-afternoon. Propping himself on one elbow he looked at Elouise, taking in every aspect of her face. Not for the first time he felt a sense of wonder at the perfection of her features. Her eyes, her ears, her mouth, her lips, all came in for the utmost scrutiny as if he wanted to commit every detail to memory. He marvelled at the shape of her neck and the way it curved into her shoulder. His gaze took in her raven hair that gently curled across her shoulder and lay over her breast.

With the tips of his fingers he began to caress the golden skin of her arm, making a circular tour of her back and the base of her neck. Elouise stirred and, without waking, moved her body backwards so that they were pressed together like spoons.

'Hullo, my love' Guillaume whispered in her ear. Elouise

said nothing but slowly turned over towards him, allowing one arm to drape across his bare chest. Guillaume brought his face closer to hers so that she could feel his breath on her skin. He kissed her eyes softly, like a butterfly landing, then moved his lips towards hers. They kissed gently for a while, barely touching each other's mouth until Elouise's lips parted and allowed Guillaume's tongue to slip between them. As their tongues touched she felt a kind of buzz that connected directly to the deepest part of her stomach. As their kissing became more intense Elouise let Guillaume's hands wander freely over her body, aware of his penis pressing against her stomach. He pushed back the cloak that covered them so that they lay naked again. Slowly he moved his head towards her breasts and began to kiss each one in turn, feeling her nipples harden beneath his tongue as a moan escaped from somewhere deep in Elouise's throat. As he stretched out his fingers to enter the patch of soft dark curls that separated her legs, Elouise gripped each side of his head and pushed herself against his hand. In her passion she sought out his erection and prompted him to enter her again. This time their lovemaking was slower and longer than the frantic urgency of before. Their bodies moved in rhythm, consumed by the pure pleasure of such an intense experience. As Guillaume's thrusts became longer Elouise crossed her legs behind his back allowing him to penetrate more deeply and fill her completely. Their breathing and moving became faster, each thrust of Guillaume accompanied by a gasp from Elouise. Their bodies pushed together, their hands and arms gripping each other tightly until finally Guillaume thrust deeper and shuddered and they both let out great sobs of abandon. It seemed as if time had been suspended. Gradually, slowly, Guillaume's hips stopped moving, but he stayed hard inside her. Elouise held him tightly and felt her spirit, which seemed to have left her body at the height of their passion, quietly return to her body.

Exhausted and tired they dozed for a while longer. Guillaume stirred and looked into Elouise's lavender blue eyes. 'I love you, Elouise, I love you so very much.' She held his gaze and smiled back. 'Thank you' she said, 'me too'.

They continued to exchange gentle kisses until Guillaume spoke again. 'Come on,' he said 'we'd better get moving before they send out a search party.' Slowly they put on their clothes and remounted the horse that had waited patiently for them all afternoon, a silent witness to their union.

At suppertime that evening, the Count announced that he was going to give a special feast the next day to celebrate Helene's eighteenth birthday. There were smiles all round the table; it transpired the Count and his wife had been planning a celebration for some time but this was the first that Helene had heard of it.

'Oh, Papa,' she cried out with delight 'That's so sweet of you. I was beginning to wonder if you'd forgotten it was my birthday. How could you keep such a secret!' she teased him.

'Well you know how much you like surprises, so your mother and I decided to keep it to ourselves. Some of your relatives will be arriving tomorrow, as well as the Count and Countess of Mirapoix and their son Roger, and all our guests here are invited too, of course.' he indicated everyone around the table with a sweep of his arm.

'Roger is coming?' she asked, her voice rising with excitement and disbelief. 'Oh my goodness, I haven't seen him since I was twelve. This is so exciting, I can't believe it!' She grabbed the arm of Elouise and tugged her from her seat. 'Come on!' she said, pulling a surprised Elouise along behind her.'We haven't much time. What we are going to wear?' It only took a moment for Elouise to realise she knew the answer to the question. She had precisely nothing to wear for such a special occasion.

CHAPTER FOURTEEN

At breakfast the next morning Elouise confided in her father.

'Helene is so excited about her birthday. We spent all evening trying on clothes, she even offered to let me wear one of her dresses, but they don't really fit and I don't want to appear rude by turning it down. I know I shouldn't be concerned about my appearance but I can't go looking like this.' She tugged at the front of her plain wool dress, 'Maybe we shouldn't go.' She looked at her father forlornly, hoping he would offer her a solution. He answered with an enigmatic smile, as if he knew something that she didn't.

'My darling child, you have been such a good daughter to me. Sometimes I forget you are a young woman and there is nothing wrong in wanting to look your best.' He held both her hands together and stroked them gently. 'I have something I must do this morning. Why don't you come and see me at midday and we'll see if we can come up with an answer to your problem.' Elouise looked at him a little doubtfully, not sure what he meant. The thought crossed her mind that he might be going to make something. She smiled to herself at the idea that he would do this for her.

'Go on,' he said, 'Go and see what Helene is up to. I'm sure she probably still needs your advice. I'll see you later.' Jean stood and left the room, leaving Elouise on her own except for the two hounds, loitering ever hopefully around the table.

In the kitchen preparations for the feast were well under way. The wild boar that had been caught a few days before in the oak forest surrounding the chateau was turning slowly on a spit. Haunches of venison, whole pheasants, ducks and rabbits were trussed and ready for roasting in the great oven usually reserved for baking bread. Piles of vegetables from the kitchen garden and mushrooms collected that morning from the fields were waiting to be prepared. Trout freshly caught from the river would soon be added to the menu and baskets of peaches and apricots from the orchard would join the mounds of soft berry fruits accumulating on the kitchen table. Outside in the courtyard the activity continued. Lamps were being checked for oil, wicks cut and dipped, and the big iron flares that hung from the walls were soaked in lamp oil ready to be lit. A muscled labourer toiled in the open air, stripped to the waist, his axe swinging and flashing in the sunlight as a pile of logs grew around his feet. Buckets of water were fetched from the cistern and pitchers of wine filled from the oak barrels that lay in the coolness of the cellar.

Through all this activity Elouise wandered, offering to help here and there. By now she knew the names of most of the people who worked in the chateau. She greeted them as they went about their tasks, but didn't stop too long, not wishing to interrupt them from their chores. There was a mood of anticipation about the place, everyone caught up in the excitement of the feast to come. Most of the staff had worked at the chateau for many years and they knew from past experience that the Count was a kind man; he would make sure they were included in the celebrations to mark his daughter's eighteenth year.

The sound of the church bells striking midday drifted up from the village below and was the signal for Elouise to make her way to the Countess's dressing room where she knew her father would be working. She knocked gently on the door and waited for permission to enter.

'Ah, here you are, my child. What have you been doing this morning?' said Jean, looking up from the tunic he had been repairing.

'Doing my best to keep out of the way,' replied Elouise with a rueful smile. 'Everyone is so busy preparing for this evening, I've never seen such a hive of activity. They're all so excited about tonight!'

She watched as her father returned to his sewing and waited a few moments before tentatively asking the question that had been on her mind most of the morning.

'Did you manage to come up with a solution to my dress problem, Papa?' She tried not to make it sound like she was reminding him in case he really had forgotten.

'Ah yes, the matter of your dress.' He said it slowly, as if he'd given the subject a great deal of thought. 'I think I may have found the answer for you.' Elouise waited nervously, not knowing what he was going to propose but suspecting he may have made something quickly for her that morning. If he had done this for her she knew she would wear it with pride, no matter what it looked like.

'Why don't you close your eyes,' said Jean, 'I have something to show you.' Elouise shut her eyes as instructed and stood still. Jean moved to the dressing screen on one side of the room and returned.

'You can look now' he said.

Elouise opened her eyes slowly and found herself looking at her father. His arms were out in front of him, holding a blue dress.

'Oh, Papa, it's beautiful,' she exclaimed, 'Where did it come from? Did you make it?' She moved forward to touch the dress and brushed the soft material against her cheek.

'The truth is, yes, I did make it,' replied Jean in answer to his daughter's question, 'but a long time ago.'

'What do you mean?' she asked, puzzled.

Jean looked down at the dress for a few moments, rubbing his thumbs slowly across the material before replying.

'I made it for your mother.' His voice was now as soft as she'd ever heard him speak.' The first time I ever saw her, I made it to match the colour of her eyes. I've carried it with me ever since you were a little girl and we began our travels together. I hoped, I knew, the day would come when you would be ready to wear her dress.'

Elouise moved towards her father and held him tightly, the blue dress pressed between them as her tears began to flow.

Jean held on to his daughter for a few moments and gently stroked her back.

'Don't cry, my child' he comforted her. 'Why don't you try it on? Besides, I've spent all morning cleaning and pressing it for you. We don't want it to get all squashed now!' he unclasped her hands from behind his neck and gave her the dress. 'Go and change behind the screen, I want to see what it looks like on you.'

Elouise hurried over and disappeared from view whilst Jean turned around and waited for her to reappear. It wasn't long before she stepped out again, nervously.

'What do you think?' She was looking down and holding out the side of the dress with one hand and twiddling a strand of her hair around one finger of the other. Jean turned around slowly and looked at Elouise. He couldn't prevent a sob rising in his throat at this image of his beloved Blanche standing in front of him. He had to put a knuckle into his mouth to prevent the sob emerging. Then he smiled, 'You look absolutely beautiful, it fits perfectly. Your mother would have been so proud of you.' The nervousness that Elouise had felt earlier dissolved. She smiled and twirled in front of her father to let him see the complete effect.

'Thank you, Papa, thank you so much,' she beamed. 'I can't believe that you've carried it with you all these years. Am I really so much like my mother?'

'Looking at you now takes me back to the first moment I saw her,' replied Jean. 'She took my breath away on that day and you have done the same today.'

They both looked at each other without speaking, each one understanding what was going through the other's mind.

'Very good,' said Jean, as if to break the spell. 'Now that we have solved the problem of a dress for you perhaps you will help me finish this pile of mending.' Reluctantly, Elouise took off the dress and put on her old clothes. Picking up her needle and thread, she tried to concentrate on her work, but her mind held the image of the blue dress and her thoughts raced ahead to the evening's celebrations.

CHAPTER FIFTEEN

The Comte and Comtesse de Quillan circulated amongst the guests assembled in the great hall of the chateau. People had been arriving all day and now everyone was gathered for the celebration of Helene's birthday. Various land-owning neighbours had arrived with their entourages, including, as expected, the Count and Countess of Mirapoix and their son Roger. Guillaume and Bruno and six of their fellow knights mingled with the guests, resplendent in their best tunics embroidered with the Count's coat of arms. Jean and Michel stood together, Michel unusually nervous at the prospect of performing in front of such a distinguished audience.

Upstairs in Helene's bedchamber the two young women were putting the finishing touches to their clothes for the evening, helped by Annie who was fussing over their hair and accessories.

'Hold still, my lady,' insisted Annie as she arranged the finely embroidered cotton that would cover Helene's hair, framing her face and fixed by a gold clasp to her shoulder. 'If you don't stop moving this pin is going to pierce your skin.' Helene, for once, did as she was instructed, and for the hundredth time checked her appearance in the looking glass. She was wearing a long dress of green and gold that complimented the delicate paleness of her skin and emphasised the golden flecks in her reddish brown hair. Around her neck she wore a gold and emerald necklace that rose up and down on her bosom as she breathed. On her feet a pair of gold coloured leather slippers completed the ensemble.

'You look really lovely,' said Elouise with genuine affection. When she'd first met Helene she had to admit she thought she was a typical empty-headed daughter of a noble, but over the course of the past few weeks the two young women had spent much time together and Elouise had come to realise that they had more in common than they had differences. They'd talked a lot about their experiences and shared their hopes and secrets until now a strong bond had developed between them.

'If I look lovely then you look truly beautiful,' replied Helene, returning the compliment. And it was true. Standing there in the blue dress that matched perfectly the blue of her eyes, and with her straight dark hair encircled by the garland of wild flowers she had made that afternoon, Elouise looked as if she could have been born into a noble family herself. She smiled and toyed with her mother's silver necklace that now encircled her slender neck.

'Thank you, kind lady,' she said to Helene. 'Now, if you're finally ready don't you think it's time we made an appearance? After all it is your birthday.' The two young women looked at each other and clasped hands, as much out of friendship as for mutual support.

'Come on,' said Elouise, teasing her friend, 'You don't want to keep that handsome young Roger waiting, do you?'

Still holding hands, they left the chamber and headed for the stairs that led down into the great hall. Annie followed closely behind making sure that nothing fell out of place.

At the top of the stairs they stopped and paused for a while, taking in the scene below and glanced nervously at each other. Then, slowly, they began to descend the curving steps until their arrival was noticed. Elouise gave Helene a little nudge to indicate that she should go first. One, then two then several heads moved in their direction until the whole room had turned to look and the chatter of conversation dried up. It was the Count who began to clap first as his daughter descended the stairs, then everyone joined in the applause as Helene continued her descent until she reached the flag stones of the hall.

Elouise remained at the top of the stairs, waiting for the applause for Helene to die down so that she could descend too, but the clapping continued and she was eventually prompted to come down when she saw Guillaume waving his arm, inviting her to join the party. Blushing at being the centre of attention, Elouise grasped her skirt and continued her own entrance into the assembled throng, torn between heading in the direction of Guillaume or finding her father. Her dilemma was solved by Guillaume who stepped forward to take her hand as she negotiated the last step. Placing her hand in the crook of his arm he could hardly contain his look of pleasure as he escorted her through the guests until they stood in front of Jean and Michel, both of whom had been watching Elouise's entrance with the look of people seeing someone clearly for the first time. Guillaume found the necessary boldness to speak to Jean.

'You have a beautiful daughter, Monsieur, and it would be my honour to escort her this evening.' Jean smiled at the earnest young man standing before him and looked with fondness at his daughter. She looked very happy beside the handsome knight and her eyes seemed to be asking for some kind of approval. 'Thank you, dear boy,' replied Jean, 'I'm sure my daughter will be most safe in your care and protection.' Guillaume took this as his signal that Jean had given his permission and, bowing respectfully to the older man, led Elouise off in the direction of the other guests.

'Well who would have thought it?' It was Michel who spoke, interrupting Jean's train of thought, 'I can't believe it's the same girl I once taught to whistle and climb trees. What a transformation! I'll never be able to ask her to help me castrate a lamb again!' Jean laughed out loud, grateful to his young friend for helping him to adjust to this new phase in his daughter's life.

The good man and the shepherd smiled at each other but inwardly they each felt different concerns for her future.

As the guests mingled and the servants began to bring food to the table, Michel moved to where he had left his lute and rejoined the young tambour player he had recruited from the village. The two had spent all day preparing the evening's entertainment. Now Michel began to strum the opening chords of one of the popular tunes of the day, not so loudly as to stop the flow of conversation but enough to provide a pleasant background as the evening unfolded. He knew from experience that no matter how high or low born the audience might be, once the food and the wine combined there would be many requests and encouragements for more songs as the evening wore on. The two musicians nodded to each other as they played and prepared themselves for a long evening.

The sound of the music was the signal for the guests to sit down around the great wooden table. The Count and his wife took the place of honour at the head of the table, Guillaume sitting to the left of his mother and Helene to the right of her father. There was no special placement for the other guests although Guillaume made sure that Elouise was next to him and Helene had insisted that Roger de Mirapoix was on her right. She'd already made up her mind that this was the best way she could continue the earnest conversation that the two had struck up together, much to the apparent pleasure of their parents.

Despite the celebratory nature of the occasion there was no formal service at the table, the guests heartily helping themselves from the mountains of food in front of them. The Count's servants were kept busy replenishing the platters and refilling the jugs of wine, all of which were destined to empty rapidly as the evening wore on.

Jean found himself sitting next to Pierre Biscaye, the Count's steward. The Countess had instructed the kitchen to make sure there was fish for Jean and now he found himself looking at the largest baked trout he had ever seen.

'I think you are allowed to eat it, not just look at it,' teased Pierre. Jean smiled at his companion. 'Do you know it's twenty years since I decided to devote my life to my faith, which included a vow not to eat any flesh except fish. In all those years I don't think I've seen a finer looking specimen than this.' He pointed at the trout with his knife, 'it almost seems a shame to eat it.'

'Have no qualms my friend, enjoy it,' Pierre encouraged, 'Think of it as the fish's gift to you.' He laughed and gave Jean a friendly slap on the back. Jean decided to accept Pierre's reasoning and took a mouthful. He chewed for a while before delivering his verdict to his friend, who was now filling both their mugs with wine. 'You were right,' he announced, 'the fish is delicious,' and they both laughed again. The two men continued eating for a while before Pierre spoke again.

'Twenty years is a long time for a man of your calling, if you don't mind me saying, particularly in the difficult times we have had. Don't you ever get worried or frightened?'

'Well I'm not frightened for myself, if that's what you mean,' replied Jean, putting down his knife. 'I'm not afraid to die because I know where my spirit will be going. But I do worry about the effect this persecution of our faith is beginning to have on ordinary people, not just those we call believers. How can something that puts neighbour against neighbour, family against family, even sister against brother be seen to be doing God's work? The Church of Rome may have decided it wanted no rival but you can't barter with people's souls. Only God can decide what happens to us when we die.'

Pierre said nothing as he chewed over Jean's words, their earnest seriousness in complete contrast to the happy scene surrounding him. He was on the point of replying when the sound of dagger on metal candlestick caused everyone to look towards the head of the table. Armand, Comte de Quillan and proud father, was getting to his feet and readying himself to make a speech.

'My dear friends, neighbours, kinsmen and family,' he began, his face beaming with pleasure and his voice booming around the great room. 'My wife and I are very grateful to see you here at the Chateau Roc on this happy occasion. It's not every day we get the opportunity to meet and mingle as we have this evening. We hope that you will stay as our guests for as long as you are able to stay away from your own hearths.'

'Tonight we are celebrating the birthday of our beloved daughter Helene who we have cherished now for eighteen summers.' The Count looked down at his daughter and rested his hand on her shoulder. 'It seems incredible that not so long ago this young lady was scraping her knees on the chateau walls and now here she is before us, a beautiful young woman, for whom I must thank God,' he paused, 'and my wife.' Helene blushed at her father's words and a burst of laughter and applause broke out from the assembled guests. The Count raised his hand and the applause subsided. 'So now I ask you to be upstanding and join me in a toast to Helene, may she have many more happy birthdays.' All the guests stood and raised their drinks and a chorus of 'Helene' rang around the room. The Count remained standing and clapped his hands to indicate he had more to say, and the guests slowly sat down again. 'As those of you with daughters will know,' he confided, 'finding a suitable gift for their birthday can be a difficult task. If it's new clothes are they the right colour? If it's a piece of jewellery is it the right shape? Well I hope tonight that Sybille and I have found something for Helene that is both the right shape and the right colour.' The guests began to look around to see what the gift might be but nothing obvious came to light. Instead the Count clapped his hands again and pointed in the direction of the main door. At his signal the huge door swung open and in the doorway stood one of the stable boys. The boy entered the room looking a little self conscious, but he had been well drilled in his part of the proceedings. He tugged on the leather rein he had concealed behind his back and led into the great hall the most splendid white stallion. The guests broke out into more applause at the sight of this beautiful horse whilst Helene put her hands to her mouth in a gasp of amazement and then stood up and threw her arms around her father's neck.

'Thank you, thank you, thank you,' she gushed with delight, 'how on earth did you keep him a secret? Where did you keep him?' But her father wasn't about to break the spell of the moment.

'Go on,' he said, 'go and meet your new steed. Talk to him and then think of a name.' Helene grinned at Roger and then crossed the room towards the horse, which stood uncomfortably in these alien surroundings and snorted his displeasure, pawing the flag stones so that sparks flew from his hoof. Helene, quickly and sensibly, had concealed a piece of fruit in her hand as she left the table and now offered it to the horse whilst she stroked its nose and breathed into its nostrils. The horse seemed to calm down and gently nudged Helene's shoulder to see if any more fruit might appear. It was obvious that a bond had already formed between them. Helene tousled the hair on the stable boy's head and shook his hand, thanking him for being such a good horseman. The boy looked rather shy at all the attention, so at Helene's whispered suggestion he was grateful to turn and gently lead the stallion out of the room and back to the stables. The door closed and Helene bowed towards her guests in a gesture of thanks and appreciation then resumed her place next to her father.

The evening was turning out to be a great success. The earlier, excited chatter as people took this rare opportunity to catch up on each other's news had given way to a more convivial atmosphere. With their bellies filled with good food and their senses softened by the wine, the guests were in a relaxed mood and gradually turned their attention to the music from Michel, who had begun singing a popular love song. He would have been the first to admit that he was not a troubadour in the true meaning of the word. That world belonged to a time decades earlier at the court of Eleanor of Aquitaine, who encouraged the sons of noblemen to write their passionate verses of courtly love. But the songs remained, handed down by word of mouth, and their essence was loved as much now as it had been then. And Michel's life as a shepherd allowed him to continue the tradition of the troubadours as itinerant players, carrying the news from place to place in verse and song.

Michel's melodic voice now sang:
'The first day, Lady, that I saw you
When they pointed you out to me,
I took from my heart all other images,
All my wishes affirmed in you.
Your smile, a look soft and tender,
Gives to me such desire, oh my Lady,
That I forget myself and the universe.

As he finished the song the guests applauded and smiled to each other, reflecting their appreciation of the performance and the effect the song had on them. The Countess in particular showed her approval of the young shepherd and encouraged him to play more of the same.

After several slower love songs some of the younger guests asked for music they could dance to and Michel agreed it was time to change the mood, after all this was a birthday celebration for a young woman. He and the tambour player struck up a faster tempo and soon a space had been cleared to allow the dancers to move. Helene wasted no time in persuading Roger to demonstrate his prowess, but Elouise needed a lot more encouragement from Guillaume before reluctantly agreeing to take the floor. She had skipped around before at various village functions but this was the first time she had taken part in a formal dance and she felt nervous and self conscious. She needn't have worried as Guillaume proved to be an excellent teacher, guiding her through the steps and steering her around the room until she felt able to relax and enjoy herself. Besides, it was the perfect opportunity to feel his body close to hers again. The guests clapped along to the music and cheered the dancers as one tune led swiftly into another.

Jean sat back and watched with pleasure as his daughter danced with Guillaume. He caught the eye of the Countess and they nodded to each other in acknowledgement of the budding relationship between their offspring.

A voice in Jean's ear interrupted his moment of parental pride. He turned to see one of the Count's servants standing next to him.

'Can you come with me, please?' said the man, 'there's someone who wishes to speak to you.' Jean stood up slowly, sensing he shouldn't draw attention to himself, and followed the servant to the doorway. Outside in the coolness of the night he found the young Borrel boy twisting his hat in his hands and looking agitated.

'Jacques, what's the matter? What brings you up to the chateau at this time of night?'

'Monsieur Jean, my father sent me. He says you're needed in the village.' The message didn't make too much sense to Jean but he could see that the boy was anxious. 'Someone's dying,' added Jacques almost in a whisper. That was all the information that Jean needed for it told him that a *croyant* needed his final blessing.

'Wait for me here,' said Jean, 'I'll get my cloak and bag. I'll only be a few moments.' He turned to make his way to his quarters when a familiar figure came hurrying up.

'Is everything all right, Papa?' Elouise had noticed her father leaving the great hall and had excused herself from Guillaume's attention. Jean could see the concern on her face.

'Don't worry, I'm needed in the village.' It was all the explanation he needed to give her. 'I'm leaving with Jacques now.'

'Shall I come with you?' she offered.

'No, there's no need for that. It's very thoughtful of you, Elouise, but I want you stay here.'

'Well at least let me walk with you to the gate.'

Jean hurried off to collect his belongings whilst Elouise and Jacques breathed in the cool air and listened to the sounds of the celebration coming from the great hall.

'Who is it?' asked Elouise, looking down at the boy.

'What do you mean?' replied Jacques.

'Who is dying?'

Jacques realised he could tell the Good Man's daughter.

'It's Madame Garouste, she has a terrible fever. My father says she won't survive much longer.'

Jean returned in no time at all and the trio set off across the courtyard towards the huge double gates that guarded the entrance to the chateau. The gates were shut firmly as always at nightime but Jean and Jacques were able to exit through the small door set into the middle of one of them.

'I'll come and see you tomorrow,' said Elouise. She stood and watched the two figures descend the steep path towards the village until they had disappeared into the blackness of the night. She bolted the door shut, shivered slightly and turned to walk back to the hall.

Elouise had only walked a few paces when a hand clamped over her mouth and she felt herself being dragged sideways. She tried to bite the hand and struggled to free herself, but whoever was holding her was too strong and forced her head backwards so she couldn't move her mouth or make a noise. Her assailant pulled her along a path that Elouise recognised led to the kitchen garden. The path was narrow and she felt her elbows and ankles scraping on the stone walls on either side. Elouise tried not to panic but to think clearly, seeking an opportunity to break free and escape. But the man kept a tight grip, resisting her struggles and dragging her further into the garden. He stopped when they had reached a secluded corner where they couldn't be seen, even by the guards patrolling the high walls. Elouise felt the man's rough face move closer to her ear and flinched as he began to whisper.

'I think its time the heretic's daughter was taught a little lesson in manners, don't you? You've been enjoying the Count's hospitality for long enough, now it's time for you to show a little gratitude.' Elouise recognised Bruno's voice immediately, and by the smell of his breath he was drunk. She struggled again to free herself but Bruno only tightened his grip around her neck with one hand and started to fumble underneath her skirt with the other. He was still standing behind her, trying to force her legs apart with his knee, and she could feel his rough hand exploring her body, his fingers probing between her legs.

In the brief moment it took for Bruno to adjust his grip Elouise seized her opportunity to bite hard into the fingers still clamped around her mouth. Bruno winced with the pain and spun Elouise around so that she was facing him. 'You little bitch,' he spat into her face, 'I was going to be gentle but now I'm going to hurt you.' He slapped her hard across her face with the back of his hand, making her stumble backwards and fall to the ground. In an instance Bruno was on top of her, tearing at her dress and trying to free himself while swatting away the blows she was aiming at his head. As much as she squirmed and struggled Elouise couldn't shift Bruno's weight from her body as his excitement now turned into an attack. Tears began to flow from her eyes, not out of fear but out of frustration that she couldn't prevent what she knew was going to happen. By now Bruno had managed to extract his penis and had begun to thrust himself towards her naked thighs. Elouise shut her eyes and bit into her lip to stop herself crying out. She wanted to deny Bruno any sense of victory.

But the penetration she was expecting didn't come. Instead she was aware of Bruno's body suddenly going limp and then falling heavily on top of her. She struggled to move out from beneath his body but he was too heavy and she had used up more energy than she realised during the attack. She became aware of something warm spreading slowly over her chest and neck. Elouise opened her eyes and saw a figure standing over her, sword in hand. It was Guillaume.

Even in the pale light of the moon Elouise could see his face was white with fury. Slowly his grip on the sword loosened and it fell softly into a bush of rosemary. Guillaume shook his head as if trying to erase an unwanted image then used his booted foot to push Bruno's body off Elouise. He knelt down beside her and lifted her into his arms and held her trembling body tightly.

'Did he...' Guillaume tried to find the right words, '... has he hurt you?' Elouise said nothing but shook her head weakly.

'Thank God I followed him. I saw him watching you when you left with your father. He may have been my cousin but the man is, was, a sadistic brute.'

Elouise said nothing again but nodded in agreement.

'We need to get you somewhere warm, we can't go back into the hall.'

Guillaume thought for a moment before deciding. 'I'm taking you to my room, there'll be a fire there and I'll get Annie to fetch some hot water and get you something clean to wear.' He stood up, still holding her in his arms, and began to make his way to the keep and his own quarters. Elouise never spoke a word, her arms dangling by her side and her head lolling backwards. To any observer she could easily have been dead herself.

CHAPTER SIXTEEN

Jean and young Jacques knocked loudly and waited for the gates to open to allow them entry to the village. The guards had been expecting them, otherwise the gates would have remained shut until first light allowed entry to any unrecognised visitors.

Jacques led Jean along the narrow paths and alleyways until they reached the house of Madame Garouste. The light from several oil lamps spilled out around the doorframe and through the small windows, making the house look like it was glowing in the dark, indicating that this was a household still awake. The door opened as soon as they knocked and they were quickly ushered inside. Several people were gathered in the smoky interior and Jean quickly recognised Jacotte Borrel and her daughter Bernardette. Jacotte made her way over to him and, without fuss, knelt and bowed her head before speaking.

'Thank God you could come. I fear Catherine has not much time with us,' she said, after Jean had blessed her.

'Take me to her,' said Jean. Jacotte led him to a small room at the back of the dwelling where a figure lay on a low wooden bed. The room was hot with very little air and he could see from the yellow light of the tallow lamp that the woman was sweating heavily with fever. Jean placed his hand on the woman's brow.

'What happened to her?' said Jean, 'how long has she had the fever?'

'She's been like this for three days,' replied Jacotte. 'She cut her foot badly in the fields; her husband thinks she trod on a piece of rusty metal, probably a broken weapon. We've tried everything to heal the cut but the fever's taken hold of her.'

Jean had seen cases like this before. He knew enough to know that if the wound did not close cleanly it would soon swell with puss and the poison would spread quickly, bringing on the fatal fever. Jean brought the lamp closer to look at the woman's foot but the sickly smell alone was enough to tell him that she would not survive.

'Catherine was a strong believer. She asked me to make sure I found you. Will you give her your final blessing?' asked Jacotte.

Jean nodded and moved around to kneel at the head of the bed. He leant forward and cradled Catherine's head in his hands.

'I will bless her soul and free her spirit,' he reassured Jacotte. He began to recite the words of the *consolamentum*. It would free her spirit to begin the next stage of its journey towards heaven. Only Parfaits, such as Jean, could be certain of a place at the side of God, but if Catherine Garouste had led a good life then her spirit would return into the soul of a newborn baby, to continue its journey to heaven. When he had finished he laid his hand on top of Catherine's head and began to lead Jacotte and the other people who had now gathered around the woman's bed in reciting the Lord's Prayer. From this moment on the woman would be allowed no food or water, the strict conditions of the *endura*, until her body succumbed to the illness.

'You must come and stay with us, Jean,' said Jacotte, as she and Bernardette prepared to leave the Garouste household. 'You can have the barn to yourself. Jacques will take you back to the chateau in the morning.'

'Bless you, Jacotte, you are a kind woman,' replied Jean. 'I'll decide in the morning if I am going to return to the chateau.

Perhaps it's time for me to think about where I go from here.'

'Then you are welcome to stay with us for as long as you need,' said Jacotte, as they made their way in the dark along the familiar path that led to the Borrel home.

CHAPTER SEVENTEEN

As Guillaume carried Elouise across the courtyard he called out to one of the servants to find Annie and tell her to bring some hot water to his room. Once inside the keep he climbed the stairs, still carrying her, until he reached the doorway to his room. He had to stand her on her feet while he opened the door then, taking her hand, he led her gently towards the hearth where the embers of a fire still glowed.

Guillaume added logs to the fire and lit two candles and placed them on the mantelpiece. Elouise stood motionless in front of the fire staring into the flames. Then she looked down at her dress and her tears began to flow. The front and one sleeve had been ripped and torn during her struggle with Bruno and now his blood soaked the fabric where his dying body had lain on top of her. Elouise pulled her arms tightly around herself and her shoulders shuddered with her sobs.

'It's over now, he can't hurt you any more,' whispered Guillaume. He wanted to hold her but only managed to rest his hand on her shaking shoulder.

'It's not that,' she said, between sobs. 'It's not him, or me. This was my mother's dress and now look at it. My father carried this dress for me for all those years and now it's ruined. Don't you understand what that means to me?' Guillaume knew enough to know there was no answer to her question, so said nothing. Elouise's sobs began to subside after this outburst and now she just sniffed between her tears.

'What's going to happen now? What's going to happen to you? You've killed your cousin because of me.'

'Nothing's going to happen right away,' said Guillaume. 'Everyone is still celebrating my sister's birthday. I will have to deal with this in the morning. As for Bruno, shed no tears for him. He lived like a pig and now he's died like a pig.' The contempt in his voice indicated all he needed to say about his cousin.

A knock on the door interrupted their thoughts. It was Annie, standing there with two pitchers of steaming water.

'Come in, Annie, let me help you with those,' said Guillaume.

Annie entered the room, took one look at Elouise and her hand shot up to cover her mouth.

'God's mercy! What happened to you?' Elouise said nothing but took comfort in the presence of another woman.

'Annie, there's been an accident,' explained Guillaume, taking control of the situation. 'I want you to help Elouise get out of her dress and bathe her, she's had a very bad experience. And you'd better keep this to yourself,' he added. 'I'll be back soon, there's something I have to do.' He left Elouise in the gentle care of Annie and hurried back to the garden, thinking about what to do with Bruno's body.

By the time Guillaume returned to his room Annie had already left and Elouise was sitting on the rug in front the fire, now clean and dressed in the cotton shift that Annie had found for her. A woollen shawl was draped across her shoulders to keep out the night chill. Guillaume crossed the floor and knelt down beside her and she turned her head towards him.

'How are you feeling?' he asked gently. He looked into her eyes to see if the hurt and anger had subsided. Elouise looked back at him, a rueful smile on her face.

'I'll be fine,' she said 'no damage done.' She reached across and stroked a stray curl of his hair. 'I'm sorry if I shouted at you earlier. I really should be thanking you for saving me from Bruno.'

'No need to thank me,' Guillaume said, 'I did what anyone would have done. I just wish I could have got there sooner, I couldn't bear the idea of anyone hurting you.'

'Sshh' Elouise placed two fingers on Guillaume's lips to let him know he needn't say any more. Guillaume reached up and took her hand in his, kissing her fingers and then kissing the palm of her hand. They looked at each other for a long moment and then he encircled her with his arms and Elouise rested her head on his shoulder. They stayed on the rug letting the fire keep them warm, the only sound the crackle from the burning logs.

'You should get some rest,' said Guillaume, lifting her head from his shoulder. Elouise nodded sleepily and allowed him to carry her and put her into bed, covering her with a sheepskin for extra warmth.

'Don't go, stay with me,' she murmured, gently patting the bed. Guillaume lay down next to her and held her until they both fell into a deep sleep.

PART TWO

CHAPTER EIGHTEEN

The early light of a June morning filtered into the room, gradually penetrating Guillaume's closed eyelids until he awoke. He stretched slowly, tugging at the blanket he had pulled over himself after the fire in the hearth had died and the air had cooled. He turned towards the sleeping figure lying next to him and gently brushed away a strand of hair that had fallen over one eye. Elouise stirred in her sleep and turned over towards him. He studied her sleeping face for a while then gently lowered his head to kiss her lips.

'Good morning, my love,' he whispered. He watched as she slowly awoke and her eyes blinked open. She smiled at him, a look of pleasant surprise on her face to see him there, and then the smile faded as the events of the previous night resurfaced. A tear formed slowly in the corner of her eye and dissolved into the pillow.

'Oh, Guillaume, you killed Bruno! What's going to happen now?'

He took her hand to comfort her. 'After I left you with Annie last night I went back to the garden and found my sword. No one knows it was me, but I'll have to tell my father, all the same. He'll know what to do, even if it means I have to go to prison.' Elouise held onto his hand and squeezed it hard as another tear rolled onto her cheek. They lay together in silence, both of them lost in their own thoughts.

'What about you?' asked Guillaume after a while, 'What are

you going to do? Will you stay here at the chateau?' Elouise pondered his question for a while, chewing on her lower lip.

'I have this feeling I need to see my father, I can't explain it but I'm worried about him. I think I should go down to the village.'

'I'm sure he's not in any danger,' Guillaume said, trying to reassure her, 'but if you're going to the village you'd better ask Michel to go with you, just in case there's trouble.' Elouise turned her face towards him.

'You're right,' she said, stroking his cheek with the back of her hand. Guillaume leant towards her, wanting to place another kiss on her perfect mouth, when a sharp knock at the door interrupted him.

'May I enter, please?' It was the voice of Annie.

'Yes, of course, come in,' Guillaume called out.

Annie entered the room carrying a large tray. 'I thought you might be hungry so I've brought some breakfast.' She put the tray down on a wooden chest and turned to look at Elouise.

'How are you this morning, dear girl? I hope the young master has been taking care of you.'

'I'm fine, really,' replied Elouise 'no damage done except to my pride, and my beautiful dress,' she added, trying to draw the attention away from herself.

'Well don't you worry about that,' continued Annie, 'I'll have that washed and mended myself, I promise you. Now it's a beautiful morning and time you two were up and about. Everyone else has had breakfast and probably wondering why you were not there. And as for you, young Sir,' she said seriously as she turned towards the door, 'your father wants to see you. Your cousin Bruno's been found dead. Probably got himself drunk and into a fight, knowing him,' she surmised. Guillaume exhaled deeply at the abruptness of this news and his head sunk back into the pillow. Elouise, gathering a blanket around her, crossed the room to pick up the tray of food and brought it back to the bed.

'Come, my handsome rescuer,' she looked at him with determination on her face, as if she'd made up her mind about something, 'we need nourishment, I have a feeling this is going to be a very long day.'

CHAPTER NINETEEN

Bernard Villac looked down from his pulpit at the villagers gathered together for Sunday Mass. Like most villages the church was one of the few buildings capable of holding a large number of people, so it was quite normal for Sunday Mass to be an opportunity to meet friends and neighbours, to catch up on all the news and even do a little business on the side. Even the Cathars in the village were not afraid to attend Mass, seeing no dilemma in their appearance at the house of a God they didn't worship if it meant they could meet their friends on their day of rest. Besides, very few people could understand the priest's Latin prayers, so they could easily ignore his words.

Villac raised his hand to try and silence the babble of noise that rose up from the congregation. Gradually, people began to take notice of him and the level of noise subsided until he had their full attention.

'People of St. Julien de Roc,' he began, trying to sound friendly, 'it is good to see so many of you here today, although' his voice tried to take on a more serious note, 'I would like to see more of you here during the week too. All of us are capable of sin any day of the week and the sooner you are prepared to admit it the sooner our good Lord can absolve you. Confess your sins to me and I, with the help of God, will set you on the path to forgiveness.' Most people had heard all this before and few took much notice of his words. Villac continued, trying to ignore the sense of apathy that floated upwards.

'It has come to my attention that one of your neighbours, a heretic by the name of Catherine Garouste, has passed away. No doubt her family will be coming to ask if she can be buried in the cemetery of this church. Let me remind you, whilst I cannot refuse her body to be buried in our hallowed ground, be assured that her bones and soul will rot in Hell, never to be received into Heaven.' Now, the priest thought, he had their attention and decided to press on with his message.

'I have received word from our Bishop, the very Bishop who blessed us with his presence on our Saint's Day, that the time has come to finally face up to the heretics in our midst and persuade them to repent. And if they won't repent then they must be cast out from our midst. My message to you is simple. Seek out the heretics and those that sympathise with them. Point out to them the error of their ways. Tell them that your Church can offer them hope and salvation, and if you do this for yourselves then your own salvation will be assured.'

He could see his words were finding their target, some of the congregation casting nervous glances around them, others shuffling uneasily and casting their eyes down towards the floor. Villac decided to press on, raising his voice and shaking his fist in the air.

'Remember that Jesus was crucified on the cross so that your souls could be saved. Go out and work for your saviour! Help those poor souls who have been led astray! Bring them back to your church that they too may be saved!' Villac slumped back in the pulpit. Oratory did not come naturally to him and he felt exhausted by his efforts. He watched as the church slowly emptied, his words, for once, seemed to have the desired effect. Amongst the crowd he noted the Borrel family leaving and made a mental note that this was one family he would be keeping a close eye on himself.

CHAPTER TWENTY

When she had finished her breakfast Elouise returned to her room, hoping no one would see her. As soon as she was dressed and had packed her few belongings she went in search of Michel. She didn't have far to look as she knew he would be somewhere in the vicinity of the kitchen. Sure enough she found him leaning back against the wall, a large plate of food in front of him.

'Lou Lou, there you are!' he called out, a big smile of pleasure on his face. 'Where have you been? You seemed to disappear last night and no one's seen you all morning. What have you been up to?' Elouise bent down and gave her musical friend a kiss on the cheek by way of greeting and returned his smile.

'It's a long story, I'll tell you later,' she said 'But now I need to find Papa. Will you come with me?'

'Of course I will,' he replied, 'do you think something has happened to him? Are you worried?'

'I don't know,' she sounded a little vague. 'I just have this feeling I need to see him. Will it take you long to get ready?'

He put down his plate, sensing her need for urgency. 'No. I'll meet you at the gate, wait for me there.' He hurried off in the direction of the room he'd been sharing, stopping just long enough to give his favourite kitchen maid a warm hug.

As Elouise crossed the courtyard she saw Helene and Roger approaching from the direction of the garden. She waved and altered her path to meet them.

'Thank goodness we've found you! We missed you,' exclaimed Helene. 'First your father leaves last night, then you and Guillaume disappear and now it seems Bruno has gone missing. What on earth is going on?' It was obvious that the truth about Bruno had been kept from Helene so Elouise decided not to enlighten her.

'Nothing for you to worry about, really,' she replied. 'I hope I didn't spoil your party.' Elouise looked at the smiling couple. 'Anyway, what about you two? You look very pleased with yourselves. What's going on?'

Helene gazed up at Roger and took his hand in hers. 'We're going to be married!' she gushed, unable to contain her excitement. 'My mother and father and Roger's parents agreed last night that we should be wed. Isn't it wonderful?' Her face showed her eager delight to be married to the young knight.

'Yes, that really is wonderful news,' said Elouise, smiling at the unabashed happiness of her new friend. 'I hope you will both be really happy. And have lots of babies too!' The two girls burst into giggles at this suggestion and poor Roger could barely hide his embarrassment.

Helene noticed the bag hanging from Elouise's shoulder. 'You're not leaving are you? Where are you going?'

'I need to find my father, I'm worried about him. Michel said he would come with me to the village.' Elouise paused for a moment,' Could you do something for me please, Helene?'

'Yes, of course. What is it?'

'I need to leave straight away,' explained Elouise 'When you see your mother could you please explain to her and give her my apologies for not coming to see her. She has been so kind to me these past weeks and I don't like leaving without saying goodbye.'

'Of course I will,' assured Helene. 'I'm sure she will understand. But what about Guillaume, aren't you going to say goodbye to him?'

'I think he might be busy with your father right now,' replied Elouise, 'besides,' she added, 'we said our goodbyes this morning.' Her voice sounded a little wistful and she couldn't help the tinge of embarrassment that began to form on her face. Helene saw it straight away and could not resist the opportunity to tease her friend.

'So that's what you two were up to last night. No wonder you couldn't make it to breakfast this morning!' She laughed and Elouise smiled back. She decided to let Helene think she had guessed correctly; she wasn't about to explain the real truth about the previous night. Elouise moved towards Helene and the two young women held each other tightly.

'Don't forget to invite me to the wedding.'

'I won't, I promise,' replied Helene as they parted. Elouise turned and gave Roger a friendly kiss on both cheeks. 'You look after her, won't you?'

'Of course I will, she means the world to me,' he replied, looking adoringly at his bride-to-be. Elouise smiled at them both then turned and made her way to the gate, hoping that Michel would be there already.

As they descended the steep path that led to the village Elouise told Michel what had happened the previous evening.

'What a bastard!' he swore. 'If Guillaume hadn't killed him I would have done it myself. That man was evil. Are you sure you're all right?' Elouise smiled at her lifelong friend.

'Yes, I'm fine. No harm done,' she reassured him, 'but I'm worried about what might happen to Guillaume.'

As they continued their descent Michel tried to lighten the mood as he described in great detail all the events surrounding the announcement of Helene and Roger's betrothal and the number of songs that he had been called upon to play. By the time they reached the gates of the village Elouise felt her spirits lifting and she turned and looked back to the chateau. A shadow of doubt clouded her thoughts and she shivered as she wondered whether she would ever see Guillaume again.

Jean was sitting outside the Borrel's barn talking to Jacotte about the message in Villac's sermon when Elouise and Michel arrived at the doorway.

'What are you two doing here?' said Jean, a puzzled look on his face 'I thought you would still be celebrating at the chateau.'

'I know, papa,' said Elouise 'but I was worried about you. I can't explain it, it's just a feeling I had. Michel said he'd come with me. It was his idea we'd find you here.'

'Well so you have, and very pleased to see you I am too, although I can't think why you should be worried about me.'

'I can,' said Jacotte, her voice was serious 'you were right to be worried about your father.'

'What do you mean?' said Elouise.

Jacotte gave them a brief summary of the events at Mass and the threats implied in the priest's words. 'It's worse than anything else we've heard from him before,' she concluded. 'We've had rumours and suspicions but this is the first time people have been told to inform on each other. I tell you, that man is trouble.' She shook her fist and, to emphasise the point, spat on the ground.

'What are we going to do, papa?' Elouise knelt in front of her father and took his hand in hers. Jean looked into his daughter's trusting face and stroked her hair. 'What Jacotte says is true,' he admitted, 'people are going to be afraid, suspicious. They will need guidance and I must be here to give it.'

'Won't it be too risky to stay here?' said Michel, asking the question that was already in Elouise's mind. 'It won't be long before the priest finds out you're in the village and he'll have the bishop's men here in days.' Jean looked over at the young shepherd and smiled. 'And what do you suggest I do, my friend? I can't leave just at the point when people may need me the most.'

'My instincts tell me to head for the hills,' replied Michel, 'but if you really want to stay close to the village then I think we should hide in the woods. We can find somewhere safe there and only those people who want to see you need know where we are.'

'Michel's right, papa,' said Elouise, wanting to reinforce Michel's suggestion.

Jean knew it was a sensible plan. 'You're right, both of you,' he sighed. 'I just don't like the idea of going into hiding. But we can't stay in the village either. It's unfair to expect the Borrel's to look after us, they've done enough for me already.'

Jacotte didn't say anything but she knew it was the right decision. If Jean continued to stay with them it wouldn't be long before some wagging tongue told the priest.

'Right' said Michel, taking control, 'let's get ourselves organised. I think we should leave straight away.'

The bells of the church were ringing out the hour of evening vespers as the trio made their way through the lower gateway and out of the village. As they walked towards the fording point on the river they passed several villagers returning home after their day's work in the fields. Some of them recognised Jean and nodded to the Good Man but none knelt before him to ask for a blessing as they might have done before. The fear of being identified as a heretic was already taking hold of the village.

Once across the river Michel led them into the forest. There was still enough daylight to find a safe place, somewhere off the beaten track yet close enough to the village. Michel was more accustomed to finding his way around the grazing pastures of the uplands but he had passed through this forest before and knew there was a woodsman's hut not far away. His memory served him well and before long the pathway led into a glade where a small dwelling was tucked under the branches of a thick oak. The hut itself was deserted, the woodsman only using it three or four times a year to gather the pieces of timber he needed to make tools, and probably do some illicit poaching, but it was dry and not too far from the river. Before they left the village Jacotte had made them a parcel of food, enough to keep them going for a day or two. And once they felt safely hidden the plan was for Michel or Elouise to return to the village for fresh supplies.

There was nothing left for them to do except go about the mundane tasks of settling into their new 'home'. By the time darkness fell they had fetched water, eaten a meal and then lay on their bedding talking quietly. The two men were soon asleep, leaving Elouise with her thoughts about Guillaume and the noises of the forest.

CHAPTER TWENTY-ONE

The priest's opportunity to find out more about the Borrel's came sooner than he expected. Bernadette was a friend of Lilianne, his house maid, and the two of them would often meet after their domestic duties were over for the day, sitting on a wall, swinging their legs and chatting. The day after Sunday Mass Bernadette had to run an errand for her mother and she found herself passing the door to the church vestry. On an impulse she decided to see if her friend was there. Bernadette knocked and entered, stepping into the cool gloom of the kitchen. There was no sign of Lilianne and she was just turning around to leave when the door to the priest's room opened and Villac entered the kitchen.

'Can I help you, my child?'

Bernadette looked at him, startled by his sudden appearance.

'No. No thank you. I was just looking for Lilianne.'

'I'm afraid you've just missed her,' said Villac. 'She's gone down to the fields to see if the laundry is dry. She won't be back for a while.'

Bernadette felt uncomfortable being this close to the priest, who represented a figure of authority to her. She shivered as a trickle of perspiration ran down her spine.

'Well I expect I'll see her later. I'd better be going,' she said and turned towards the door.

'Wait, my child,' said the priest. 'Aren't you one of the Borrel family? Which one are you?' His voice had taken on a tone of friendliness that didn't come naturally to him. Bernadette felt fixed to the spot, like a rabbit in bright moonlight.

'Bernadette,' she replied, looking down at her feet, not wanting to look at the priest.

'Well isn't that a coincidence?' continued Villac, still trying to sound friendly, 'we both share a saint's name, so we have something in common already.' Bernadette didn't know how to reply so decided to say nothing. She just wanted to get away from this man who was making her feel ill at ease.

'Why don't you come and sit at the table here with me?' suggested the priest, knowing that she would find it difficult to refuse. Bernadette edged over to the table and perched awkwardly on the chair next to the priest.

'I believe you know the Garouste family?' Villac began.

'Yes' replied Bernadette.

'Were you at their household when Madame Garouste passed away?'

'Yes' was all she could say.

'And who else was there? Your Mother?' probed the priest.

'Yes, maman was there. And my brother too,' she added as an after thought, thinking that the priest was just being nosey.

'And was anyone there from outside the village? A stranger perhaps?'

'A man called Jean was there. He's not from the village, but he's not exactly a stranger,' she replied truthfully.'

'And who is this man Jean? Why was he there?' the priest continued with his gentle enquiry.

Bernadette thought for a while before replying. 'He's one of the Good Men. My mother sent for him at the chateau. She said Madame Garouste needed to see him because she was dying.' Villac's eyes lit up at this piece of information that confirmed his suspicions about both Jean and the Borrel family. He decided to press on with his questions.

'And did you see this man with the Garouste woman?' he asked, the friendliness in his voice now disappearing.

'No I didn't. I was sent out of the room and told to wait outside.'

Villac said nothing but continued to stare at Bernadette. He was admiring her round face and plump, firm features and an idea began to form in his mind.

'Come with me, my child, I want to show you something,' he indicated she should follow him into his room. He closed the door behind them and told her to sit on the bed. Then he took something out of the draw of his bedside table and sat down next to her.

'This man you call Jean is not really a good man. He's one of the leaders of the heretics and he is a danger to your family. Do you know what happens to heretics and the people that help them?' Bernadette was beginning to feel frightened and shook her head.

'Let me show you,' said the priest and revealed what he had in his hand. It was an image of a man being burnt at the stake. He had found it during his training to be a priest. Something in it, maybe the way the smoke curled around the man's agonised head, appealed to him and he had decided to keep it. Bernadette looked down at the crude illustration and started to cry. Her vulnerability only increased Villac's excitement and he started to stroke her thigh.

'Now you wouldn't want this to happen to anyone in your family, would you, my child?' Bernadette sniffed back her tears and shook her head again, unaware of Villac's hand as it slipped under her tunic.

'So you'll tell me if you see this so called 'good man' again, won't you?' Bernadette nodded.

'And you want your family to be safe don't you?' Bernadette nodded again.

'That's good, my child. Now you must do something for me.' Villac's breathing became heavier and he used his weight to push Bernadette back onto the bed. His hand tore at the clothing beneath her skirt and she could feel his thick fingers probing inside her. Villac moved on top of her, pushing her legs apart with his knees and pulling out his stiff penis with his free hand. Bernadette tried to struggle from under him but he was too heavy. She screamed as he forced himself into her but her cries seemed to excite Villac even more and he plunged deeper, destroying her innocence. 'That's a good girl,' he panted into her ear between thrusts, 'this will keep your family safe from ending up like that man in the fire.' Tears streamed from her eyes but Bernadette would not cry out again; she'd seen animals acting like this in the field and she knew it would soon be finished. She didn't have to endure the pain for too long before Villac arched his back and let out a loud groan then slowly rolled away from her. When his breathing returned to normal he sat up without looking at her.

'Go now, my child, and let this be our secret. You have done well for your family. And you will tell me if you see this man again, won't you?' Bernadette sat up feeling dazed and confused but nodded her agreement. Pulling her clothes around her she half walked, half stumbled to the door and let herself out. She reached the sunlight, sobbing with shame, and hobbled away from the church, away from the vile priest who shared the same name.

CHAPTER TWENTY-TWO

Jean had only been in the forest a few days but already a steady stream of people had started to come to the woodsman's hut to seek his guidance.

On his first visit back to the village Michel had told Jacotte where they were hiding and it didn't take long for the whereabouts of the secret location to be shared amongst the *croyants.* Some of them made the journey from the village but others broke off from their work in the fields to make the short distance into the woods.

They all wanted to know the same thing. How were they to keep their souls, and indeed their bodies, safe from this new threat from the priest?

It was true that from time to time a few believers had come to the notice of the church and been threatened with excommunication, or worse, if they didn't repent. But for the most part these people had lived in peaceful times, left alone to continue worshipping in their own way, the brutal persecutions of the crusades now fading from first-hand memory into folklore. However the Roman church was still a mighty powerful institution, influencing the lives of Catholic and Cathar alike. It owned property and land, collected taxes and controlled the details of a person's life throughout birth, marriage and death.

'How can we trust our neighbour?' 'Who will look after my fields?' 'What do we say to the priest?' 'How can we protect our families?' 'How will God protect us?' These were the questions that needed answering.

Elouise watched Jean as he tried to calm his worried visitors, knowing the words he would use, how he would reassure them, trying to make them feel more secure.

'Remember, God is in your heart. He is with you every day. Believe in God and he will protect you. Trust each other and be true to your beliefs, hold your faith. Keep your lives pure and simple and your spirit will enter Heaven. You do not need to ask for forgiveness for God knows your sins and has already forgiven you'.

Jean didn't have an answer to every question and he could tell that these people were more frightened than any he had seen before. For the first time for many of them their faith was under pressure. He realised that for some people the easy way out would be to accept whatever punishment was given to them and return to the established church for protection.

'It's not easy, is it Papa?' Elouise watched as the last of the day's visitors left the glade.

'No, my child, it isn't.' Jean stood up from the upturned log he had been sitting on. 'They are frightened, and when people are frightened they need more than words. They need to feel safe and I can't give them that safety.' Jean sighed his frustration, 'Only God can make them safe.'

Elouise slipped her arm around her father's waist and held him tightly.

'Come on' she said, 'you need a rest. Walk with me to the river and we'll dip our toes in the water.' Jean nodded his agreement, smiling at his daughter, and allowed himself to be led through the trees and down to the riverbank.

Back at the village Bernadette and Lilianne were sitting in the sunshine after supper, enjoying a moment's rest from their chores.

'Have you told anyone else?' It was Lilianne's response to her friend's story about what had happened with the priest. Bernadette shook her head and sniffed. It had been difficult enough telling her friend about the priest's questions and his attack on her body. 'What should I do?' she said, tears welling up, 'I daren't tell my mother, the priest said he could only protect my family if I kept it secret.'

Lilianne thought for a while before answering. She'd already decided not to tell Bernadette about her own sordid experiences with the priest and now an idea was beginning to form in her head. 'Don't say anything, not yet anyway,' she advised, 'Let's wait and see what the priest does next.'

What began in Lilianne's mind as an idea had now hatched into a plan. 'Is this good man, Jean, is he still at your home?' She made the question sound as innocuous as she could. Bernadette was still lost in her own misery. 'No, thank goodness, he's hiding somewhere in the woods. At least we don't have to worry about him any more.' This was just the information Lilianne needed. Now she really did have something important to tell the priest. Something so big that she could bargain with him to leave her alone forever.

CHAPTER TWENTY-THREE

The Bishop of Pamiers dismissed the messenger with a perfunctory sign of the cross followed by a curt wave of the hand. The news from the priest at St. Julien was interesting but he needed some time on his own to think about what action he should take. His own master, the Cardinal Archbishop of Albi, had issued the edict that the Cathars were to be pursued more vigorously, and the Dominican Brothers had increased their pursuit of the heretics with their own methods of inquisition.

When Lilianne had told Villac about the *Bon Homme* hiding in the woods he had wasted no time in sending a message to the Bishop. He was hoping the information would keep his profile sufficiently prominent to make him a candidate for promotion, away from this dreary village.

Having praised Lilliane for bringing him the information Villac, suddenly aroused, was taken aback when she refused to submit to his sexual needs. 'No,' she had said with an unexpected confidence ,'this is valuable information I have given you and in return I want you to leave me alone. I will continue to work for you, but you will not make me do those other things ever again.' Frustrated, Villac had had to agree to her defiant demand, but in his mind he decided this would be an ideal time to start looking for a new housekeeper.

The Bishop continued to mull over his options. He could, of course, have the heretic arrested and hand him over to his superior, like a cat leaving a dead mouse at the door of its master.

But he realised the benefits this might bring could be fleeting, at best. He might even be rebuked for allowing the man to have preached within his domain for so long without capture. He decided, instead, to have the man arrested and brought to his abbey where he could ask questions in his own time. At the very least it might lead him to uncover other heretics, thereby adding numbers to his offering to the Cardinal. Or, at the very best, he could take the credit for persuading a *Parfait* to renounce his beliefs as an example to his followers, thus delivering a significant victory to the Archbishop and at the same time enhancing his own reputation.

Pleased with this decision the Bishop wasted no time despatching his sergeant-at-arms and two priests to the forest surrounding St. Julien with orders to arrest Jean de Rhedones, on suspicion of being a heretic.

It didn't take long for the news that Elouise was hiding in the forest to travel to the chateau and reach the ears of Guillaume. He had been in an anxious state ever since they had parted and this news did little to allay his concerns.

'Why are they hiding?' he had asked his mother. 'Why didn't they came back here to the chateau, surely they would feel safer here?'

Sybille recognised the state her son was in; the pacing, nervous, helpless anxiety that love can induce. She remembered the same anguish when Armand had been forced to flee into the hills after the murder of his brother. Her distress had not subsided until she had been reunited with him after almost two months of waiting and searching.

'You must remember that Jean would put his religious duty before his own safety,' she tried to calm her son, 'and Elouise will have a fierce loyalty to her father, an instinct that will not permit her to dwell on her own feelings.' She put her hand on her son's arm, trying to reassure him that some part of Elouise would still be thinking about him.

'Besides,' she continued, 'if what we hear is true then all of us must be mindful of the fear that is being spread. It seems we are entering a new era of persecution and it won't be long before the Inquisition comes knocking on our door too. Then will be the time for us to stand up for our beliefs.' She said all this with an air of calm, almost serenity, as if she was seeing into the future.

She looked at her son again and tried to give him something practical to think about. 'Why don't you ride down to the forest and see if you can find them?' she suggested 'at least you'll be able to satisfy yourself that they're safe and you could take them some food and blankets too.'

Guillaume smiled at his mother and kissed her on both cheeks. 'You're right,' he said, pleased to have been given some activity to occupy his mind and also appreciative of his mother's understanding of his feelings. 'I'll leave right away.' He stood and bowed politely then hurried off to fetch his horse and find some supplies. Sybille watched the retreating back of her son and wondered, not for the first time, what might develop from her son's obvious deep feelings for the Good Man's daughter.

Guillaume forded the river and made his way through the cultivated fields on the opposite bank before entering the forest shade. Riding through the village he had waved at many of the people he recognised, people who had watched him grow up, but this time he had sensed a different atmosphere. Whereas before they would have welcomed him with warm words and a friendly greeting, now his wave was returned with a half-raised arm and a thin smile of acknowledgement, as if the villagers were preoccupied within their own little world. He had stopped at the Borrel's household and spoken to Jacotte briefly, long enough for her to tell him where to find Jean and Elouise. He knew exactly where to go, he'd seen the woodsman's hut before on his hunting trips, and now he steered his horse along the path that led to the clearing, his heart beating faster at the thought of seeing Elouise again.

Turning a corner the branches gradually parted and he entered the glade. Elouise was sitting on the far side in deep discussion with her father and it was a moment or two before they realised they had company. Almost immediately she stood up and, recognising who it was, rushed across the grass to meet him. Seeing her running towards him, Guillaume swung his leg over the saddle and jumped to the ground. She reached him just as he landed and they fell into each other's arms.

Jean was taken aback at the intensity of their embrace. Elouise had told him nothing of the events after he had left the chateau. He realised the two young people had feelings for each other, that was obvious when he had watched them dancing at Helene's birthday celebration, but this spontaneous display of passion was something he hadn't seen in his daughter before. He watched, partly bemused, partly concerned, as they walked hand in hand towards him. Guillaume's horse following faithfully behind, pausing to dip its head and nibble on the lush, fresh grass.

'Guillaume, how wonderful to see you,' said Jean as he stood to greet the young man. 'How did you find us?'

'Madame Borrel told me. I remembered this hut from my hunting trips.' Guillaume let go of Elouise's hand and began to untie the bundle attached to the saddle. 'Look, my mother has sent food and warm bedding for you.'

Jean accepted the parcels of food and the thick blankets, 'Your mother is a good woman, it's very kind of her to think of us.' He could sense that the two young people wanted to be together. 'Now that you're here perhaps you could help Elouise fetch some water.'

'Of course' replied Guillaume, 'I'm only too pleased to help' he grinned and looked around to see Elouise, who seemed to have read her father's mind, already holding the empty leather flagons.

'Come on,' she said. 'I'll show you the way.' And she began to half walk, half run towards the path that led to the river.

'So, what happened about Bruno?' Elouise sat on the riverbank, her chin resting on her knee as she watched Guillaume fill the flagons. Guillaume forced the stopper back into the last of them and sat down next to her.

'My father was really angry to find out that Bruno had been found dead in the garden. He was upset that the news would overshadow the announcement of Helene and Roger's betrothal. At first he thought that Bruno must have been in a drunken fight with one of the other knights, but when I confessed it was me who killed him, and the reason why, he began to calm down. He'd known all along about Bruno, especially his problem with drink and women.' Guillaume paused and his anger began to resurface as he recalled Bruno's attack on Elouise. 'My father cautioned me about the fine line between defending a woman's honour and being blinded by love but, in the end, he decided we should keep the matter within the chateau walls. He instructed two of the knights to bury him next to the chapel and our own chaplain said a prayer.'

'What about his family? Won't they need to know?' asked Elouise.

'No. There's no one to tell. Bruno was an orphan, his father was killed at Minerve and his mother died soon after. My father took him in when he three years old and he had lived with us ever since.'

Elouise rested her head on Guillaume's shoulder and stroked his arm.

'You poor boy. It's still a terrible burden for you, to have killed someone you grew up with.' Guillaume clenched his fist and shook his head. 'I couldn't bear to see him hurting you,' was all he could say.

They sat for what seemed a long time, watching the river flow by, their bodies leaning against each other.

'What about you?' Guillaume broke into her thoughts. 'Are you and your father safe here in the forest? And where's Michel?'

'We're fine here, you mustn't worry about us,' she reassured him. 'The only people who know we're here are those villagers who need to speak to my father. And Michel has only gone for a day or two at the most. He needed to make sure his sheep were still being looked after up in the pastures.' Elouise continued, keeping her voice positive. 'My father has sent word to the village that he will hold a special prayer meeting here tomorrow morning. After that I think we shall be moving on, probably to Bugarach. My father's needed in other places too, you know.'

Guillaume turned to look at her. 'I can't help worrying about you, I love you.'

Elouise reached across to push the hair away from his eyes and stroked his stubbly cheek. 'And I love you too. You are my handsome, strong protector.' She dazzled him with a smile and he began to feel aroused by the intense gaze of her eyes. He leant towards her and she let her lips meet his. They kissed for a long while and she felt him drawing her closer. The kiss brought back memories of the last time they had lain by a riverbank and she could sense herself wanting him inside her again.

'Mmm, that was nice,' she murmured as she drew back from him, 'but I think we should be getting back before my father decides to come and find us.' Guillaume stood up rather reluctantly but held out his hand to help her to her feet. Together they collected up the bulging flagons and headed back to the glade.

Jean was adding wood to the small fire they had kept alight

since their arrival in the forest. He looked up as they returned with the water. 'Are you going back to the chateau, Guillaume, or will you stay and eat some of this wonderful food your mother has sent us?'

'If I may, I will stay and eat with you,' replied Guillaume, 'besides, I understand Michel is away so perhaps you will allow me to offer my services as a guard for tonight.'

'I have no concern we need guarding, my boy,' replied Jean 'but I'm sure Elouise will sleep safer knowing you're here to protect us, won't you Lou-Lou?' Elouise knew her father was teasing her but decided not to rise to the bait.

'If Guillaume has offered to stay with us then it would be rude not to accept,' she said, trying hard to disguise her pleasure at the thought of having his company for longer.

They ate their meal sitting around the fire, Jean asking Guillaume all about his childhood at the chateau and in return telling him stories about Elouise growing up on their travels. He painted a picture of a tomboy with constantly grazed knees and knotted hair, climbing trees and cuddling lambs, but Guillaume could tell by the fondness in his voice that he was fiercely proud of the beautiful young woman who sat between them.

As the night fell and the heat from the fire began to fade Jean made his excuses and retired to the hut to sleep, but not before kissing his daughter goodnight and giving Guillaume a surprisingly strong squeeze on the shoulder. 'Goodnight and God bless,' he said to them, 'and don't let the fire go out.'

Elouise and Guillaume lay side by side, wrapped up in blankets, looking up at the stars in the ink black sky. 'What do you make of all this?' It was Guillaume who spoke.

'What do you mean?' she asked 'the stars up there? How did they get there?'

'No' he sighed, 'You know what I mean. All these new threats from the Bishop, and the priest. You and your father having to hide away'. He paused then added 'and us too. What do you think will happen?'

'What happens will be what God wants to happen. We must put our trust in Him.'

'I wish I had your strength of belief,' he replied.

'You do my brave knight, you just don't know it's there.' She squeezed his hand in the darkness. 'Don't worry, everything's going to be fine. Now try and get some sleep.'

By the middle of the next morning nearly forty villagers had filled the glade. They knelt on the grass in front of Jean, who, sitting on the upturned log, was reading verses from his Gospel of St. John. When he had finished he stood up, clutching his wooden staff, and blessed them all. All week he'd been giving them answers to their questions but now his congregation just needed to feel the security of their faith. As the ceremony ended people began to rise slowly to their feet. One or two walked over to wish Jean and Elouise a safe onward journey but most of them began to head towards the path that led back to the village.

From such tranquil moments everything afterwards seemed to happen very quickly. Suddenly there was a shout from the forest and the bishop's sergeant rode into the glade followed by the two priests and Villac, who immediately pointed at Jean. The small crowd fell back as the sergeant advanced in the direction of the priest's outstretched arm.

'Jean de Rhedones,' he called out 'By the power invested in me by the Bishop of Pamiers I am here to arrest you.'

Jean looked up at the sergeant. 'And what is the charge?' he asked calmly.

'The charge is heresy!' the man shouted and turned towards the priests. 'Seize him and tie his hands' he ordered.

'Hold there!' It was Guillaume who called out, his sword unsheathed. 'Before you take him you will have to take me first.'

He made to move towards one of the priests, but Jean held out his arm to signal that he should advance no further. 'Let there be no violence.' He gestured to Guillaume to put away his sword then turned back towards the sergeant. 'I will come with you, in peace,' he declared.

Now it was Elouise's turn to act. She rushed over to her father's side 'If he goes then I go with him,' she said defiantly, gripping her father's arm tightly. Jean turned towards his daughter, 'I won't let you do that,' he said gently 'You must stay here, my child, it's me they want not you.'

'You'd do well to heed his words,' the sergeant said, looking down from his horse 'And you too, Sir' he added pointing in the direction of Guillaume, 'Otherwise I'll be back with more men and we'll arrest the lot of you.'

Jean's hands were tied together and he was attached by a short rope to the sergeant's horse.

The whole episode had taken no longer than it takes a boy to climb a tree. The sergeant and the priests began to move out of the glade with their prisoner in tow. A stunned silence fell on the villagers and Guillaume held a tearful Elouise in his arms. Only Villac stayed to enjoy the scene, a satisfied smirk on his face. Just before Jean was hidden from view by the trees he turned and kissed the palm of his hand and raised it towards his daughter.

It was a gesture she had never seen him make before.

CHAPTER TWENTY-FOUR

Jean's arrest was not an isolated incident. Throughout the Razes region, between Foix and Carcassonne, similar arrests were taking place as part of the concerted effort to suppress once and for all the Cathar heresy. The cells of the Abbeys and the Dominicans soon began to fill with *Parfaits* and *croyants,* held for questioning in the expectation that they could be persuaded to abandon their faith and return to the Catholic church. And if persuasion didn't work then torture was always an option to help them change their mind and confess. Often the arrests were an opportunity for neighbourly scores to be settled as long standing grievances turned into religious accusations. Communities began to turn in on themselves as accusing fingers were pointed between former friends and even family members.

It was a time of suspicion, a time when fear returned.

After Jean had been taken in the forest Guillaume's immediate thought was to bring Elouise back to the chateau, but she had other ideas.

'I can't stay with you at the chateau,' she reasoned, 'It would be like I'm hiding; I'd be making myself a prisoner.'

'Then what are you going to do? Where can you go that will be safer?' his voice expressed his frustration at her stubbornness.

'Guillaume, I don't know yet,' her voice rising with her own vexation, 'but I do know I have to do something to help. I haven't followed my father all these years not to realise that this is more important than my own safety.'

Guillaume breathed out deeply, realising he was not going to be able to change her mind.

'Well at least let me take you back to the village. You can't stay out here in the forest on your own,' he reasoned, 'perhaps Madame Borrel will let you stay with her tonight.'

'Yes, of course. You're right' Elouise said, softly this time.

Guillaume busied himself tightening the straps on the saddle then mounted his horse. 'You will let me know what you decide to do, won't you?'

Elouise grasped his hand as he pulled her up behind him. 'Don't worry, I'll get word to you somehow. At least I'll know where to find you.' She put her arms around him and hugged his back as they moved off. 'Although when I'll see you again I just don't know,' she thought to herself, gripping his back tightly. At least he couldn't see the deep frown that settled on her face.

Jacotte Borrel was more than pleased to have Elouise as a house guest once more. 'Now don't you worry,' she reassured Guillaume, 'we'll take good care of her.'

'And you'll get word to me as soon as you know where she goes, won't you?'

'Yes, of course, young Sir' said Jacotte. 'Now you should be getting back to the chateau before they close the gates.' She left the young lovers to say their goodbyes, Guillaume holding Elouise tightly in his arms and stroking her hair. 'If you won't let me look after you then at least promise me you'll ask Michel to be with you wherever you go.' Elouise nodded into his shoulder 'I promise.' She tilted her head up to him and they kissed each other deeply. 'Go on,' she said as their lips parted, 'before I change my mind.' Guillaume turned towards the door, looking back once as he remounted his horse. Elouise stood and watched as he left, her hands clasped to her heart. Soon all she could hear was the sound of hooves echoing off the alleyway. She shivered in the warm night air then slowly closed the door.

By the time Michel returned to the Borrel's he'd already heard the news about Jean's arrest. It was the reason he'd come back sooner than he had anticipated.

'Well I don't think it's safe for you stay here either.' They were sitting in the hayloft of the barn where Elouise had slept for the past two nights discussing their options. 'There are plenty of people who know you and it won't be long before one of them decides to redeem themselves by talking to the priest.' Elouise said nothing for a while, trying to think of the best thing to do. 'What do you suggest, then?'

'We need to disappear for a while. At least until we know what's happening to your father.'

'Go on' she said.

'We'll go up to the high pasture, keep to the mountain paths, stay in the shepherd huts.'

'And how can I help my father if I'm hiding in the hills?' a trace of irritation in her voice.

'Because there are plenty of villages between here and Foix. We'll visit one whenever we need to. That way you can sell your potions and keep in touch with other *croyants* and we'll be able to get the latest news about your father at the same time.'

'What about your sheep?'

'Ah, don't worry about them, they'll be fine where they are. Besides, I'm paying Andre good money to look after them!' he laughed.

Elouise had to admit it was a good plan. 'You're right,' she said, jumping off the hay. 'Get your things together, Michel. I'll tell Jacotte we're leaving straight away.' Michel couldn't help smiling at her abrupt instructions. This was the second time in as many weeks she'd asked him to drop everything to go with her.

He could have told her he'd follow her to the ends of the earth if she asked him. 'Best not to tell Jacotte where we're going, just in case,' he advised instead.

'God be with you,' said Elouise as, once again, she bade the family farewell. She turned to Claude, 'Next time you go to the chateau please get word to Guillaume. Tell him I'm safe and with Michel. Tell him I'll see him soon, he'll understand.' Claude nodded and reassured her he would pass on her message. 'You just be careful, Miss, and take good care of her, Michel' he added.

Bernadette had been standing at the back of the small family group but now rushed up to Elouise, bursting into tears. 'I'm really sorry about your papa,' she said between sobs. Elouise wiped away the young girl's tears, wondering why she was so distressed.' Now then, you mustn't cry,' she said gently 'it wasn't anyone's fault.' But Bernadette could only cry harder, carrying the secret that she believed would save her family.

CHAPTER TWENTY-FIVE

'Come on Lou Lou, not much further.' Michel stopped on the path to encourage Elouise to keep walking. Since leaving St. Julien they had climbed the hills to the south west of the village then descended to cross the River Aude at Cavirac, the only fording place after the river raced through the gorge further upstream. Now they were heading back into the steep hills south of Quillan. Michel planned to follow the high country route towards Belcaire but he knew they'd need another day at least to reach there. Even though it was only late summer there was already a freshness in the air and he knew that it would get colder before night fell. They were aiming for one of the huts and Michel wanted to reach it before the sun dipped down behind the hills to the west.

Elouise caught up with her companion. Most of the day they'd walked in silence, each of them settling into their own pace and lost in their own thoughts. 'I'd forgotten how fast you walked,' said Elouise stooping with hands on thighs to get her breath back after the long climb.

'Nonsense,' teased Michel, 'I think you've gone soft after your stay at the chateau.' He knew she could usually keep up with him so he put her slowness down to her worries about Jean. 'We'll soon be at the hut and then we can eat and rest up for the night.' They carried on together side by side, Elouise calling out the names of the plants and birds along the way and Michel, as always, keeping one eye on the weather.

As they crested a rise on the hillside pasture the low outline of the stone hut came into view, a flock of sheep already penned into the walled enclosure. A wisp of blue smoke emerging from a hole in the roof indicated that someone was already in residence. They increased their pace and soon covered the short distance to the doorway.

'Hullo!' called out Michel into the gloomy interior 'anyone about?' 'Who's there?' enquired a voice from inside.

'It's me, Michel, and Elouise, daughter of the Good Man Jean.' A stocky figure emerged from the smoke filled room. 'Come in, come in,' said the shepherd, whose name was Henri. 'Come and help me get this fire going, I think the wood must be damp.' Between them the two shepherds added more kindling and blew onto the embers until the fire was burning strongly enough to cook a meal.

'I'm sorry to hear about your father,' said Henri, adding more wood. 'I saw Clement on the high pass yesterday and he said he'd seen your father with the sergeant and the priests passing through Lavelanet.'

Elouise pounced on this morsel of information 'How did he seem, did he say anything?'

'I'm sorry Miss, I don't know,' replied Henri 'but he did say that your father was walking with much dignity and that quite a few people knelt as he went past, much to the annoyance of the priests.'

'Typical,' thought Elouise, knowing that her father would want to give courage to others even when he was being forced to walk at the end of a rope.

A stamping of feet at the doorway signalled the arrival of another shepherd looking for shelter for the night. 'Who's that?' called out Henri. 'It's only me!' came the shouted reply. Michel recognised the voice immediately and a happy smile spread across his face.

'What are you doing here?' Michel called out, 'I thought you were over the mountains in Catalonia.' Alain entered the room, ducking his head under the low doorway. 'Yes, I know, but some of my sheep got sick so I thought I'd turn back. I didn't want to lose any more going over the mountains.'

'Well I'm sorry to hear about your sheep but I'm really glad to see you.' Michel took a pace across the room and gave his friend a warm hug. 'Come and sit down, we've just got the fire going. Elouise is here too, she's just gone outside to fetch some water.'

'So, still babysitting the girl.' Alain teased his friend.

'No, you know it's not like that. Her father's in real trouble, he's been arrested by the Bishop, they've taken him to Pamiers.'

'God help him,' exclaimed Alain, 'How's Elouise taking it?'

'With her usual defiance and recklessness,' replied Michel. 'She wanted to go over there and debate it with the Bishop but I've told her we need to keep a low profile for the time being. There's no point both of them getting arrested.'

'Wise words' said Alain to his friend. 'Still it must be tough on her.'

Elouise entered the room, a large pail of water in each hand.

'Alain!' she said with pleasure, dropping the pails to the floor, the water splashing over the rims as she ran to greet him. 'What a lovely surprise!' She kissed him on both cheeks. 'It's such a long time since we've all been together. This calls for a special supper, I'll go and see what food Henri and I can muster.' She picked up the heavy pails and made her way to find the older shepherd, leaving the two friends to catch up on the rest of their news.

Supper turned out to be rabbit stew accompanied by bread and cheese, with wild berry fruits picked from the bushes on the hillside. Henri had managed to find a flagon of wine, which was having the effect of keeping the conversation flowing at a high level of excitement. Henri and Alain wanted to know all about Michel and Elouise's stay at the chateau and teased them about their elevation in social status. Henri quizzed Alain about market conditions on the other side of the Pyrenees whilst Elouise was keen to know what was happening to the *croyants* in the Catalan lands. Were they being persecuted as they were now in the Razes? The two shepherds expressed their disgust at Jean's arrest and promised to help Elouise in whatever way they could. But they were also keen to know about her friendship with Guillaume, or as they called him, her 'knight in shining armour'. Thinking about her lover made her tummy flip over, which in turn made her blush as she resisted their requests for more details. The conversation continued to flow around the table and for a while their spirits were lifted in a mood of mutual support and friendship.

But now, the meal over, the three men and Elouise sat in mellower mood around the hearth, each lost in their own thoughts, their faces lit by the flickering flames of the fire.

Michel reached across to pick up the lute that was never far from his side, and began to pick out a few notes. The notes turned into melancholy chords, which, as he strummed, revealed a beautiful melody. Then, in a soft clear voice, he began to sing:

I call my lady Sunshine
Because she spreads around her
Rays of happiness
That I may bathe in
And reflect

Elouise felt her throat tighten and a tear began to well up in the corner of her eye as she listened to the words. She turned towards Michel. 'That was really beautiful. Did you write it yourself?' Michel looked at her, and nodded, a shy look on his face, too embarrassed to admit that the song was one of his own.

'Is there any more?'

Michel shook his head, 'Not yet, I'm still working on it,' he said and continued to strum the melody.

'Well whoever she is she's a very lucky lady,' said Elouise 'I hope you get to play it to her one day'. Michel smiled at the daughter of Jean, but couldn't bring himself to tell her that he had composed the song for her.

That night, four people curled up to sleep on the straw spread across the floor. Elouise lay awake, listening to the breathing of the three men. Pascal had fallen into a deep sleep almost as soon as the lamps had been extinguished and the fire damped down. She looked over at Michel and Alain, nestled together under the same blanket, their heads almost touching. Maybe it reminded her of her own night with Guillaume and her new feelings of love for someone else, but for the first time she wondered how close to each other the two friends might be. As her eyelids lowered and she drifted off to sleep she smiled, hoping they felt the same happiness that she felt for Guillaume, her 'knight in shining armour'.

CHAPTER TWENTY-SIX

Jean watched the daylight fade through the window set high in the thick stone wall of the small room. He had been held in the wide wall, the *murus largus*, of the Abbey at Pamiers ever since he had arrived three days earlier. Food and water arrived at regular intervals, though he declined to eat any of the meat, eggs or cheese that were brought to him as these were the products of procreation and therefore eschewed by all *Parfaits*, a fact his captors probably knew. A blanket had been provided for the simple wooden frame that served as a bed and an oil lamp allowed him the comfort of reading his well-thumbed copy of the gospel of St. John. His visits to the outdoor latrine, accompanied by a guard, gave him the opportunity to stretch his legs and enjoy a few moments of fresh air. If it hadn't been for the fact that his door was locked from the outside no one would have considered him to be a prisoner. He amused himself with the thought that he felt like a prize specimen, a rare butterfly, to be studied at leisure at a later date.

It was a further two days before Jean was taken, unfettered, to see his captor. He stood at one end of a long room in front of the Bishop and noted the two clerks sitting at a raised desk to one side of the room.

The Bishop sat alone at a refectory table concentrating on the remains of what seemed to have been a substantial lunch. He wiped his mouth on the thick linen napkin tucked under his chin then reached out his hand to pick up the goblet of wine that sat next to his plate. He took two long swallows before replacing the goblet carefully onto the table. Bejewelled fingers plucked the napkin from his throat, letting it drop onto the plate, then the hand gave a dismissive wave, the signal for the novice priest waiting in the shadows to emerge and clear the remains of lunch from the table.

The Bishop looked up at Jean, giving the impression that he had not even noticed him being ushered in to the room. He folded his arms across his chest.

'So, Jean de Rhedones, we meet again. Although this time you do not have the protection of your noble friends at St. Julien.'

Jean met the gaze of the Bishop and returned it with polite, yet firm, interest.

'I have no need of protection nor indeed do I seek it,' replied Jean, his blue eyes focussed directly into the Bishop's own black pupils.

'Does it not concern you that you are my prisoner?' asked the Bishop.

'I have no concerns for myself,' replied Jean, still holding the Bishop's gaze. 'You may hold this body but you cannot capture my spirit.'

'Brave words,' replied the Bishop 'but I wonder if you will still be so brave when I have finished with you.'

'That will be for you to determine, not me,' said Jean, an enigmatic smile settling on his mouth.

'So you're not afraid to die,' continued the Bishop, 'even if you are sent to the flames? You know that only flames can purify a heretic?'

'That's your belief, Bishop, not mine.'

'Are you not afraid of the pain of burning?'

Jean paused before replying, as if trying to find a simple way to explain something complicated to a child. 'It is your church that preaches pain, not mine. My God will take the pain of the fire upon himself; I would not feel the flames.'

The Bishop breathed out a long sigh and decided to take a different approach. The clerks at their desks paused, pens in hand, waiting for him to start speaking again.

'A simple man might say,' he began 'that our two churches share certain similarities. We both believe in God and the Devil, in good and evil.'

Jean smiled back. 'But you are not a simple man, Bishop. You believe that God created the world and man within that world, and if he does not live his life according to your rules then that man will go to hell, the domain of the devil'. Jean paused before continuing, 'I believe that God exists as the ultimate good spirit and that the devil is an evil spirit who created this world to trap other good spirits in the shape of man and prevent them from returning to God's side. The earth we live on is already hell, a hell we can only escape from by the purity of our thoughts and deeds'.

The Bishop absorbed this view for a while before speaking again.

'You talk about rules but surely you must believe in the concept of sin?'

'Not in the same way as you do,' replied Jean. 'You preach that if a man commits one of your sins and does not repent then his soul will go to hell, so he is ruled by fear. We say that to be alive on this earth is a sin itself, therefore everything is sinful. But our God, being good, absolves all sin, even before it has been committed.'

'So every Cathar soul goes to heaven?' suggested the Bishop, throwing Jean a challenging look. Jean smiled again.

'No, it's not that easy. The Devil has made man weak and open to temptation. If he chooses to lead a good and honest life then we believe his spirit will return into the soul of a newborn child. And if he continues to reject temptation his spirit will become purer until it is ready to ascend directly to heaven.'

'And if he does succumb to temptation?' enquired the Bishop.

'Then his spirit will return in the form of a lower life form, perhaps a rat, a snake or...' Jean could not resist the opportunity '...even a parish priest.'

He watched as an angry red flush surfaced on the Bishop's face.

'You would do well to remember you are my prisoner, Jean de Rhedones, and not the Archbishop's. He has had men burnt for such arrogance.'

'I'm sure he has,' replied Jean, unimpressed by the Bishop's blunt threat. The two men looked at each other, neither speaking.

Finally the Bishop broke the silence, tired of the debate. 'Take him away,' he ordered, motioning to the guard who had been standing by the door throughout the lengthy discussion 'We will continue this another day.'

The guard led Jean out of the room and along several stone corridors and down flights of stairs before arriving at a different room from the one he had occupied before. He was pushed with unnecessary force through the doorway. Jean stooped in the centre of the room and surveyed his new surroundings. The room was small, dark and damp. The straw on the floor smelt of mildew and only the faintest movement of cold air seemed able to penetrate the small metal grill set into one corner of the wall. There was no table and no chair, and only a rough pallet to serve as a bed. Jean decided to ignore the severity of his new surroundings and tried to make himself comfortable on the straw instead. As he drifted off to sleep Jean made a mental note to ask one of the guards for his belongings in the morning.

If Elouise could have seen the circumstances in which her father was being held it would have made her even more frustrated by her own situation. Her unswerving objective had been to reach Jean as quickly as possible but her ambition was tempered by the sound advice of the friends around her. The simple fact was that she had now acquired something of the status of a fugitive herself.

As the daughter of a well-known *Parfait* – now in the hands of the Bishop – there would be many people willing to point a finger at her if they thought it would help them avoid the attention of the Dominicans. If Elouise was noticed in any of the villages en route to Pamiers there was a strong chance she would be denounced to the nearest priest. These were the villages she had spent her life travelling through and she was as well known as her father to their occupants. Her shepherd friends advised her to stay out of the villages and remain in the hills with them. They had a freedom of movement that was denied her and they could bring her any news. As frustrating as it was, she was obliged to accept their advice.

The colder air in the mornings was a clear sign that autumn was on its way. Elouise kept herself busy helping the shepherds and collecting the herbs and leaves to make the ointments and potions she used to dispense on market days. 'I need to keep myself occupied,' she explained to Michel one morning, 'what else am I going to do with all this energy?' Despite her concerns about her father, she had never felt better in her life. She used her new vitality to clean thoroughly whichever hut they happened to be staying in. Like most men, the shepherds liked their huts to be warm and comfortable but they were not so bothered about cleaning floors and washing pots. By contrast, it didn't take Elouise long to have the place looking clean and tidy, usually persuading one of the men to fetch fresh supplies of straw to renew the bedding. Michel and his companions began to appreciate this new level of comfort, especially if there was a fresh stew in the pot. It soon became obvious that the number of shepherds needing to stay in the hut increased whenever word got round that Elouise was in residence. She couldn't deny she enjoyed their company and, she reasoned, the more people who arrived the better the chance of news about her father or perhaps Guillaume. More than six weeks had passed since she said goodbye to him and she knew he would be worried about her. She made up her mind to ask Michel if he would return to the chateau and let Guillaume know she was safe and to find out if his family had any better information about her father.

That night, as she lay under her blanket, she became aware of an odd sensation in her nipples. She touched her breasts and noticed they seemed harder and more sensitive than usual. As she pondered this new feeling she lowered her hand and let it rest on her stomach. She couldn't help noticing that it too seemed different, slightly swollen. She fell asleep wondering what had brought about these changes and reasoned that they were probably due to her recent increase in workload, including all the cooking and cleaning for the shepherds. It didn't occur to her for one moment to imagine that she might be with child. Nor would she have known that at precisely the same moment a young girl in the village of St. Julien was experiencing exactly the same changes in her body.

CHAPTER TWENTY-SEVEN

Michel had agreed, reluctantly, to Elousie's request to return to the chateau. He didn't like the idea of leaving her but he couldn't disagree with her reasoning that the Count might have some influence over the fate of her father. It took him the best part of three days to make the journey and when he arrived he was given a warm welcome by Guillaume. A hot meal was soon on the table in front of him; Guillaume barely containing his good manners to allow Michel to finish eating before plying him with questions about Elouise.

'So tell me, my singing friend,' he asked, as Michel wiped his plate with a chunk of bread. 'How is Elouise? Is she safe? Is she well?'

Michel chewed and swallowed before replying. 'Don't worry, young sir, the lady is safe in the hills. And in fine form too. In fact I have never seen her looking so well. She is positively glowing! Goodness knows what you have done to bring such colour to her cheeks!' Guillaume looked bashful at this gentle teasing but was pleased nevertheless to hear such good news about his love. 'I'm grateful to you for bringing me this news, Michel, and for giving Elouise your protection too. I tried to persuade her to stay here but she insisted on wanting to help her father'.

'I know' replied Michel, 'she can be a very determined young woman when she wants to be'. He paused before continuing 'Is there any more news about Jean?'

Guillaume looked across the table at Michel. 'We should go and talk to my father if you've finished eating.' The two young men left the warmth of the kitchen and made their way to the Count's private chamber. Guillaume knocked on the thick oak door and waited for his father's permission to enter. 'Father,' he said as they entered the room, 'Michel, the shepherd, is here. He's asking if we have any news of Jean de Rhedones'.

'Come in, my boy,' boomed the Count 'Come and warm yourself by the fire.' He signalled for Michel to join him. 'Did you bring your lute with you? I've never heard of a shepherd being such a wonderful entertainer. You were marvellous at my daughter's birthday, you have a real gift for music!'

'Thank you, my lord,' replied Michel, surprised by the informality of the Count. 'It was an honour to play for you and your daughter'.

The Count's friendly face took on a more serious look. 'So, you want to know if we have any more news of the *Parfait*? Well the truth of the matter is not very much. I had one of my men travel to Pamiers to find out what was happening and to see if we might be able to negotiate his release, but the most he could tell me was that Jean remains a prisoner of the Bishop.' He paused and looked directly at Michel. 'At least that means he's still alive. It seems the Bishop is determined to make an example of Jean one way or another'. The Count stared into the fire for several moments. 'Just between the three of us I have to say I fear for his life.' His words hung in the air like a cold fog. In truth Michel had not expected much else but he had made a promise to Elouise to find out what he could.

'How much time do you think we have?' he asked.

'To be honest with you, my boy, I don't know. In my experience these interrogations can go on for weeks, even months. Who knows what the Bishop has in mind for Jean? One thing is for certain, he won't miss an opportunity like this to impress the

Archbishop or indeed the Pope himself.' The Count poked at a log in the fire, sending a shower of sparks up the chimney, then turned to his son.

'Guillaume, why don't you make sure Michel is comfortable for the night. I'm sure your mother would like to see him in the morning'. The Count grasped the shepherd's hand, 'Goodnight, young man, and thank you for coming. I'm sorry we don't have better news for you about the Good Man but at least my son will be happier knowing that Elouise is safe and well.'

Not long after breakfast Michel found himself seated in the dressing chamber of the Countess listening to her describing the changing mood in the village. 'It's strange but people have stopped smiling,' she said, 'There's an air of suspicion around the place as if everyone's looking over their shoulder. I've seen people wearing the yellow cross of penance; it's hard to know who to trust anymore.' Her sadness made her look even more beautiful to Michel's eyes and he would have liked to have consoled her in some way, maybe stroking her hand, but he knew this would be crossing an impossible line. Then, as if shaking off an unwanted image, her eyes brightened and she turned and smiled warmly at the shepherd. 'Guillaume tells me you have been looking after Elouise and that she's safe and well. At least that's one piece of good news; he's been very worried about her. I had to tell him it would do more harm than good if he tried to find her.'

'He shouldn't worry so, my lady' replied Michel, 'Elouise is very strong. Besides, I wouldn't let anything bad happen to her'.

'No, I'm sure you wouldn't, she's very fortunate to have you to protect her. You're a very good young man, Michel.' Sybille leant towards him and patted his arm as if to endorse her words and Michel could not stop himself from blushing. 'Come,' she said, as if to save his embarrassment 'I see you have your lute, why don't you play something for me?' Michel reached behind him for the instrument that was never far from his side and was just about to begin when there was a gentle knock on the door.

'Mother? Are you in there?'

'Yes, yes,' replied Sybille, 'come in, my darling.' Helene appeared through the doorway. 'Michel was just about to play something. Come and sit with me and we'll listen together.' She patted the cushion next to her and Helene, directing a friendly smile at Michel, joined her mother.

Michel began to strum slow chords and then started to sing, his voice soft and low. This was not a song of celebration but a song of sorrow. Not of love unrequited but of lost causes and beaten battles. It was a song from the past but one that seemed to reflect the mood of the present and the uncertain times ahead. As his voice sang of slain heroes and broken dreams the mother and daughter held each other and tears began to flow down their cheeks as they listened to the familiar, but seldom heard, words. After his song had reached its crescendo and his voice had diminished to a final desperate whisper a silence descended on the room and the three people in it.

After several long moments Sybille finally spoke. 'That was beautiful, Michel, but very sad. Don't you have something brighter to raise our spirits?' Michel looked at the mother and daughter, uncertain how to reply to their request. Finally he found the courage to speak, 'Not today, my lady. I don't think I can find a happy song inside me. Besides, I should be going. I have people I must see in the village.'

'Yes, of course,' replied Sybille, 'We mustn't keep you. It was very good of you to play for us.' Michel stood up and Sybil took his hand and held it in both of hers. 'God be with you, Michel. I hope it won't be too long before we see you again.' Helene came over and stood next to her mother. She leant forward and kissed Michel gently on the cheek, 'Say hullo to Elouise for me. Tell her we are all thinking about her.' Michel thanked them both and bade them farewell. The thought crossed his mind that it could be some time before he saw the chateau again.

It didn't take long for Michel to make the steep descent to the village. As soon as he had passed through the gate he made straight for the Borrel residence. Stepping through the entrance to their small yard everything seemed normal and familiar. A few chickens scratched and pecked at the ground and a pig grunted as it nosed through some discarded vegetable peelings. A thin plume of smoke emerged from the hole in the roof, the smell of burning wood mingling with the pungent aroma from the dung heap in the corner of the yard.

Michel knocked on the door out of politeness and waited for permission to enter. He would have expected a friendly 'Come in, come in whoever you are,' but this time he heard a concerned voice call out 'Who is it?'

Michel recognised the voice of Claude Borrel and registered a mild surprise that he was at home and not working in the fields. 'It's me, Michel,' he replied, leaning his face closer to the wooden door. He heard a bustling inside as if someone was being pushed out of the way and then the door opened wide and he was immediately enveloped into the ample arms of Jacotte Borrel. 'Michel, come in, bless you,' she said as she released her grip and grasped his face between her hands and planted a kiss on both cheeks. 'Come and tell us all your news. Are you hungry? thirsty? Bernadette pour some wine for Michel and fetch some bread and cheese.' She said all this in one burst and Michel smiled self-consciously as he allowed himself to be pulled into the room. Soon bread, cheese and wine were in front of him as he sat at the table with Jacotte and Claude seated opposite. By the time he brought them up to date with news of Elouise and their time in the high pastures and of his visit to the chateau and answered all their questions there were only crumbs left on the plate in front of him.

It was gloomy inside the room and Michel had noticed that whilst he had been talking Bernadette had remained seated in the corner, listening but not taking part in the conversation. He nodded his head towards the girl.

'What's the matter with Bernadette?' Claude and Jacotte exchanged a hard look between themselves before Claude spoke. 'She's only gone and got herself pregnant, the silly little madam' As he said this he turned towards his daughter, his face a mixture of anger and sadness.

Jacotte pulled at her husband's arm. 'Don't be too hard on her, you heard what she had to say.' Jacotte turned her head towards Michel, wanting to include him in the situation.

'What do you mean?' he asked gently. Jacotte sent a sympathetic glance towards her daughter before answering. 'She won't tell us who did it, who the father is. She keeps mumbling about protecting the family, though from what, god only knows. Claude thinks it must be one of the village lads who's scared her into keeping quiet.'

'Yes, and when I find him I'll rip his balls off!' Claude spat the words out as he grabbed his hat and headed for the door. 'I'm going to feed the goat.'

Michel slid off the bench and went over and sat down on the floor next to Bernadette. He put his arm around her shoulder, 'Are you alright?'

She sniffed and nodded and turned her face up towards his. The reddened rims of her eyes told him how much she'd been crying.

'I can't tell them,' she whispered, 'he promised me they wouldn't be punished if I kept quiet and didn't tell them who he is. What else can I do?' Her question didn't need an answer as she leant against Michel's shoulder and began sobbing again, but he couldn't help thinking that it must have been a man with some power, rather than a boy, to make such a threat to a simple, innocent girl. Jacotte interupted his thoughts.

'It's getting dark, you'll stay the night, won't you?'

'Of course, Jacotte, you're always most kind' replied Michel.

His mind continued to ponder Bernadette's predicament. He made a promise to himself to find out who could have taken such ruthless advantage of the Borrel's daughter.

CHAPTER TWENTY-EIGHT

'Why don't you just commit suicide? Wouldn't it be the easiest way to release your spirit?' The Bishop was beginning to get exasperated with the progress of questioning Jean. They had been bouncing dogma backwards and forwards for the best part of three weeks and he was still no closer to getting Jean to recant or even give him the names of other Cathar sympathisers.

Jean, despite the weakness brought on by the deprivations of his cell and a diet of bread and water, managed to raise a smile. 'Then who would look after my flock? There are still many who need my guidance. No, to take my own life is not an option, but when the time comes I shall be happy to leave this earthly body.'

'And take your place at the side of God, no doubt' sneered the Bishop.

Jean refused to rise to the bait. 'Not necessarily,' he said, smiling serenely, 'even St Paul had to go through thirty reincarnations before he was admitted to Paradise.'

The Bishop could stand the debate no longer. He signalled to the clerks to stop writing and waved to the guard to take Jean back to his cell. 'God help you, Jean de Rhedones. You are forcing me to make a very grave decision.' The guard pulled up Jean by an arm and dragged him to his feet; he was getting too weak to walk by himself. As they reached the door Jean turned around. 'Then make your decision, Bishop, and live with it. One day you will have to answer for it.' The guard pulled Jean roughly through the door, leaving the Bishop to sit and debate with himself what to do with Jean. One thing he had decided for certain, he was not going to hand over such an obstinate prisoner to the Archbishop. It would be seen as a sign of his own failure to extract a confession.

It took Michel three days of hard travel to reach Elouise. The weather was deteriorating and more than once he'd been forced to stop and shelter as flurries of icy rain and snow blew through the high pastures. Usually by this time of year the flocks would have been taken down to the lower slopes. He wondered just how his own sheep were coping with being kept for so long with barely enough food. Suddenly the fact that they needed to be moved gave him the solution as to how he and Elouise might reach Pamiers.

'Michel, Michel, at last! I've been so worried about you. Come and warm yourself.' Elouise had sprung up to greet him as he came through the door of the hut, a cold blast of air swirling in behind him. Michel threw off his cloak and stood in front of the fire, turning slowly to allow the heat to penetrate his body. Elouise busied herself over the stove, filling a bowl of stew for her friend.

'So, tell me the news. Did you find out anything about Papa?' The eager anticipation on her face made it difficult for Michel to reply, knowing that he didn't have the answer she was looking for.

'The Count couldn't really tell me much,' he measured his words carefully. 'He had one of his men go to Pamiers but he wasn't allowed to see your father. It seems that Jean is still being held by the Bishop, which at least means he's still alive.'

Elouise had already come to that conclusion. She brushed some crumbs from her lap trying not to let her disappointment show. Eventually she spoke again. 'And did you see Guillaume?' she asked softly, 'How is he?'

'Yes, of course I did, Lou-Lou,' replied Michel. 'He's fine, although very worried about you and missing you too. He wanted to know how you were and I told him you were looking really well, all things considered. His mother asked after you too. She seemed reassured when I told her you were a very capable young woman. Actually what I should have said was that you are a very headstrong young lady.' He laughed as he said this and he was glad when Elouise smiled back at him. He continued to eat, enjoying the taste of the rabbit mixed with the herbs that Elouise had added. 'Oh yes, there is something else,' he realised, pulling a bone between his teeth. 'You remember the Borrel's daughter, Bernadette? Well she's pregnant but she won't tell anyone who the father is. Seems he's threatened her family with some kind of punishment if she tells them his name.'

Elouise's hand flew to her mouth. 'Oh no! that's awful,' she exclaimed, 'the poor girl, she's so young too. Who could be so evil?'

'Well I've had three days to think about that, too,' said Michel 'and my money's on that priest in the village, the one that limps.'

'What makes you say that?'

'Well, the mood in the village has changed. People are getting suspicious of each other now that the Catholics have decided to crack down on the *croyants*. Who else is in a position to threaten a family like the Borrel's, especially one that makes no attempt to hide its beliefs? Besides, I seem to remember that Bernadette had a friend who works for the priest, maybe he has a weakness for young girls.'

'The bastard.' Elouise spat out the word, to the surprise of Michel, who had never heard her swear before.

While Michel had been telling her about Bernadette there was one word that seemed to trigger something inside Elouise. Pregnant. Suddenly certain events seemed to add up. She remembered missing her monthly flow, her breasts had begun to feel a swollen; certainly her appetite had increased. 'Oh, my God,' she thought, 'that's it! No wonder I've been feeling different, I must be pregnant too. I'm going to have a baby!' The realisation sent a flush to her cheeks and a hundred thoughts racing through her head. She managed to resist the temptation to blurt out her conclusion to Michel. 'The last thing I need now is a man getting all protective over me,' she decided. Instead she bit her lip and allowed herself half a smile and half a frown as she digested this unexpected new development in her life.

The next morning Michel explained his plan to Elouise. 'You want to get to Pamiers to see your father and I need to get the rest of my sheep to lower ground, so here's what I suggest. We get the sheep off the mountain and take them to market at Pamiers. I know it's not the nearest market but it will give us an excuse to be on that route. And in case there's a problem with anyone recognising you we'll dress you in some leggings and put a cap on your head. You'll look just like a shepherd boy. What do you think?'

Elouise smiled and hugged her friend. 'I think it's a great idea. I don't know where I'd be without you.' She couldn't resist a smile to herself at the thought of what might have happened if she'd been further into her pregnancy. It would have been a lot more difficult to disguise her as a boy. 'I'll go and get food ready for the journey. I think we should leave straight away, don't you?' Michel looked out of the small window at the gathering grey clouds and nodded his agreement.

They decided to keep to the higher paths where possible, making their way from one hut to the next, instead of descending the hills and following the valley to Pamiers. It would take them longer but they would avoid passing through any villages and they would have somewhere to shelter at night. They set off in good spirits, two childhood friends accompanied by a flock of bleating sheep, all of them glad to be on the move again.

CHAPTER TWENTY-NINE

The smoke from the tall candles that helped to illuminate the proceedings drifted up slowly in the cold air towards the ceiling of the Abbey's grand hall. The Bishop of Pamiers in his purple robes and gold mitre sat at a large table flanked by a dozen of his fellow inquisitors, administrators and other priests. In front of him lay several sheets of parchment on which were written in precise detail all the questions and responses collected over the weeks involving the case against the accused. The Bishop picked up one sheet and studied it carefully before replacing it slowly on the table. He looked up at the prisoner kneeling on the cold flagstones a few paces in front of him, two guards standing a pace back from the man's shoulders.

'Jean de Rhedones,' began the Bishop 'I ask you for the final time, will you recant your heretical life? Will you stop leading others into your misguided beliefs? Will you return to the one true church and save your soul from damnation?'

Jean looked up at the Bishop. His face was haggard and unshaven, his body was weak from lack of food but his eyes remained clear and bright. His spirit had not been broken. 'I cannot,' he replied, 'I believe in neither your hell nor your purgatory therefore your church's salvation is of no consequence to me.'

The Bishop absorbed the reply, looking at Jean for several moments.

'Is that your final word?'

'It is,' replied Jean.

The Bishop turned his head from side to side as if conferring with the others at the table then looked directly at Jean.

'Stand him up,' he ordered the guards. They each placed a hand under Jean's armpits and pulled him upright.

'Jean de Rhedones you have been found guilty of heresy, the punishment for which is death. You will be executed neither by the rope nor by the blade but by burning at the stake, the only remedy that is guaranteed to purify the heretical.' He paused to see what effect the verdict had on Jean but it drew no reaction from the prisoner. 'You will be handed over to the town authorities and they will see that the sentence is carried out. May God have mercy on your soul.' The two guards pulled Jean backwards and dragged him towards the door but he kept his gaze locked onto the Bishop's eyes, not in defiance but with a look that expressed forgiveness. The Bishop couldn't return Jean's stare and was forced to look down at the parchment in front of him. He picked up a quill and slowly put his signature to the document. A candle and wax were soon provided and he pushed his signet ring with careful deliberation into the molten red pool to seal the verdict.

Anticipating Jean's refusal to recant, the Bishop had already given instructions to his clerks to prepare the death warrant in advance.

Jean slumped onto the thin layer of filthy straw that served as both floor covering and bedding in his cell. A jug of brackish water and a few hunks of stale bread were the only nourishment he had been given in the past few days. He couldn't remember the last time he had felt anything warm in his stomach. He wasn't at all surprised at the Bishop's verdict, in fact he'd been expecting it and he certainly wasn't afraid to die. The prospect of his spirit freeing itself from this hell on earth and flying upwards to join the good God in Heaven was central to his belief and he knew he would be following many others who had found similar freedom at the stake. Nevertheless there was sorrow in his heart. Sorrow that he would not see his daughter again and yet more sorrow for his beautiful Blanche who had been taken from him on the day Elouise had been born. The only comfort left to Jean was his battered copy of the gospel of St. Paul. There was not enough light in his cell to read but it soothed him just to rub the leather covers with his thumb and imagine the words inside.

He wondered how long he would have to wait before his jailers came to fetch him from his cell for the last time. 'I'll miss my verbal sparring with the Bishop,' he thought to himself, a wry smile spreading across his sunken face. 'Given a bit more time I may even have been able to convert him, instead.' The thought amused him enough to let out a loud laugh, a sound that the guard positioned outside his door found strangely alarming, coming as it did from a condemned man.

Elouise and Michel continued their journey until they could see the spires and towers of Pamiers appear out of the gloomy afternoon. They stood and gazed at their destination for a few moments, the chill, frosty hills behind them and the sheep quietly grazing at their feet. 'Not far now, Lou-Lou' said Michel, 'We should press on and get there before they shut the gates at dusk.'

It had taken them fifteen days to get this far, keeping to the green-oaked woods of the hillsides and skirting the hamlets and villages along the way. One morning they had caught a glimpse of the formidable fortress at Montsegur, its sinister walls rising up from the stark peak, before it disappeared from view in a swirl of dark cloud. It had taken them two days extra to skirt Foix, deciding to take a longer westerly path to avoid the large town. It gave Elouise a strange feeling to be so close and yet not visit the town where she'd been born. But the advantage of their chosen route was that they met very few people on the way. There were hardly any other shepherds about at this time of year and the few souls they had seen were farmers or their wives making their way to the local market. They exchanged greetings but had not stopped for longer conversations, each seeming keener to reach their respective destinations. Elouise's disguise therefore had not been strictly necessary, but she maintained the pretence, if only to keep Michel happy.

'Where are we going to stay?' asked Elouise as they began walking towards the town.

'Don't worry' replied Michel, 'As soon as we get through the gates I have a friend who will look after us.'

'You never fail to amaze me,' teased Elouise, 'Do you have friends in every town between here and Quillan?' Michel smiled at his travelling companion, still beautiful even in her disguise as a shepherd boy.

'Well, you know me, I like to make friends with all sorts of people.' She laughed at his reply and once again felt safe and secure in the comforting care of her good friend.

They reached the gates of the town just as the flaming torches were being fixed on top of the walls.

'And what might be your business in Pamiers?' enquired the watchman at the gate.

'We come to sell our sheep at market,' replied Michel.

'And do you have lodgings in the town?' continued the guard.

'Yes sir. We are expected by my good friend Pascal Escoy who lives near the Abbey Square.' The man seemed to be satisfied with Michel's answers. 'Come on then, hurry up and get those sheep in quickly' he ordered gruffly, 'I have to shut these gates now.'

Michel and Elouise herded the sheep through the portal and up the narrow street towards the centre of town. As she turned around Elouise saw the heavy gates being closed and locked behind her. She quickened her pace to keep up with Michel who was concentrating on keeping the sheep heading in one direction. It had been some time since he had been in Pamiers but he found the way easily to Pascal's and was soon knocking on the door of his friend's house.

'Michel! What a lovely surprise! I had no idea you were coming to Pamiers,' said the well dressed man who opened the door to them.

'Well don't tell that to the guard at the gate,' replied Michel as he busied himself with getting all the sheep through the side entrance and into the yard. As soon as the flock was settled Elouise and Michel followed Pascal into his home. The warmth of the interior soon penetrated their cold bones and Elouise began to realise how tired she felt.

'And who is this charming young boy you are travelling with, Michel?' Elouise realised she was still wearing the cap as part of her disguise. Slowly she pulled the cap from her head and allowed her long, dark hair to tumble around her shoulders. Pascal could not prevent a look of amused shock appearing on his face, raising his eyebrows as he turned to look at Michel.

'Allow me to introduce Elouise de Rhedones, daughter of the Good Man Jean,' said Michel. At the sound of his visitor's name the look on Pascal's face turned instantly from amusement to one of serious concern. He was about to say that he knew about her father but decided in a split moment to keep that information to himself. 'By the look of her,' he thought to himself, 'the last thing the poor girl needs is bad news'. He quickly recovered his composure and resumed his duties as host. 'Come, both of you and warm yourselves by the fire while I find you something to eat, you must be starving. You can tell me all your news when you have eaten and rested.'

Elouise and Michel needed no second invitation to slump in

front of the fire and Pascal had to wake them when he returned with two large bowls of steaming stew. Having devoured the hot food the two travellers were too tired to talk and they agreed it would be better to sleep and wait until morning.

Elouise arose fully rested and found Pascal busying himself in the cramped kitchen. The smell of fresh bread filled her nostrils and an inviting platter of cheese lay on the table. 'Ah, there you are my sweet guest. Please sit down and help yourself,' said Pascal, ushering her towards the table. He continued stirring a pot hanging over the fire.

'Where's Michel? He's not still asleep is he?' asked Elouise, pulling apart the bread and chewing on a sizeable crust.

'Up and gone,' replied Pascal.

'Gone? Gone where? 'she said, suddenly anxious.

'Don't worry, young lady,' he reassured her. 'He's taken the sheep to the market place. He was hoping to get a good price for them. He left early so as not to disturb you.'

Elouise chewed slowly, concentrating on balancing a bite-sized piece of cheese on top of a chunk of bread. She looked at Pascal; he seemed older, more sophisticated than Michel's usual friends. 'So, how do you know Michel?' she began, 'You don't look much like a shepherd.' He laughed, 'That's because I'm not. I hate sheep, horrible eyes!' He shuddered with mock horror and made Elouise smile. He came over to the table and sat opposite her, pouring himself a tumbler of wine mixed with water.

'I make musical instruments and give a few lessons, that's how I met Michel.' Elouise said nothing but her eyes asked him to continue. 'I was in the market place one day, buying some eggs if I remember correctly, when I heard someone singing. The voice seemed to be coming from the direction of the sheep pens, which I thought unusual, so I followed the sound. There was

Michel, strumming a few chords and singing a simple song. He was obviously popular, judging from the applause from the small crowd that stood in front of him. He'd even collected a few coins in a hat on the ground.' Pascal paused, reliving the scene in his mind. 'It was obvious he had a good voice, but his playing was a little crude to say the least. I waited until he'd finished and his audience had dispersed, then I approached.

'I told him I'd enjoyed his song but his playing could do with some improvement. I remember he smiled and laughed; he had a beautiful smile, and wasn't at all upset at my criticism. He told me he had taught himself to play and was really only a beginner. So, I introduced myself and told him what I did and offered to teach him how to play his instrument properly. He came and spent some time with me to begin with and then he'd come and see me whenever he came to Pamiers. He used to come two or three times a year but this is the first time I've seem him for a long time.' Pascal looked wistful, saying nothing but twisting the tumbler from side to side. Elouise looked at this man who obviously cared for Michel very much and realised how little she really knew about her friend.

'I hope he won't be too long,' she said, bringing the two of them back to reality. 'I need him to help me find out what news there is of my father. We have to get to the Abbey.' Pascal looked across at the beautiful young woman and reached out a hand to touch her arm. 'Elouise, there's something I need to tell you. I couldn't tell you last night, you looked exhausted. Your father...,' he struggled to find the right words, 'the rumour in the town is that your father has been sentenced to die for being a heretic. I'm so sorry.' Elouise looked at Pascal in disbelief, the blood draining from her face.

'No, no, that can't be right, it can't be true,' her hands covered her face and she couldn't prevent a deep sob emerging. 'I need to get to the Abbey, I have to see my father, I need to see him now!' she started to stand up but the shock of the news made her sway and she clutched the edge of the table to steady herself. Pascal swiftly moved around and held Elouise. She clung to him, her tears flowing into his shoulder. He stroked her hair and tried to soothe her. 'I think you should wait for Michel to return. Then we can decide what's the best thing to do.'

'Does Michel know?' she asked quietly.

'No, my dear girl, I had to tell you first.' But, as he continued to comfort the sobbing young woman, the thought struck him that Michel would probably have found out for himself by now.

Almost immediately the door flew open and Michel burst in, the cold rain dripping from his cloak, wet hair plastered across his face. One look at the scene in the room and he could see that Elouise knew about Jean. Pascal let go of her and allowed Michel to take over the comforting role.

'Lou-Lou, I'm so sorry. I just heard the news in the market. I came back straight away, I didn't realise that Pascal might already know, I was too tired to think last night.' His tears mingled with hers and the two of them held each other tightly. Gradually Elouise composed herself and stepped back from Michel, a determined look on her face.

'I need to find my father. Will you help me?' The two men looked at each other and nodded slowly.

'Of course we will,' said Michel. 'There must be something we can do to stop this.'

Elouise smiled at the innocence of her friend. 'My dearest sweet Michel, don't you see? This was always possible the moment they took my father in the forest. He would have known that too. The important thing for me now is to see him.'

'What about you, Elouise? Will it be safe for you to see your father?' asked Pascal, realising that a *Parfait's* daughter might be an added prize for the Bishop and his inquisitors. 'I've already thought of that,' she replied, and grabbed the cap she'd worn yesterday. 'I'll just have to become a shepherd boy again, won't I?'

Despite his protests it was agreed that Pascal wouldn't go with them to the Abbey. Michel explained, with good reason, that it might not be safe for a resident of the town to be making enquiries about the condemned man. Better that he and Elouise should go alone in case there was any trouble, then they would need somewhere safe to hide.

Elouise and Michel left the warmth of Pascal's hearth without delay. Bending their heads into the driving rain they made their way along the narrow streets that led to the Abbey.

'You'd better let me do the talking,' said Michel as they approached the arched doorway, 'No point in giving yourself away.' Michel knocked several times before a panel in the door slid open and a face appeared. 'What do you want?' the face enquired in a gruff, unfriendly voice.

'We'd like to see the condemned man please,' replied Michel calmly.

'And why would that be?' the man sounded suspicious.

'I have a message for him from a relative in Foix. Someone I met on my way here to sell my sheep.' The disembodied face looked at the pair of bedraggled strangers for a few moments.

'Well you're too late,' came the reply. Elouise's head jerked upright at these words and she was just about to hurl herself at the gate when Michel cut in front of her.

'What do you mean, too late?'

'I mean he's not here, he's been taken to the town jail. They'll be burning him as soon as this weather clears up'.

The two of them didn't wait to hear any more but hurried from the Abbey, only stopping to ask a surprised woman for directions to the jail.

'My poor father, I must see him, I need to see him!' Elouise was beginning to lose her self-control as she and Michel huddled together in a doorway deciding what to do next.

'Wait here, I've got an idea,' said Michel and he ran towards a shop across the street. He reappeared a short while later clutching a small brown sack.

'What have you got in there?' said Elouise.

'I've bought some food for your father, I thought it would be the simplest thing to do. And I've got a flagon of eau-de-vie in case it's needed.'

'But my father doesn't drink strong liquor,' said Elouise, not believing that Michel could make such a simple mistake.

'It's not for him my dearest shepherd boy, but it might come in handy to bribe the guards.' Elouise thanked Michel silently for his calmness and allowed herself to be pulled across the street towards the jail.

This time they had no difficulty gaining entrance and, with the help of Michel's bribe, a guard was soon leading them down a dank, cold corridor towards one of the cells. The guard stopped in front of a low door and selected a key from the chain that hung around his waist. The ancient door had swollen in the damp conditions and he had to heave his shoulder against it before it would open. 'You've got visitors!' he said loudly, without entering the cell, then turned to the two young people. 'See that lamp on the wall?' he pointed at a crude tallow lamp that rested in a niche, it's flame flickering in the chill draught, 'When that wick needs trimming your time's up.' He didn't wait for a response but turned and hurried back up the corridor, keen to renew his acquaintance with the gift of liquor.

Elouise hesitated briefly in front of the cell and then entered, Michel just behind her. 'Who is it? Who's there?' Jean could only see the outline of two people.

'It's me, father,' said Elouise softly 'Michel's here too.'

She rushed to Jean who was struggling to get up from the

floor. 'Oh papa! my poor papa!' she clung to Jean and held him tightly. Jean could do nothing to prevent the tears rolling from his eyes as he held his daughter.

'Elouise, my dear sweet child, and Michel too. How in all wonder did you get here?' He regained a little of his composure and held Elouise at arm's length and, for the first time in what seemed a long while, smiled down at her. Elouise looked up into his face, stifling a cry of shock as she took in his gaunt features and ragged grey beard, then stood up on tiptoe and kissed him gently on both cheeks.

It was Michel's turn to embrace Jean and then, sensibly, offer the food they had smuggled in. As they sat on the musty straw watching Jean chew slowly they explained how they had travelled across the hills and made their slow way to Pamiers. Jean seemed genuinely interested in their journey, asking questions and recalling journeys of his own through the same region. But he knew he was only delaying the inevitable. He could see the crumpled look on Elouise's face and the sad way she looked at him. He wanted to calm her obvious distress.

'Elouise,' he began, 'You know what's going to happen, don't you?' She nodded and put on her bravest face. 'Many have gone before me and this is just the end of my journey in this world. I would never choose to leave you but I'm not afraid to die.'

Elouise reached out to hold her father's hand. She had to swallow hard before she was able to speak.

'I know,' she said, gripping his hand tightly as if to reassure him. 'You have taught me well. I don't want to lose you but I know you, of all people, will be going to a better place.'

The three of them sat in silence until Michel, noticing the dying lamp on the wall, nudged Elouise. 'We have to go,' he said gently. Jean placed a hand on both their heads and blessed them.

'Is there anything you need, anything I can get you?' asked

Elouise, still anxious for her father. Jean thought for a moment before replying.

'Yes, you can bring your scissors and give this grey beard a good trim.' He forced a smile, 'and some clean clothes would be welcome too.'

'Of course, papa' she said, grateful to have another chance to see him, 'I'll come back tomorrow.'

Father and daughter embraced once more then the two young people turned to leave the cell, the footsteps of the returning guard echoing off the damp, sombre corridor.

CHAPTER THIRTY

Elouise left Pascal's house early the next morning. She took a pair of scissors with her and some money borrowed from Michel. The rain had stopped and a weak sun struggled to brighten the damp streets and alleyways as she made her way towards the centre of town and the premises of a cloth merchant. Elouise had to knock loudly before the merchant appeared at the doorway. 'We're not open yet,' said the owner with obvious annoyance, looking at Elouise, still in her disguise as a shepherd boy. 'What is it you want?'

'Forgive me, sir,' said Elouise, in as low a voice as she could manage, 'I need to buy a shirt.' The mood of the merchant changed at the prospect of selling a ready-made garment rather than just some material. 'You'd better come in then,' he said, fumbling with the lock and pulling open the door. Elouise entered the shop and the man proceeded to lay out several garments for her to inspect. He continued to stand behind the counter, wondering if this shepherd boy could afford such an item. Elouise ignored his obvious suspicion and slowly examined each shirt. Eventually she made her choice. 'I'll take this one,' she said, holding up a long shirt made of fine white linen. 'How much is it?' The shopkeeper made a mental calculation of a figure, doubled it, and told her the amount. Without hesitation Elouise brought out some coins from a small leather pouch and laid the money on the counter. 'Will you wrap it for me please?' 'Certainly, young man,' said the merchant, his mood rapidly improving with the swiftness of the transaction. He busied himself folding the shirt inside a length of muslin and tied the package together with string. 'Can I show you anything else?' he enquired with greedy enthusiasm, thinking that this could turn out to be a very good morning's business.

'No thank you, sir,' said Elouise politely, picking up the package and heading for the door. As she left the shop she heard the owner calling out behind her,' Come again, won't you!'

Elouise hurried towards the prison. Her route took her across the main square and she shuddered when she saw a group of men carefully placing bundles of wood around the thick wooden stake that had been hammered into the ground. She pulled the cap lower over her eyes and forced herself to look away. When she reached the prison gate the same guard they had seen the day before answered her urgent knocks.

'Oh, it's you again,' said the guard, looking at the slight figure in front of him. 'I hope you've bought more liquor with you.' His ugly tone made it clear that if she hadn't then this was as far as any visitor was going. Elouise said nothing but took his hand and pressed several coins into the palm, closing his fingers around them. She smiled at him and started walking towards Jean's cell. The guard watched her for a moment then looked down greedily at the coins she had smuggled into his hand, surprised and puzzled at the generosity. But, as he ambled after her to open the cell door, it didn't stop him muttering behind her back 'You'd better make the most of it, he'll be burnt to a cinder before this day's over!'

Elouise ignored the taunts of the guard and rushed into her father's arms as soon as they had been left alone. They said nothing, but drew comfort from each other's embrace. After several long moments Jean held Elouise at arms length and looked directly her, sending as much love as he could with his eyes. 'There's something I'd like you to do for me,' he said eventually, 'although it is a little unorthodox.'

'Of course Papa, tell me what you need,' replied Elouise.

'I'd like you to bless me with the words of the *consolamentum*.' Elouise looked up at her father, never expecting such a request. This was the most sacred Cathar blessing and could only be given by a *Parfait* to a believer to whom death was a certainty.

'Don't worry,' said Jean smiling and sensing the doubt in his daughter's mind. 'I'll tell you what to say; besides, I'm sure our Good Lord will understand if my spirit arrives next to him blessed by the hand of my own daughter.' Elouise returned her father's smile, proud that he should entrust her with such an important role.

'But first,' he said, as if to lighten their mood, 'I need you to trim my beard. I hope you remembered to bring your scissors.'

Elouise spent a while cutting and trimming the white whiskers that had spread across her father's face until the normal appearance that she remembered so fondly returned. As she concentrated on the task in hand she realised that she couldn't tell him that she was pregnant. She knew that if she put this knowledge into her father's mind, it might deflect him from his chosen path. She swallowed hard as she arrived at this difficult decision but felt relieved that she could let her father go without giving him such a burden.

'There,' she said, stroking the soft beard on his cheek, 'you look just like your old self again, as handsome as ever. Now put this on.' She turned and picked up the package, undid the string, and shook out the garment, holding it up for his approval. Jean took the new shirt from her hand and held it up against himself.

'Perfect' he said. He turned around to take off his grimy rags and pulled the new shirt over his head, tugging it down until it reached below his knees. He turned again, arms outstretched as if to say 'Will I do?' The whiteness of the fresh linen glowed in the gloomy cell and to Elouise's amazement her father seemed to shine in front of her.

Jean stepped towards Elouise and then knelt in front of her. 'Put your hands on my head and repeat my words,' he commanded gently. Elouise did as she was instructed, repeating faithfully the phrases of the most holy blessing, willing them to flow through her hands and into her father's soul. When the blessing was over Jean stood up slowly and held his daughter by both hands. His eyes shone with confidence. 'Now you must go, my beloved daughter. When our spirits meet again we will both be in heaven.' Elouise could barely bring herself to look at her father, fearing that she would let him down by bursting into tears. But the look in his eyes gave her the courage to smile and her face reflected his love.

'You have been a truly wonderful father; I shall always, always love you. May God be with you.' Now it was Jean's turn to swallow hard and force back the tears that sprang to his eyes. At that moment he knew that Blanche would have been so proud of their daughter.

Nothing further needed to be said and Elouise turned away from her father and left the cell. She held her head straight and high as she walked back along the corridor, past the bemused guard and out into the bustling town towards Pascal's house. But anyone who looked at her closely would have seen the steady flow of tears that streamed across her face.

Michel and Pascal wanted to know all about Elouise's visit to her father. She told them about the shopkeeper and how she had bribed the guard with money. When she got to the part about Jean asking her to bless him they could see how emotional it was for Elouise and the two men took it in turns to comfort her. By the time she had finished speaking they were all holding each other tightly and sharing her grief.

As the afternoon wore on a steady stream of people passed Pascal's small window heading towards the town square. Far from being sombre their mood seemed to be one of curiosity and excitement. Elouise had already made up her mind there was no way she was going to watch her father be taken to the stake. They had said their goodbyes, she knew where his spirit was going, and she had no need to see his mortal body suffer in the flames. Instead she and Michel had made the decision to leave Pamiers that day and make their way back to St. Julien de Roc and the safety of the chateau. They tried to persuade Pascal to travel with them but he chose to stay in his own home. But they couldn't prevent him buying as many provisions for their journey as they could carry. This time they planned to ignore the risk of discovery and take the direct route to St. Julien; they were keen to put some distance between themselves and Pamiers before nightfall.

Elouise embraced Pascal, thanking him for his kindness and understanding. Pascal kissed her and turned towards Michel. He looked down into the eyes of his young friend and gently brushed the fingertips of one hand against Michel's cheek. 'Goodbye, dearest boy, you take good care of yourself, and this young lady too.' Michel reached up to take Pascal's hand and kissed it gently, 'Don't worry about us, we'll be fine,' he said, as pupil and tutor held each other.

Pascal insisted on walking with them to the city gates and stood and watched as they passed the sentry and headed south towards Foix, following the river on their right hand side. At a bend in the path they turned together and waved once at Pascal, still standing at the gate, waiting until they had disappeared from view.

In the main square in front of the prison a large crowd had gathered to watch the execution. A pile of wood as tall as two men had been built in a rough circle around the stake. A ladder rested against the collection of timbers. People jostled with each other to get a better position and a murmur of anticipation rose from the crowd. Suddenly the noise increased in volume as a door in the prison wall opened and Jean emerged, led by two guards. The crowd parted to allow a pathway towards the pyre and Jean, barefoot and wearing only his new white shirt, walked steadily towards the stake. He ignored the jeers and taunts from the crowd and those closest were amazed to hear him singing. He sang a hymn of joy. As they reached the pyre one of the guards put his foot on the lowest rung of the ladder and indicated with a nod of his head that Jean should climb. Jean obeyed the order and the guard climbed up behind him. As he came into view of everyone the crowd began to surge forward and the level of noise increased again. The guard began to tie Jean to the stake, first his hands behind his back and then a rope around his ankles. Having made a show of testing the knots the guard carefully descended the ladder and pulled it away. Jean, still singing to himself, surveyed the crowd, his eyes coming to rest on a man standing directly below and in front of him. The man extended his arms slowly at right angles to his body and raised the palms of his hands, signalling for silence from the crowd behind. As the noise abated and the crowd finally stood in silence the man looked at Jean and began to speak.

'By the power invested in me as chief magistrate of Pamiers I declare that you, Jean de Rhedones, have been found guilty of heresy, the punishment for which is death. If you choose to recant and admit your guilt then you will be given a swifter death, if not, then your body and soul will be cleansed by the flames.' The magistrate looked up at Jean, 'How do you choose?'

Jean, looking down at the man, said nothing and continued singing, but louder this time.

The magistrate looked past Jean's shoulder towards a group

of figures standing on a balcony overlooking the square. Watching the scene below him the Bishop stood still for several moments, then slowly nodded his head once in the direction of the magistrate, before crossing himself. The official saw the signal and indicated to the men standing either side of the wooden pile to proceed. Each man held a bundle of kindling sticks that were already soaked in pitch. Now the sticks were pushed into the pots of burning embers that stood at the men's feet. As soon as the kindling had caught alight the men stepped forward and plunged their torches into the base of the pyre. For a while nothing seemed to happen. Then, slowly, a few wisps of blue smoke emerged from the top of the pile. The smoke drifted in all directions before the fire took hold and a thickening grey cloud began to engulf Jean. The crowd cheered as the first flames appeared. Jean, despite the hot smoke that seared his throat and forced his eyes to close, continued to sing as loudly as he could, strong in his faith and content in his destiny. The flames broke through the topmost layer of the pyre darting like snakes' tongues around his feet. The hem of Jean's shirt singed then burst into flames, the flimsy material transformed in moments into charred flakes that floated upwards on the hot air. Jean, his naked body now exposed to the flames was, mercifully, already unconscious. It was not to the heat of the fire that he finally expired but to the lack of oxygen for breathing, as it was hungrily consumed by the roaring flames. The crowd, perplexed by the lack of agonised screams, became subdued and stood with varying looks of curiosity and disgust as Jean's corpse blackened and burnt in the flames. Soon the only reminder that this had once been a human body was the stench of burning flesh that hung at head height over the slowly dispersing crowd.

On a hillside some distance from the town Michel turned and looked back. He could see the pall of black smoke that rose steadily upwards above the rooftops. He held Elouise tightly as she concentrated on the path ahead, forcing herself not to turn around.

CHAPTER THIRTY-ONE

The news of Jean's execution spread quickly through the villages and hamlets that sheltered along the narrow valleys of the Razes. This hidden region of steeply wooded hills and mountain pastures had enjoyed an era of relative calm during the twenty years since the last crusade. Most of the population had never experienced a burning in their lifetime. The poorness of the land and the unwelcoming terrain had allowed Cathar and Catholic to live in neighbourly harmony, with little interference from the outside world. Only the occasional zealous priest, like Bernard Villac of St. Julien, tried to make a reputation for himself by stirring up conflict and suspicion, but their threats would usually fall on pragmatic ears. Why cause trouble for a neighbour when you have just borrowed his axe or lent him your plough?

One man, however, took great interest when the news reached him. The Archbishop at Albi saw the death of a *Parfait* as the spark he needed to finally rid himself of this irritating Cathar thorn in his side. Immediately he wrote to the Pope in Rome and the King in Paris requesting their support to put down, once and for all, the heresy that had been allowed to breathe and grow, hinting, he added, through their neglect. As he waited for replies to his request the Archbishop wasted no time in issuing instructions to increase the pursuit of anyone displaying signs of heretical beliefs, whether true or imagined. Officials and inquisitors fanned out across the archdiocese on a mission to visit every priest in every village to remind them of their duty to identify those suspected of rejecting the holy sacraments of the Catholic Church.

As Elouise and Michel turned east and headed back towards St. Julien they would have been unaware of the dark shadow that had begun to creep down from Albi, oozing slowly into every corner of the landscape like thick, cold oil.

CHAPTER THIRTY-TWO

'Michel, there's something I need to tell you.' The two weary travellers had stopped to rest, sitting on the dry stone wall of a sheep pen. The food provided by Pascal had nearly gone and they were chewing on the last remnants of bread and a few crumbs of cheese. Since leaving Pamiers they had hardly spoken to each other except to discuss the best direction and where to spend the night. Elouise trudged along a few paces behind Michel, lost in thoughts of her father and trying to recall every memory of their life together. Michel kept an eye on the weather, alert to the cold air and clear sky that signalled the first frosts of winter. Even when they stopped long enough for him to strum a few chords he didn't seem able to raise a smile from Elouise.

Michel turned to look at his companion. He'd seen that look on her beautiful face before and knew that she had something serious to say.

'What is it, my dearest girl?,' he said, waiting for her to speak. Since the death of Jean he felt he needed to be even more responsible for her now, like a father figure.

'I'm going to have a baby.' Her voice expressed a mixture of determination tinged with uncertainty. For once Michel was lost for words.

'When?' was all he could manage.

'Sometime in the new year, before springtime' replied Elouise slowly, as if her thoughts were already in that season. Michel chewed and swallowed his last mouthful before carefully asking his next question. 'Did you tell your father?'

'No, I couldn't do that to him.' She looked directly at Michel and, as the first tear began to roll down her cheek, he stepped towards her and held her tightly and they clung to each other for several long moments.

'Well, what are we going to do now?' He said it in such a way that Elouise suddenly realised that telling him had been a huge relief, a weight lifted from her shoulders knowing that her best friend in the world shared her secret. For the first time in days a smile spread across her face.

'Well I ought to tell the father, don't you think?' she said, a touch of humour returning to her voice.

'I'm presuming Guillaume,' said Michel with mock seriousness. Elouise couldn't help blushing as a vivid image of her passionate afternoon with Guillaume formed in her mind. She said nothing, but grinned and nodded at Michel. 'I knew it!' he exclaimed, 'I knew it when we were up in the pastures. All that energy and you glowing with good health. I even told Guillaume how fantastic you were looking!' Elouise knew he was teasing her but was pleased that he seemed to have taken the news so well. She was glad that she would have Michel to lean on in the months to come.

'Come on,' he said, gathering up his satchel and lute 'let's see if we can get to the chateau before nightfall tomorrow. I'm sure there's going to be one very handsome young man who'll be very pleased to see you.'

They set off again, hand in hand, along the path that curved around the hillside between the green oak trees.

That night they rested with friends of Michel in a village less than a day's journey from St. Julien. As they sat around after supper they learnt of the news trickling in from other villages; about the inquisitors stirring up suspicion and of *croyants* being rounded up and taken away for questioning. There were even rumours of families packing up their animals and belongings and leaving home to escape the persecution. As they lay down to sleep in the warm barn the brief, happy mood that Elouise and Michel had shared that afternoon was already turning into one more sombre and worrying.

Early the next morning, approaching the crest of a hill on the path that led to St. Julien, the towers of the chateau gradually came into view. Elouise and Michel stopped for a while, taking in the familiar scene. Beneath them flowed the river, appearing and disappearing between the canopy of trees that clung to its steep banks. Further upstream they could make out the sloping fields that surrounded St. Julien. From this distance it was easy to see how the walls and rooftops of the village followed the dips and rises of the hilltop on which it sat, as if trying to merge with the natural shape of hill itself. And rising up directly behind the village, like a guard on permanent duty, stood the massive bulk of the Roc. The walls of the chateau at its summit seemed to emerge seamlessly from its sheer rock face. It was a truly powerful sight and one that had deterred many potential invaders in the past.

It was only eight weeks since they left the chateau, but to Elouise it seemed like a lifetime. She sighed and looked at Michel. 'Come on,' he said, reading her mind 'if we get a move on we can reach the chateau before nightfall. And I'd like to call on the Borrel's on the way.'

She fell into step behind him as the path descended back amongst the trees towards the river. It had begun to rain and before long even their thick woollen cloaks were soaked by the dripping leaves that spanned the path above their heads. By the time they finally emerged from the forest and into the fields that led up to village they were wet, cold, hungry and feeling altogether miserable. It had been a long journey back to the village.

There were few people about as they passed through the gateway. Even the watchman on duty seemed reluctant to stand about too long in the rain to ask them what business they had in St. Julien. They hurried through the damp, smokey alleyways, eager to get to the Borrel's dwelling. There they were welcomed warmly, as always, by the bustling Jacotte and ushered towards the fireplace to shed their cloaks and warm themselves. The news of Jean's death had already reached the village.

'My poor sweet girl' said Jacotte, bringing a bowl of hot soup to Elouise. 'Your father was truly a good man amongst all the Good Men. May his spirit be with God.' Elouise smiled and clasped the bowl with both hands, feeling its warmth penetrate her chilled fingers.

'How are things in the village?' How is Bernadette? Michel told me,' she added, hoping that she hadn't betrayed a confidence.

'She's well,' replied Jacotte, 'although she still won't tell us who the father is. Keeps saying she's protecting us, though from what I can't imagine.'

Elouise glanced around the small room. 'Is she still here?'

'Oh yes' said Jacotte, 'spends most of her time in the barn, trying to keep out of her father's way. Only comes in to eat. At least there's nothing wrong with her appetite.' Her voice expressed an understanding and sympathy for her young daughter's condition.

'Do you think she'd talk to me?' asked Elouise.

'You can try, my dear, no harm in that,' Jacotte replied, ladling more soup into each of their bowls.

When she had finished eating, Elouise stepped across the threshold of the barn, her eyes adjusting to the fading light. She made out the figure of Bernadette sitting on the straw, her arms clasped around her legs, chin resting on her knees.

'Hullo, Bernadette,' her voice friendly 'it's me, Elouise.' She crossed over and sat down next to the girl. 'I've been talking to your mother. She says you haven't lost your appetite.' Bernadette didn't smile at the little joke and continued to stare ahead.

'I suppose she asked you to find out who did it, didn't she?'

Elouise paused before replying. 'No, she didn't. She's just worried that whoever it is has frightened you so much that you won't even tell your mother.' Bernadette turned and looked at Elouise miserably.

'He made me promise; said if I told anyone then my family would be in serious trouble. How can I tell them if it means something bad will happen?' The young girl sniffed and fresh tears began to roll down her stained cheeks. Elouise leant towards the girl and put her arm around her shoulder, pulling her closer until her chin rested on top of Bernadette's head. The girl sobbed quietly, grateful for the sympathy. Elouise continued to comfort Bernadette and recalled Michel's suspicions about the priest, '... someone in the village with power' he'd said. She waited a few moments before she spoke again. 'Would I find him in the church?' she asked gently.

Bernadette stiffened and nodded twice.

'Don't say any more,' she said, 'but I promise I'm going to help you, and your family. I'm not going to let any harm come to you. Will you trust me?' Bernadette lifted her head and looked at Elouise, feeling a sense of relief that she'd found a friend at last. A smile lit up her face for the first time in weeks and she nodded several times.

'Now, can you keep another secret?' said Elouise, looking in mock seriousness at the girl. Bernadette suddenly became anxious again at the thought of having to bear another burden, but the expression in the eyes of Elouise told her not to worry.

'Yes, of course,' she replied, 'What is it?'

Elouise took hold of the young girl's hands and gently

squeezed them in her own. 'Well,' she said slowly, looking directly at Bernadette 'I'm going to have a baby too!'

'No, never!' was all the young girl could say in shocked response, then quickly gathering her thoughts 'Does anyone else know?'

'Only Michel' said Elouise.

'He's not the...' but before Bernadette could finish the question Elouise jumped in.

'No, no. Michel's my best friend but he's not the father.'

Bernadette thought for a moment. 'Then we've both got a secret!' she announced, grinning with delight. The two young women laughed and hugged each other.

Their shared comforting was interrupted a few moments later by the voice of Michel at the doorway. 'Elouise, it's getting late. If we want to get to the chateau before darkness we need to leave now.' His voice sounded strangely worried and urgent.

'Michel, what on earth's the matter?' said Elouise, breathing heavily.

Since saying goodbye to the Borrel's the pair had hardly spoken as they hurried through the quiet village and exited from the upper gateway. Now they were climbing the steep, winding path that led to the chateau's entrance. The village was already far below them, a cluster of roofs radiating outwards around the church tower. Michel paused and turned, waiting for Elouise to catch up. 'Something's happening and it doesn't sound good, Lou-Lou.' His gaze went past Elouise and down to the village.

'What do you mean?' she said. A gust of cold wind ruffled her dark hair and made her shiver.

'Claude and Jacotte think they may have to leave the village, and they're not the only ones. They've talked with the other *croyants* and it seems everyone is worried they will be the next on the list for questioning. Apparently the priest has become quite fanatical and is threatening more and more people with a visit from the inquisitors. Claude reckons the nasty creep is relishing his new powers.' Elouise listened to her friend but said nothing for a while, his words confirming their suspicions.

'You were right about one thing, Michel!'

'Right about what?'

'It's him, the priest. He's the one that did it!'

'Did what?'

'The reason Bernadette is pregnant. He's the only one in the village with the power to threaten her family unless she kept quiet about it. You were right to have your doubts about him.'

'The limping, catholic bastard,' was all Michel could think to say, looking with renewed disgust at the church below.

Elouise continued speaking, determination in her voice. 'We're going to have do something to help the Borrel's, and the others.' The serious look on her face suddenly reminded him of her father.

'What have you got in mind?' he said, knowing that she would already have a solution.

'They need a protector. I'm going to ask the Count to take in the Borrel's, and any other Cathar family that is frightened to stay in their own home. We have to turn the chateau into a safe haven.'

'Sounds like we may have a lot of persuading to do. Perhaps you'd better make a start on Guillaume first. Once he hears your news he'll want to protect you for certain, that's what knights do.' He said it with a smile and Elouise couldn't help herself from smiling back.

'Come on,' she said, holding out her hand, 'help this pregnant lady get to the top.' Michel took her hand and gently pulled her along. Daylight was disappearing rapidly as they finally reached the sheer walls of the chateau, passing through its huge gates under the vigilant surveillance of the two guards on duty.

'You will speak to your father, won't you? And your mother too?'

Elouise and Guillaume lay naked side by side, holding hands under the heavy woollen bed covers. When she had returned the evening before Guillaume had been amazed, literally, to see her. Of course he had been praying daily for her safe return but he'd never expected her to arrive unannounced like this. There had followed a flurry of greetings amongst the family and a hastily arranged supper to welcome back the two travellers. Sincere condolences had been expressed over the death of Elouise's father but the evening had not been allowed to descend into melancholy. Michel had even been persuaded to sing some of the old songs and they all joined in to sing the choruses. There was a strong mood of togetherness.

Finally, after everyone had retired to bed, the two young lovers had tip-toed along the cold flagstones to Guillaume's bed chamber. They'd leapt between the cold sheets and spent most of the night making love to each other until their passion had been satisfied. Exhausted and content, Elouise had finally told Guillaume about the baby she was expecting. His reaction made her laugh and cry at the same time. He'd been happy, amazed, concerned, upset and happy again, all in the space of a few moments. Then they had slept, curled up together like puppies.

Now the cold light of a winter's morning brought reality back to their situation. Guillaume stretched, enjoying the feel of his thigh sliding against hers, and thought about his answer. He'd been listening to Elouise for some time as she expressed her concerns about the Borrel family and the other villagers. 'I think we should both go and see them,' he concluded. 'We'll talk to them this morning, after breakfast.'

A knock on the door alerted them to the entrance of Annie, bringing in hot water and a towel. This time Elouise did not bother to hide under the sheets, knowing that the maid would already have seen her unslept bed and arrived at the obvious conclusion.

'Good morning Annie, thank you' said Elouise.

'Good morning, Miss, good morning, young sir' replied the maid, making a show of pouring the water into a bowl, unable to suppress a wide grin forming on her face.

'Will there be anything else?'

Elouise looked at Annie, slightly embarrassed 'Do you think you could get me some clothes please? I can't go creeping along the corridor in Guillaume's shirt.' The two women smiled at each other, Annie pleased at having something helpful to do.

'Of course, miss. I'll go straight away so you won't be late for breakfast. The Count and his good lady are already downstairs.' The maid hurried from the room leaving the young lovers time for one long kiss before they too made haste to get ready for the day ahead.

The Count and Countess sat alone at the table, the dogs circulating as usual. 'You look deep in thought this morning, my dear. What are you thinking about?' the Countess stroked the back of her husband's hand.

'Rumours,' replied her husband, chewing thoughtfully on a slice of ham.

'What kind of rumours?'

'The kind that spell trouble. Every day one of my men comes back with more stories of unrest. The whole region seems to be in the grip of fear. I tell you, Sybille, this is not going to blow over.'

He was about to continue sharing his thoughts with his wife when Guillaume and Elouise descended the stairs together and entered the room. Guillaume walked around the table kissing his mother and father, but Elouise stood back, unsure how to greet them.

'Come and sit next to me, my dear,' invited the Countess,

sensing her unease and patting the bench beside her. 'Did you sleep well? You must be exhausted after all you've had to cope with.' Elouise smiled at the Countess, grateful for her genuine concern. For a moment she had a sense of what it would have felt like to have had a mother. She'd always been able to talk to her father, and she'd shared many secrets growing up with Michel, but except for Clementine when she was fourteen, she'd never really had another woman to talk to, as a daughter to a mother. Those conversations,she knew, would have been different to any other.

Elouise and Guillaume helped themselves to food; their love-making had given both of them an appetite. Guillaume concentrated on his breakfast for a while before speaking.

'Father, we need to talk to you.' The Count's nod to his son indicated that he should proceed. Guillaume looked at Elouise for support, and then continued. 'Elouise has been telling me how things have changed in the village, how she's heard about the same things happening in other places since she and Michel left Pamiers. People are worried, scared...' His voice trailed off, not sure how to continue. The Count looked at Elouise then back to his son.

'What sort of things?'

'People are frightened. They feel threatened.' It was Elouise who spoke. 'I've heard of families leaving their homes for fear of being persecuted.' 'My friends, the Borrel's, are already under threat from the priest. There are people in the village who no longer trust their neighbours. People are turning against each other to save themselves.' There was frustration in her voice and she could feel her cheeks burning with anger. The Count listened carefully to the intense young woman sitting next to his son.

'And what do you suggest we do about it?'

Elouise fixed her blue eyes directly on the Count, her voice gentle but determined. 'They need protection, my lord, your protection.'

The Count got up from the table and stood in front of the fire, rubbing his hands with the warmth from the burning logs. He turned around and looked in turn at his wife, his son and the young woman who had so obviously captured his son's heart.

'What you say young lady confirms what I have already heard. What you ask for is a lot more difficult. It would be dangerous for all of us, particularly my family.' He paused for a while, the look on his face showing the difficulty he was having in making a decision. Eventually he moved to his wife's side and lifted her hand into his, indicating that this was a decision he was making on behalf of them both.

'In reality I do not see myself in the role of Protector, but I do see we have a duty to look after those who are unable to defend themselves.' The Count made a sweeping gesture with his arm around the room, 'I would say to those people 'Come to the chateau and let our walls protect you.'

Sybille looked proudly at her husband as he turned his attention towards Elouise. 'Tell your friends the Borrels they are welcome here at the chateau, and tell them to let their friends know too.'

'Thank you, my lord, that is a very noble offer; you are indeed a good man.'

'No, young lady,' replied the Count, smiling now 'It was your father who was the Good Man.'

The Countess stood up next to her husband and kissed him tenderly on the cheek. She was grateful for his decision and knew that he had made it, in part, to ease her own conscience. They started to leave the room when Guillaume spoke again.

'Father, mother... there's something else we need to tell you.' The young couple stood side by side, hand in hand, but looking more serious than happy. The Count and his wife looked at each other then waited for the young man to continue, thinking perhaps that a betrothal might be in the air.

'It's Elouise…she…we…are going to have a child.' He tried to keep his eyes on his parents but couldn't help his gaze falling to the floor. It was a habit from childhood when he knew he'd done something that wouldn't meet with their approval. Elouise folded her hands demurely in front of her. Sybille looked at her husband again, trying to read what was in his eyes, but she couldn't prevent a smile spreading slowly across her face.

'Well,' she said, trying to sound serious 'It is usual to make the birth announcement after the happy couple have been betrothed.' She tugged at her husband's arm and they moved towards Guillaume and Elouise. 'But we live in different times, I suppose,' she pulled Elouise towards her and embraced her. 'So, my dear, welcome to the Quillan family. We are going to have to take very good care of you and your baby.' The Count gave his son a look of mock disapproval then laughed and slapped him heartily on the back. 'Well you didn't waste much time did you, my boy?' he continued laughing, 'You've hardly seen much of each other at all!' His remark made Elouise blush and she noticed that Guillaume was looking bashful too, but relieved, at this unexpected response from his parents.

The Count made his way to the door, thrusting his head out to find someone to fetch him some good wine. 'This calls for a celebration!' he announced, much to the amusement of the young maid waiting by the door, who was unused to receiving such a request so early in the day.

CHAPTER THIRTY-THREE

It took a while to convince the Borrels that the safest place for them would be the chateau. They were reluctant to leave their home but Jacotte reasoned with her husband that she would rather see the family stay together than be torn apart by accusations from their neighbours. Besides, he could still tend the fields below the village and the crops would be essential to the chateau. So the Borrel family piled what belongings they could onto their cart, rounded up the animals, bolted the door to the yard and made their way up the steep path to the Roc that towered over the village.

They weren't the only ones. At first just a trickle, but before long a steady stream of *croyants* and their families climbed to the safety of the chateau. Most of them came from St. Julien but as the winter wore on and the word spread, so other families made their way from neighbouring villages and further away. By the time December arrived there were almost two hundred souls inside the chateau. Makeshift dwellings were constructed against the thick interior walls. Hens, ducks and geese scratched their way through the grounds, pigs snorted and grunted outside the kitchens, goats and sheep were kept in newly erected pens and the few cattle that the villagers owned became a welcome source of milk for the whole community. Most of the arrivals had brought with them their winter stock of grain and the chateau's ovens were kept alight constantly with the demand for fresh bread.

Far from being sombre the mood amongst the refugees was buoyant. They were people brought together by a common crisis and they drew strength from each other. They felt safe and out of reach of the Church that sought to pursue them. Amongst them moved the few *Parfaits* that had remained in the region, always ready with words of encouragement or consolation, or with practical help if needed. There was a collective sense of purpose and a positive energy seemed to envelop the chateau like a protective cloak.

The Comte de Quillan, however, did not share in this mood of relative calm and contentment. He had always been sympathetic to the Cathar way, believing it to be a benign influence on the local populace and one which its followers could relate to easily. It brought harmony to their daily lives and their spiritual needs. He also knew that his wife was a strong believer and had brought up their children to believe in the Cathar approach to life and to death. Already she was becoming a focal point for their 'guests' as she moved amongst them, tending and caring wherever it was needed most.

But he was a pragmatic man too. He knew that by opening his gates to so many believers, heretics in the eyes of the Church, he would be drawing attention to himself and his chateau. It would be seen as a hotbed of dissent and, once word of his challenge to the religious authorities reached the ears of those in power, he would become a problem that needed to be resolved.

As usual he wasn't far from the truth in his interpretation of the situation.

Further to the north, at Albi, the Archbishop was indeed considering his options. Word of this exodus of Cathars began to reach him daily from his spies in the region, but on balance he was pleased with the information. If the heretics wished to leave the protection of the Mother Church, giving up any chance of being resolved of their sins, then they would only have themselves to blame for the hell that awaited their souls. The fact that so many of them were now congregated in one place gave him another, more radical, idea. The Archbishop authorised letters to be sent to Innocent IV in Rome and Louis IX in Paris asking for their help and support to eradicate, once and for all, this menace of heretics. His request was nothing less than their permission to launch a final crusade against the Cathars.

CHAPTER THIRTY-FOUR

Elouise spent most of the day mending an ever-growing pile of shirts, skirts and breeches belonging to the chateau's new inhabitants. Her back and fingers ached from threading, sewing, patching so many garments and her eyes were sore from focussing for such a long time without a break. The daylight was beginning to fade as she put aside the shirt she was mending and straightened her back, rubbing her hand across the base of her spine to bring some relief. The baby growing inside her was also having its effect on her body. She closed her eyes, looking forward to the moment when she could lie down and rest, amusing herself to feel the small thrusts and kicks that signalled the movements of her increasingly active child.

A blast of cold air from the opening door rushed across her face and made her open her eyes. She smiled as the tall figure of Guillaume crossed the room towards her, the light from the low sun behind him throwing a halo around his head.

'Have you been here all day, my love?' His voice conveyed the concern he felt for her. 'I don't suppose you've had any rest either, have you?' He knelt down beside her and rubbed her back. Elouise closed her eyes and let out a sigh of appreciation.

'I'm fine,' she said 'besides, there's so much to do'. She decided to change the subject of her wellbeing, taking Guillaume's hand in her own and stroking his fingers, 'What have you been up to all day, anyway, your hands feel so cold.'

'I've been on top of the southern walls, above the main gates;

it's freezing up there. Father thinks it would be prudent to strengthen our defences, so we've been erecting a palisade in case the gates are attacked.' In fact the Count had initiated a whole series of defensive measures in the past few weeks. Carpenters and stonemasons had been crawling all over the chateau's walls urgently repairing any damaged sections and constructing wooden platforms and towers to repel any potential attackers.

'Do you really think that might happen? Might they just not leave us alone?'

Guillaume looked up into Elouise's face, 'Don't worry,' he said, rubbing away the frown on her brow with his fingertips 'I'm sure it won't come to that. Don't forget my father's been through times of conflict before. Maybe he's right to be cautious.' They looked at each other for a while, neither of them speaking, as if trying to reach into the other's mind.

'Come on,' said Guillaume finally, 'time to get you something to eat and then you should rest, you both need it.' He smiled at her and stroked her growing belly. Elouise put down her needle and folded the last shirt onto the pile beside her. She allowed Guillaume to help her out of her chair and, with their arms around each other's waists, they made their way and out into the cold air of the early evening. She was pleased he had come to fetch her.

That night in bed, as they lay side by side enjoying the afterglow of their love-making, Guillaume summoned the boldness to ask Elouise a question, one that had been on his mind for some while.

'Elouise?' he began, into the darkness.

'Yes.'

'Can I ask you something important?'

'Go on.'

'Do you really love me?'

'Of course I do.' She paused. 'Was that your question?'

'No.'

Elouise said nothing, waiting for him to continue.

'I'm not sure your father would have approved.'

Elouise remained silent, willing him to say more.

'Well I've been thinking, given the circumstances, whether we might consider ...' He searched for the right words, 'whether we might make a commitment to each other.' Guillaume held his breath, waiting for a reply.

'Is this because I'm pregnant?' said a small voice in the dark.

'No, no of course not!' he came back, indignantly 'I love you and I want everyone to know that. I know these are difficult times but I want to share my life with you. I want us to face life together. I want our child to know he's part of a loving family. I admit it would please my mother and father too, in fact I think everyone could do with cheering up right now.'

Elouise thought for a while. 'Well you were right about one thing.'

'What's that?'

'My father would never have approved. Don't get me wrong, I know he liked you very much and he wanted me to be happy, but marriage did not exist in his eyes. When he became a *Parfait* he believed we should abstain from sex altogether and not have children at all, that way there'd be fewer and fewer babies borne into this hell on earth until eventually there'd be no one here at all. To be honest, I'm not sure how I feel about your proposal.'

Guillaume said nothing for several moments.

'I didn't say a marriage. I said a commitment. We could make it a simple ceremony where we could express our feelings for each other and let everyone see, even in times like this, how love is something pure, something to be celebrated. Don't you think that would be good?'

There was a long pause before Elouise lent over, sliding

her arm across Guillaume's chest and kissing him on the lips.

'I think it's a wonderful idea; thank you for asking me.' She snuggled up to him for extra warmth and Guillaume let out a sigh of relief.

Elouise was talking to Michel. It was the day after she and Guillaume had been to see the Count and Countess to tell them of their wish to have a ceremony of union. The Count had huffed and puffed for a while. In fairness he had his mind on more pressing matters and he was uncertain of the legality of such a ceremony given that Elouise could be carrying an heir to the Quillan line. But his wife managed to soothe his ruffled feathers. Being a strong Cathar she would never have agreed to any Catholic endorsement of the union even though, as a young bride herself, she herself had been obliged to obey the wishes of her father. She persuaded the Count that if the young couple exchanged their vows in front of independent witnesses then they would be deemed to be legal promises in the eyes of the law. (The Count later ran his wife's rationale past his Seigneur, who confirmed that such verbal promises would be considered to be valid and binding, just like any contract). And so Guillaume's parents gave the young couple their blessing, and with much gladness too. A date was arranged for the ceremony – December 21st, just two weeks away.

'So, will you help me?' continued Elouise. She and Michel were sitting down with their backs leaning against the chateau wall, enjoying a brief moment of warmth from the weak winter sun. 'I want it to be simple, not too serious, more like a celebration, but romantic too.' Michel turned to look at his life-long friend, now more radiant than ever, even with a serious frown on her face.

'Of course I will, Lou-Lou, don't worry so much; just tell me what you have in mind.'

And so began two weeks of feverish preparations. News of the impending event spread rapidly through the chateau's growing community. As Guillaume had predicted, everyone's mood was lifted; the uncertainty of their situation and the chills of winter were dispersed, at least for a while, by the anticipation of the event to come.

Elouise and Michel spent many hours together devising the ceremony and deciding how it would be staged. They agreed there should be a strong musical content; that would be Michel's responsibility, and, despite the winter season, the ceremony should be held outdoors in the open air, not in some gloomy chamber, so that everyone could be part of the occasion. Elouise and Guillaume would write their vows to each other to be witnessed by everyone present and they would ask one of the *Parfaits* to give them a simple blessing. The Count, to his credit and much to his wife's great pleasure and amusement, decided to declare the event a 'public' holiday, to be followed by a grand feast. There remained only one decision for Elouise, a simple yet important one for her. She asked Michel to do her the honour of being the one to escort her to the ceremony.

The twenty first day of December arrived. A sharp frost had left its silvery white coating on every surface, so that when the sun eventually rose the whole chateau seemed to sparkle. Elouise and Guillaume had decided to spend the night apart; she in last minute arrangements with Michel and he in a rousing evening with his fellow knights.

Annie, the maid, knocked on Elouise's door and carried through a tray of food. Seeing that Elouise was still asleep she put the tray down gently and busied herself stoking the embers of the fire, adding more logs to bring some heat to the cold room. Elouise stirred at the noise and gradually opened her eyes.

'Good morning, Annie' she said sleepily, stretching her arms then pulling the covers up to her chin.

'Good morning, Miss,' replied the maid 'Did you sleep well? Are you hungry? Look, I've brought you some breakfast.' Annie picked up the tray and carried it over to the bed, waiting for Elouise to sit up and wrap a shawl around her shoulders before placing it on her lap. Elouise looked at the food and decided she was suddenly very hungry.

'You haven't changed your mind about what you're going to wear, have you?' asked Annie as she busied herself around the room. Elouise had given the matter a lot of thought. At first she had decided to wear her mother's blue dress. Annie had washed and repaired it carefully so that it now looked as new as when it was first made. But it was still the dress she was wearing the night that Bruno had attacked her, leaving it soaked in his blood. Even though there was no longer any trace of that shocking evening Elouise realised she couldn't carry the memory of that event into the ceremony. Instead, she had decided to make her own dress. Her skills with needle and thread were certainly up to the task, and with Annie as her eager assistant they had created a beautiful gown; one her father would have been proud of. It was simple yet elegant, made from the finest cream silk, a gift from the Countess, with gold trimming around a low, square neckline. When she tried on the finished garment for the first time Annie had gasped in admiration, not just at the wonder of their creation but at the amazing beauty of Elouise. To Annie she looked like the princess of her imagination and tears of joy had fallen from her eyes. The dress now hung in the big wardrobe, waiting for its mistress.

'No, of course not, Annie,' replied Elouise. 'I shall wear the dress we made together.' Annie smiled with satisfaction.

'Well, Miss, there's a lot to do. You finish that breakfast and I'll go and fetch some hot water for your bath. Then we'll get started on your hair.' Annie hurried out of the room leaving Elouise to enjoy a few more moments in the warmth of the bed.

Outside was already a hive of activity. In the courtyard in front of the keep a raised circular platform had been built, large enough to accommodate thirty people. Wooden posts had been set at regular intervals around the edge and each post was linked to its neighbour by another pole across the top, creating a series of arches around the platform. Michel was in full flow supervising the final decorations. Men and women on ladders were intertwining sprigs of pine and holly and binding them to each upright, the bright red berries of the holly standing out against the dark green of the leaves. The arches were similarly wrapped in foliage and from the top of each pole fluttered a gathering of white ribbons. A path of crushed white shells had been laid from the great doors of the keep up to three steps that led onto the platform. The platform itself was covered in thick tapestries of deep red and gold borrowed from the walls of the great hall and now put to temporary use as floor covering. A semi-circle of chairs placed around the edge of the platform completed the simple furnishing.

Michel took several paces back and surveyed the scene, rubbing his chin thoughtfully. After a moment or two he clapped his hands and smiled; he seemed to be pleased with the overall effect and hurried off in search of his fellow musicians to arrange a final rehearsal.

Elsewhere around the chateau people were either enjoying a day off from their usual chores or helping in the kitchens to finish cooking and baking the celebration feast. There had been several foraging trips into the woods around the chateau, hunting for the wild birds and animals that now simmered in the cooking pots, to be served later alongside the suckling pigs roasting on spits. Trestles and tables were already dotted around the grounds ready to take the weight of the many dishes that would be laid out as soon as the ceremony was over.

Even at this late month of the year there was still warmth in the winter sun and there was a mood of happiness and well being amongst the inhabitants. It could have been any village celebration, except for one significant detail; the ever vigilant guards patrolling along the top of the chateau's walls. A glance upwards would be enough to remind anyone that this was not a typical village day.

The ceremony was due to begin at noon, but with only a short time to go before the bell signalled the middle of the day, Annie was still fussing over Elouise's headdress. 'Hold still, Miss, otherwise this crown will never stay on.' The 'crown' she referred to was made up of a garland of delicate white winter flowers. Elouise had decided to wear her hair up; Annie had suggested it would highlight the fine bone structure of her neck and shoulders and, on a practical level, take the eye away from the expanding bulge that was now apparent below her waistline. Annie was getting flustered trying to fix the flowers. 'There,' she said at last, guiding another pin into the arrangement with her nimble fingers, 'that should fix it, let's have a look at you.' She climbed down from the chair she'd stood on to work on Elouise's hair and took a couple of paces back. 'Beautiful. You look absolutely beautiful; the young Master is a very lucky man.' Elouise smiled back at her helper.

'Thank you, Annie, I don't know what I would have done without you.' She moved towards the young maid and held her, the two women embracing for a long silent moment. Elouise picked up her mother's necklace from the dressing table and held the silver heart between her fingers. She closed her eyes and tried to imagine her mother, the woman she had never seen. Slowly she brought the heart to her lips and kissed it. Opening her eyes again Elouise gestured to Annie to help her fasten the necklace. At that moment a gentle knock at the door signalled the arrival of Michel. He entered the room wearing his best clothes and carrying a delicate posy of wild white flowers.

'Hullo, Annie, is she ready?' Annie stood back to let Michel see for himself. He crossed the room and took hold of Elouise by both hands.

'Goodness me, Lou-Lou, you look absolutely stunning. No one could mistake you for a poor shepherd boy now.' Elouise blushed at the compliment and smiled, leaning forward to kiss her best friend on both cheeks.

'You don't look so shabby yourself. Are those flowers for me?' she teased, squeezing his hands. This time it was Michel's turn to blush.

As the bell struck noon Elouise emerged from the doors of the keep on the arm of Michel and stepped onto the white path. On the platform sat Guillaume together with those friends and family who had been able to attend the ceremony. Around the platform and lining the pathway stood almost the entire population of the chateau, relaxed and smiling. Only those on essential guard duties were unable to take part in the celebration.

Despite the winter month Elouise chose to wear neither shawl nor cloak, relying on an inner glow to keep her warm. She allowed Michel to lead her along the path, smiling and giving little waves to all the faces she recognised in the crowd. Elouise and Guillaume had both agreed that this should be a day of happiness and joy, with no place for ritual or formality.

As she approached the steps Guillaume rose eagerly from his chair, his resplendent knight's uniform almost bursting with pride. When Elouise stepped up he walked across to take her hand from Michel and led her to the centre of the floor. Michel, meanwhile, moved to sit with his fellow players around the edge of the circle and picked up the chords of the gentle refrain they had been playing.

All eyes were now upon them as Elouise and Guillaume turned to face each other. Elouise handed her posy to the equally pregnant Bernadette, whom she had insisted be part of the ceremony and with whom she was now a firm friend. The *Parfait*, who was seated next to the Countess, stood and approached the couple, his dark cloak in stark contrast to the paleness of Elouise's dress.

He spoke loudly and clearly. 'I believe you have something you both wish to say in front of all the people gathered here,' he gestured with both hands to take in the entire crowd. The young couple continued to face each other holding hands. Then Guillaume let go of Elouise and placed his right hand over his heart. He took a deep breath and began.

'I, Guillaume de Quillan, promise to love you, Elouise, for ever. I promise to honour you and care for you as long as there is breath in my body. I will protect you and cherish you and let no one come between us. I say this in front of all these people that they may be my witness.' The air was silent for a moment or two before someone started clapping and then everyone seemed to be clapping and cheering at this emphatic declaration of love. Guillaume smiled and nodded to Elouise as if to indicate it was her turn now.

Elouise smiled back, less nervous than she had been before, and placed her right hand over her heart.

'I, Elouise de Rhedones, promise to love you, Guillaume, for ever. I promise to honour you and care for you as long as there is breath in my body. I will comfort you and cherish you and let no one come between us. I say this in front of all these people that they may be my witness.' This time there was no pause before a great cheer went up from the entire crowd. The Countess reached across to squeeze her husband's hand and, on the other side of the platform, Michel strummed his lute as tears of happiness and pride welled from his eyes. The *Parfait* allowed the cheering to continue for a while before indicating to the young couple that they should kneel before him. Elouise and Guillaume turned and knelt as he placed his right hand on Elouise's head and his left hand on Guillaume's. Without being asked to the crowd knelt as well. The *Parfait* had no experience of such a ceremony, nothing like it existed in the Cathar faith; he'd even had doubts as to whether he could bless such a union. But he was a pragmatic man and had come to the conclusion that no harm could come from such an open and honest declaration of love. And so the Good Man blessed Elouise and Guillaume, or more truthfully their spirits, for in his heart he believed it was the purity of their souls that had guided their declarations to each other.

When they both stood up the cheering began again. Guillaume held Elouise in his arms and kissed her tenderly. He took her by the hand and led her to his mother and father, who immediately embraced the very happy couple. Handshakes and kisses were shared with all the people on the platform before Elouise and Guillaume walked a circuit around the perimeter, waving and smiling to all the crowd, who waved and smiled in return.

It was time for the celebrations to begin. Food was served and music played as everyone took this rare opportunity to forget what was happening outside the chateau walls and pretend, for a short time, that life had returned to normal. As the afternoon drifted into the early winter evening bonfires were lit and people started to dance. Elouise, wrapped in a thick shawl against the cold night air, walked hand in hand with Guillaume visiting each fire, joining in the celebrations and receiving the heartfelt congratulations of each cluster of people. It had been a day none of them would ever forget.

As the night wore on and the celebrations gradually dwindled people began to drift back to their makeshift homes. Guillaume decided to take Elouise up to the top of the fortified wall, to the place he had made his first clumsy attempt to kiss her. This time there was no hesitation and they kissed and held each tightly in the cold wind.

'Well, would you believe it; just look at that,' said Guillaume.

Elouise, who had her head buried deep into his shoulder, murmured sleepily 'What is it, my love?'

'It's snowing!'

Elouise opened her eyes and a snowflake landed on her lashes, melting immediately onto her upturned cheek. She opened her mouth laughing and let the next flake settle on her tongue. By the time the young couple had descended the stairs and made their way to the keep they were covered from head to toe in snowflakes. It was if a giant hand had sprinkled them with crystal confetti.

CHAPTER THIRTY-FIVE

Christmas Eve, and the Archbishop of Albi was looking at the two elaborate parchments on the desk in front of him, debating which one to open first. One bore the seal of King Louis IX the other that of Pope Innocent IV. His messengers had returned within days of each other and he had forced himself to wait, with mounting excitement, to read the two letters together.

Being a good Christian, he reasoned, he decided to break the seal to the Pope's letter first. It contained several closely spaced paragraphs and he read each line carefully, his fingers moving along the lines and his lips forming the words. When he'd finished he set the parchment down and sat back to digest the content. In essence the Pope agreed that the matter of the Cathar heresy needed to be dealt with. However he deemed it a local matter and one that the Archbishop should be able to cope with himself, albeit with His Holiness's tacit approval. He promised to send a papal legate to add credibility to the proceedings but could send nothing of practical use, such as money to pay for troops. He did, however, allow the Archbishop to raise funds by increasing the price of religious indulgences and holy relics.

The Archbishop picked up the King's document next.

Louis, naturally, was sympathetic to the Archbishop's request. Hadn't his father and grandfather marched with their armies in two crusades to rid the region of Cathars twenty years previously? (At the same time helping themselves to the wealth of any local nobles who had harboured the heretics). But times had changed, and though he wouldn't say it in writing, the king didn't need to conquer parts of his own domain anymore. The vast estates of the disgraced Count of Toulouse had eventually come to the King, not through conquest, but by marriage and inheritance and the majority of the region's nobles owed allegiance to him. The King, like the Pope, saw this as a local issue. But, in a gesture of support, he offered to send a small force of twenty knights to assist any troops that the Archbishop might be able to assemble. He also gave his permission for local taxes to be increased to help pay for the troops.

The Archbishop read both letters again and came to the conclusion that their content was much as he expected. He had their blessing but little in the way of practical support. He was going to have to drive this campaign himself. 'At least,' he concluded, 'there'll be no one to interfere with my plans'. He put down the letter and rang the bell to signal his clerks. His orders would be sent out on Christmas Day.

The snow that had begun to fall the day that Elouise and Guillaume exchanged their vows continued throughout the next week. Now every roof, tower and rampart was covered in a thick white layer, and the grounds within the walls had been churned into a quagmire of slush and mud. Raised pathways of timber had been built to make it easier to move from one part of the chateau to another. The temperature struggled to rise above freezing and for the most part the inhabitants were content to do little more than tend to their livestock and stay close to their fires.

In the great hall of the chateau the Count was sitting at the refectory table with his closest advisors and some of the knights. They greeted each other with the normal daily courtesies before waiting for the Count to speak.

'Gentlemen,' he began, 'the news that is reaching me is not

good. Our knights have been riding out for several days and returning with increasing stories of zeal and fanaticism. It seems the Archbishop is determined to raise a force by whatever means available. He'll promise a simple man a safe entry to heaven or sell the rights to honour a family name in churches throughout the region. Nobles and merchants are falling over themselves to pay for the Archbishop's cause, so the days of peaceful co-existence with our fellow citizens seem to be well and truly over.' The Count paused and looked at the stern faces around the table, allowing the impact of his words to sink in. 'Make no mistake gentlemen, we are now the prey, something to be exterminated. I estimate that before the end of this new month of January we can expect their force to gather around the chateau. We must prepare ourselves for an attack or a siege,' he paused again, 'either way, what we need is a plan.'

'What about food? How long can we last?' asked one of the men. The Count turned to his steward, Pierre Biscaye, and indicated to him to reply. Pierre looked calm, 'Our stores are full with grain and dried meats. We have plenty of livestock for fresh meat and chickens for eggs. We still have root vegetables and feed for the animals.'

'And water?' continued the man.

'Our *citerne* is full to the brim and as long as the snow melts or it continues to rain our supply should be replenished,' replied Pierre.

'What are we short of?' asked another.

'Firewood' said Pierre. 'The ovens and fires need feeding constantly and we are low on stocks within the chateau. We need to organise gathering parties to fetch as much wood as quickly as possible. We should also send out men to hunt for food, anything that can be used in the pot.'

The Count said nothing for a while before asking the question that was on everyone's mind.

'And how long do you think we could hold out for, Pierre?'

'In theory we could last for months, my lord. We will need to ration supplies, of course, but we have enough to feed every mouth for many weeks to come. But it's important we let everyone know that once we shut our gates we must be vigilant about the functions of our bodies. To my certain knowledge a besieged chateau can suffer more through sickness than lack of food'.

'Thank you, Pierre.' The Count smiled at his friend then turned towards his son. 'Tomorrow, Guillaume, I want you to take some men and go down to the village and bring back any supplies that you can obtain. But do not use force. Only deal with those who are still sympathetic or who are prepared to sell, is that understood?'

'Yes, father.'

The Count turned his attention to one of the other knights. 'Olivier, I want you take a party and destroy any crops still on our lands that might be of use to the enemy. Then bring back as much firewood as you can carry. No need for it be used to warm the arses of those that would do us harm!' He smiled and the group of men smiled back, encouraged by his humour.

'Does anyone else have a question?'

One of the knights raised an arm. 'My lord, suppose it's not a siege. What if we are attacked?'

The Count brought his fist down so hard upon the table that the dogs dozing at his feet were instantly alert. 'Then we will fight back!' he roared and his eyes flashed in a way seldom seen before. 'These walls are thick and our slopes are steep. It will be difficult to get more than a few men at a time close enough to attack. They will try and breach the gates so that is where we must concentrate our defence. As long as our patrols stay vigilant we have the weapons to repel any attempt, day or night.' His confidence seemed to encourage the men and the mood relaxed visibly, except for one knight who had followed the proceedings without speaking. Now he cleared his throat.

'My lord, is there not another way to avoid both a battle or a siege?'

'And what might that be, young Guy?'

'We could give the Cathars to the Archbishop.'

The other men looked shocked at the boldness of the statement and turned to see the reaction of the Count, who said nothing for a few moments.

'A brave question, sir, and one that needed to be asked. It would indeed be a simple solution to our problem. But, alas, one I could not countenance. We have offered these good people our protection and that is what we will do. Besides' he added, his voice stirring with emotion, 'it would mean giving up my own wife and that I will never do.'

The Count let his words sink in before delivering his final thoughts. 'Let none of us be under any illusion. Whether we protect the Cathars or give them up, this chateau and those who defend it will not be allowed to survive. We must defeat our enemy or expect no mercy.'

The Count stood up to signal that the meeting was over.

Michel gave Guillaume a friendly wave as he watched him preparing to leave for the village. He was on his way to see Elouise, a flagon of warm soup held tightly against his chest as he bent his head against another flurry of icy snow.

He knocked on her door and waited for permission to enter.

'Who is it?' came a small voice from inside.

'It's me, Lou-Lou, Michel.'

'Come in, Michel, there's no need for you to knock.'

He entered the room to find Elouise lying on her bed.

'You look tired, Lou-Lou, is everything alright?'

'I'm fine, really,' she said, smiling and reaching out for his hand 'but this young fellow inside me is making my back ache. I just thought I'd lie down for a while.' Michel looked down at his friend and gently stroked her hair.

'Well you just rest there. Look, I've brought you some of cook's special soup, it'll do you good.' He busied himself pouring the hot, thick liquid into a wooden beaker. 'Here, sit up and drink this.'

Elouise did as she was instructed, grateful for his concern. The soup soon warmed her insides, her back stopped aching, and she began to feel much better. She watched her friend as he paced slowly around the room, absentmindedly picking up things and putting them down again. She thought of the years they had spent roaming the hillsides and wondered if he was feeling in some way trapped.

'Are you frightened?' she said.

'Frightened of what?'

'You know, what might happen to us if we really do get attacked.'

Michel stopped his tour of the room and sat down at the end of the bed, a wide smile on his face. 'Me? frightened? Why should I be afraid with so many handsome knights to protect us?'

'Be serious,' she admonished, 'don't tease me.' The smile faded from his face and he looked at her intently.

'I don't know what's going to happen,' he began, quietly, 'I've never been in a situation like this before. Part of me feels like running for the hills, finding somewhere safe to hide. But I know I won't do that; I feel I have a purpose here, so I suppose I'll stay and see it through. I don't think I could leave you here, anyway.' He looked sad for a while then a smile lit his face again and he gently squeezed her leg. 'Besides, who'll look after you if I don't, eh?'

They laughed and she held out her arms to give him a big hug.

'You're a very special person, my dearest shepherd boy. I don't know what I would do without you.'

She held him tightly but couldn't see him squeeze his eyes shut or feel the tears that trickled down his cheek, falling one by one onto her shoulder.

Guillaume and a fellow knight led a party of twelve men. There was no one to challenge their entry at the gate and the narrow road that led to the centre of the village was deserted except for a few dogs scavenging for scraps of food. The dogs looked up at the men as they passed, hoping but not expecting, something edible to be thrown their way. Of the three hundred souls who had once made up the population of St. Julien less than a hundred remained, either too infirm, too stubborn or too devoted to the church to leave. The rest had sought refuge at the chateau or had melted into the surrounding hills.

What was once a vibrant community was now divided and turned in on itself; minds that were once open and friendly had become suspicious and accusing, all in the name of religion.

The men set about retrieving what stores of food they could from their former homes whilst Guillaume and his companion sought out any of the few remaining villagers who might be persuaded to exchange food for payment. Polite as they were in their task they met few who were willing to bargain. Eyes were averted or doors left unanswered as they made their way through the village. As the two knights rode slowly back to the main square Guillaume caught sight of a limping figure emerging from the church. Villac had been in the tower, keeping an eye, as usual, on the coming and goings in the village and had seen the men enter. Guillaume spurred his horse forward to catch up with the priest.

'So, priest', he called out 'still spying on your parishioners? Who are you pointing your finger at this time?' The priest halted his shuffling walk and turned to look up at Guillaume.

'Well, if it isn't the young master,' he sneered, lips pulled back from ugly yellow teeth. 'I hope your father knows what he's doing giving all those poor misguided souls so much hope. Doesn't he realise it's not just the Archbishop he's upset but the Pope and the King of France too? Surely it would be the honourable thing to send them back to me and let my church offer them the salvation they deserve?'

'What would you know about honour, you pathetic specimen?' said Guillaume, looking down at the priest. 'By all accounts no young girl in this village was safe from your version of salvation.' The priest took a step backwards and his face went pale as he realised that Bernadette must have broken her promise not to speak. He decided to go on the attack, 'That family is evil,' he shouted, 'they have spread their heretical ideas throughout this village for many years. You shouldn't believe what a heretic's slut tells you.' He then made the mistake of pressing the matter further. 'Besides, if what I hear is true, there is another heretic's daughter who carries your very own seed.'

Guillaume leapt from his horse, drawing his sword in one movement, and pushed the priest back into the wall of the church.

'You miserable little worm,' he hissed through clenched teeth, 'I'd be doing the world a favour if I ran this sword right through you. You're not fit to wear the cloth that protects you; you are a disgrace to any religion, yours or mine.'

'Guillaume, leave him be,' said the other knight quietly, looking down on the scene. 'Let others deal with him; his blood would not be worth the stain on your reputation.' Guillaume glared at the priest for a moment then pushed him away. 'Keep out of my sight,' he warned, 'next time I could be on my own.' The priest, visibly scared, said nothing but slunk away, his lame leg scraping along the stone path.

Guillaume remounted and the two knights waited for the other men to return. As the grey wintry light faded the party passed through the deserted gate and made its slow way back up the steep path to the chateau, four of the men struggling with a cart heavily laden with sacks of provisions and the others carrying whatever they could over their shoulders. By the time they reached the chateau the torches had been lit at the gate, their light flickering off the stone walls.

Passing beneath the great archway with the gates shut firmly behind him Guillaume couldn't help wondering if he would ever cross that threshold again. He decided to keep that thought to himself.

CHAPTER THIRTY-SIX

It took nearly seven weeks for the Archbishop to muster sufficient support for his crusade; for in his own mind this was how he thought of it.

The twenty knights and their supporting party had arrived from Paris and were now barracked within the walls of Albi. Rumours of the Archbishop's money had been enough to persuade a mob of hardened mercenaries to gather in the city, some travelling from as far as Spain, each man willing to hire out his services for coinage and the prospect of looting. In return for the promise of religious favours and the sale of dubious relics, many local nobles and merchants had provided enough funds to recruit men from the surrounding villages; even the prisons had been emptied of petty criminals and thieves, their sentences temporarily terminated. The Archbishop's fund, combined with the persuasive powers of the Dominican brothers, had procured a force of some eight hundred men and assorted camp followers. It was a long way from being an army but the Archbishop and his advisors felt sure that with the aid of the knights and mercenaries it was a sufficient force to deal with one recalcitrant chateau.

All it lacked was a leader. After deliberating over which of his cronies it should be, the Archbishop decided the honour should be bestowed on one of the most generous of the local nobles. And so the Comte de Lacaune, a man with little previous military experience, was chosen to carry the white, purple and gold colours of the church on its mission to settle, once and for all, the problem of the heretics.

On the morning of February 10th in the year 1244, with banners and flags unfurled, the Archbishop's crusade set off from Albi en route to St. Julien de Roc. With good weather and no delays the journey south should take no more than seven days.

News of the force's departure soon reached the ears of the Comte de Quillan. His knights still had access to the surrounding countryside and their horses could travel at greater speed than a walking army. Tactics based on the reported strength of the approaching enemy were discussed at length. A flurry of orders was issued to make sure the chateau was secure and that all defences were in place and weapons checked and tested. The inhabitants of the chateau were placed on immediate rationing for food and water and given instructions about where to assemble in the case of attack. A double duty of sentries was put in place to patrol the walls throughout the day and night, with signals that each sentry could recognise in the dark.

Several of the young men from the village, including Bernadette's brother Jacques, volunteered for the dangerous task of undercover observers. This involved being lowered over the walls at night, hiding in the undergrowth surrounding the chateau during the daytime to watch for any enemy activity, then being raised back over the walls the following night to report. They were under no illusions that this was deadly work; if captured they could not expect to be allowed to live.

Amidst all this activity Elouise's pregnancy was taking its natural course. She and Bernadette, now close friends, talked about the experience they were soon about to share.

'Are you scared?' asked Elouise one morning; the two young

women were seated at a table sorting out a heap of vegetables, selecting those that could be stored and those that needed to be cooked.

'Scared of what?' replied Bernadette, not sure if Elouise was referring to the impending birth of their babies or the far more worrying arrival of a besieging army.

'Having a baby; the birth,' said Elouise quietly. Bernadette could see from the expression on her face and the look in her eyes that her friend was worried. Although the younger of the two, this was Bernadette's opportunity to reassure her older friend.

'No, not really. From what I've seen it seems fairly simple.' It was true that Bernadette had lived with, and been close to, other women who had given birth. She'd even helped to deliver some of the neighbour's babies and had watched the farm animals produce their young. She was well aware that pain could be involved, and she also knew that Elouise's own mother had died giving birth. Bernadette decided not to mention the pain.

'We'll be fine, I'm sure. We're both young and healthy, they'll probably have us patrolling the walls straight afterwards!' She managed a laugh and Elouise, to Bernadette's relief, lost her worried look and joined in the laughter as they both imagined climbing the walls for guard duty with their new babies on their backs.

That night, as she lay with Guillaume, Elouise recounted her conversation with Bernadette. He, with absolutely no experience of childbirth, could offer little in the way of practical support. He could only reassure Elouise that she would be fine, that she shouldn't worry and that he would be there to comfort and look after her. Elouise squeezed his hand in the dark to thank him for his gentleness and understanding but she couldn't sleep; the image of what her own mother must have gone through was too difficult to dispel. Lying there in the darkness she called silently to the spirit of her father to help her baby be born safely.

Loud shouts from the guards on the wall woke Guillaume and Elouise and he was out of bed and into his tunic before she had rubbed the sleep from her eyes. It was barely light but the sound of running footsteps meant that others were already moving around. 'What do you think it is?' asked Elouise, holding the heaviness of her belly with one hand and manoeuvring her legs over the side of the bed.

'I don't know, but the guards wouldn't have raised the alarm unless it was something serious.' Guillaume was pulling on his boots and fastening his sword around his waist as quickly as he could.'I want you to stay here until I find out what's going on.' He ran for the door and disappeared from sight. Elouise raised her legs back into the bed and pulled the covers up to her chin. She lay there and listened to the commotion outside.

Guillaume raced up the steps to the top of the wall and saw his father talking to the guards. Once he had taken his first look over the battlements he could see why the alarm had been raised. The guards had become aware of unusual activity in the village when they had seen torches and flares moving about. Now, as daylight increased, they could make out the movements of groups of men, together with large numbers of horses and carts moving through the village. Soon the narrow walkway that circuited the length of the chateau's walls was crowded with men looking down at the village. Guillaume stood next to his father and noticed the Count's clenched fists resting on the cold stone of the battlement.

'What do you think, father?' asked Guillaume as they stared down at the village. The Count said nothing for a while, his eyes absorbing the scene.

'Well, my boy, they've certainly gained an element of

surprise.' His warm breath whitened in the cold air as he spoke. 'We knew they were getting close but it's unusual they should travel by night. They must have felt it was better to press on to the village than make camp again out in the open.'

'What should we do now?' continued Guillaume, asking the question that others had on their mind.

'Nothing, besides observe,' replied the Count. 'They'll need to organise themselves first. They won't be doing anything for a while, save to let us know they're there. But our guards must report the moment any of their men look like leaving the village. I want to know about every single movement from now on.' The Count turned, smiling, and threw his arm around his son's shoulder in a gesture intended to reassure all the men gathered on the wall. 'Come on my boy, let us go and eat a good breakfast together. Never mind the rations, this could turn out to be a long day.' The Count and the rest of the men descended the stone steps back to the courtyard and headed for the great hall, leaving the guards to concentrate on the enemy below.

News of the arrival of the Archbishop's army spread rapidly throughout the chateau. There was no panic but a mood of reflection mixed with uncertainty descended on the inhabitants. People carried on with their daily tasks, trying to raise each other's spirits, but for the main part most kept within their own family groups. The few *Parfaits* that had made their way to the chateau continued to move amongst them, offering prayers and blessings.

Elouise soon realised that Guillaume was not going to return with any news. Eventually it was Annie who came to the room and brought her up to date with the events of the morning. Annie was unusually flustered.

'God forbid if the Archbishop gets his hands on us. We'll all be done for!' She fussed around Elouise, helping her to get washed and dressed, even though Elouise was perfectly capable of doing it herself.

'Don't fret so, Annie. Do you really think the Count is going to let that happen? You'll be perfectly safe here, I promise you.' This seemed to calm Annie down.

'Well if you say so, Miss, but I can't help worrying all the same.'

Elouise decided to change the subject. 'Have you seen the Countess this morning, Annie? She promised me she had a remedy to help me with the baby and I've a feeling I might be needing it soon.' Annie smiled with fondness at Elouise.

'Whatever remedy she may have I don't think you need it yet, my dear girl. That baby will come when it's good and ready, and not a day before!'

Later that morning Elouise made her way to the Countess's chamber, carefully avoiding the icy puddles that had been left by the previous day's rain. She knocked at the door and waited for permission to enter. She found the Countess seated by the small fire, warming her hands, and crossed the room to greet her. 'Come here, my child, how are you feeling?' The two women embraced and Elouise sat down.

'I'm fine, really, though I think I've had enough of carrying this weight around.' Elouise placed both hands under her belly and lifted it gently. The Countess smiled in sympathy, recalling her own pregnancies with Guillaume and his sister. She missed her daughter very much but was relieved that she and the Count had been able to get word to Helene, insisting that she remain at Mirapoix with her fiancé's family; she could imagine her daughter arguing to return to the chateau to be with her own kin but Sybille knew she was in a safer place.

'Well it won't be long now I'm sure. Have you thought of a name yet for your baby?' In truth Elouise had given the matter little thought but now, suddenly, the answer became perfectly clear. 'I will name her after my mother, Blanche,' she answered.

'And if it's a boy?' enquired the Countess, gently.

'Guillaume, of course,' said Elouise, and the Countess smiled again.

The two women stared into the fire for a while, each lost in their own thoughts. It was the Countess who broke the silence. 'What do you think your father would have said about what's happening to us now?'

Elouise furrowed her brow as she thought about her answer.

'My father, as you know so well, was a very religious man. He taught me that the more simple and pure a life we can lead the sooner our spirit can reach heaven. He also told me I should put the needs of others before my own. I think if he were here now he would be praying that the chateau would remain strong and that the Archbishop would eventually see reason and leave us in peace.'

'And if the chateau should fall?'

'Then I think he would try to find a way to let us leave unharmed...even if it meant sacrificing himself. He was not a man afraid to die for what he believed was right.' The Countess let Elouise's words hang in the air for a few moments before speaking again.

'And what about you; would you be prepared to die for your faith?'

'Yes, of course' replied Elouise firmly, 'I would rather die for my beliefs than be forced to live without hope for my soul. Could you?'

The Countess looked down at her folded hands. 'No, I couldn't' she said quietly 'I have already made that decision.' 'But you,' she continued, 'now that you will have a child...'

Elouise knew what the Countess meant and couldn't hold back the tears that began to cloud her eyes. 'That's just too difficult for me right now,' she replied, her voice beginning to shake.' I have no experience of babies. I love Guillaume with all my heart but I didn't plan to be having his child, it just happened. How can I be responsible for bringing a child into this sad world?' By now her tears were flowing freely 'And yet, and yet, how could I deprive a child of its mother, I of all people, who never had one of my own!' Her shoulders heaved with sobs and the Countess gently pulled Elouise towards her, encircling the sobbing girl with her arms and allowing her to shed her tears. 'My poor child,' she said, stroking Elouise's hair, 'what dilemmas we mothers give ourselves! You are a young woman with deep feelings and I'm sure when the time comes you will make the right decision.'

CHAPTER THIRTY-SEVEN

During the next few days the plan of the Archbishop's army unfolded. It was clear that a straightforward attack on the chateau could not be attempted. The slopes leading to the gates on the western wall were too steep, and too slippery in the snow and ice to allow any sizeable group of men to advance. The steepness of the Roc, and the rough ground around it, made it impossible for the chateau to be attacked by any rock-hurling trebuchet, although this didn't prevent an attempt to build one, balanced on top of a wooden platform that was being constructed within firing distance of the walls. The other flanks of the chateau were protected by their own natural defences, namely the sheer sides of the Roc, rising from the river below, upon which the walls had been built as if growing from the very stone of the land itself.

To any military eye the chateau seemed impregnable.

The best tactic available to the Comte de Lacaune would be to lay a circle of men around the chateau, controlling all possible points of entry and exit and gradually squeezing the life out of any resistance. He had the advantage of the village, and its water supply, to use as a base for his camp. He could even requisition the many empty dwellings that had been left behind by their fleeing residents to house his men. His main problem would be to find sufficient provisions to feed his army; in this regard the needs of the besieger and the besieged were very much the same.

It was impossible, of course, to completely encircle the chateau with troops. The nature of the land, with its steep ravines and sheer drops, meant that breaks in the line were inevitable and it was such gaps that could often become the weak points of any siege. But Lacaune had his duty to perform and so, taking the advice of the more experienced members of his party, he gave the orders for the siege to be laid and waited for the signals to tell him that his men were securely in place. Once he was sure that all preparations had been completed and his men were in position the Count retired to his headquarters to plan the next stage of the accepted rules of engagement for a siege. He and his advisors worked through the night and, when satisfied with their deliberations, had one of the travelling clerks draw up the document on parchment; it would be the formal offer to the chateau to surrender.

The next morning, as the weak sun slowly rose over the peaks to the east, the guards on the wall watched as two horsemen, one carrying the Archbishop's flag, emerged from the village gates, making their way slowly up the path that led to the chateau. One of the guards ran to the knight responsible for the watch and he immediately gave the order to alert the Count. Before the two horsemen had reached half way to the chateau the Count stood on the wall observing the scene.

'They'll soon be in range of our bowmen, my lord. Shall I give the order to shoot?' said a knight by his side. The Count held up his arm, a signal that no command should be given.

'No, sir. They have not come to fight, they have come to talk.' He stood staring for a while then motioned to his son. 'Guillaume, get yourself ready and take Guy with you. I want you to go out and meet them.'

It was strangely silent as the huge doors of the chateau slowly opened and Guillaume and his companion urged their horses out beyond the safety of the wall. The sun reflected off Guillaume's armour; one hand held the reins, the other resting on the hilt of his sword. Next to him Guy increased his grip on the banner of the Comte de Quillan, then the two knights steered their mounts carefully down the steep slope to meet the approaching horsemen. From his position on top of the wall the Count could see the distance between the two parties reducing until they stood facing each other. The horses seemed to sense the mood, pawing the ground nervously. He watched as Guillaume nodded formally to the knight mounted opposite him. A few words seemed to be exchanged and then a small package was handed to Guillaume. The rendezvous was over and both pairs of horsemen turned and made their way back to their respective camps, this time urging their mounts to move more quickly. In no time at all Guillaume had passed back through the gates and was hurrying to meet his father with the message.

Guillaume sat at the table with the other men, waiting for his father to finish reading the document. The Count had spread the parchment in front of him and read it twice before looking up.

'What does it say, father?'

The Count didn't answer but pushed the parchment towards his steward to read. The two men looked at each other, determination on their faces.

'Gentlemen,' began the Count, 'It is much as I expected. They are offering a safe passage for everyone to return to their homes on condition they renounce their heretical beliefs and submit themselves to whatever penance the Archbishop deems suitable.'

'And on what terms?' asked one of the knights.

The Count looked at the men around the table, 'The immediate surrender of the chateau, with myself and my family to be taken into custody on the orders of King Louis.' The men looked at each other but said nothing.

'When do they need an answer?' asked Guillaume. 'I'm ready to ride out again.'

The Count looked fondly at his son. 'If they don't have our response before this evening they will assume we have rejected their terms.' He turned to address all the men.

'Loyal friends, I cannot make this decision alone. You must all have your say, and if any man feels we should accept their terms then do not be afraid to speak, I shall not feel the less towards you'. None of the men seemed to want to be the first to say anything and a silence fell around the table. Then one of the younger knights, Cedric, spoke up.

'My lord, I do not accept their terms. If we cannot bring about the failure of their siege then I am willing to fight for my beliefs. I would rather die and take my chances with God than give my soul to the Pope; I say reject their offer!' The Count couldn't help smiling at the young man's passion and soon the whole group was nodding in agreement amid shouts of 'Aye!' and banging of fists on the table.

'You do me a great honour,' said the Count, 'I am very proud of you all.'

He paused. 'Now I think we should devise an answer of our own to send to the Archbishop.'

Later that afternoon, as the wintry sun began its descent behind the hills to the west, six bowmen stood on the battlements, the tips of their arrows wrapped in cloth soaked in oil and pitch. Each man dipped his arrow into a flaming torch and took aim. The volley of burning arrows sped through the darkening air and found their target; within moments the wooden platform and half built trebuchet on which it stood were on fire.

The Count, standing with the bowmen, looked down at the flames with satisfaction. 'I think they have their answer now.'

And so began the siege. Days turned slowly into one week and then another, with little activity on either side. The only constant was the cold rain of early spring that soaked everything and seemed to penetrate to the very bone. The men surrounding the chateau were wet and miserable, their faces splashed with rain as they looked upwards at the impenetrable walls. Some days they couldn't even see their quarry when the damp, heavy clouds descended and covered the chateau and the Roc it stood on, and they were left to stare into a grey, swirling mist.

Inside the chateau, despite the cold and the rain and the churned up mud, spirits remained high. The water supply was constantly replenished and as many people as possible had been moved into the great hall and throughout the other chambers of the chateau. This closeness brought about a growing sense of camaraderie amongst the inhabitants and the *Parfaits* were able to build on this togetherness with preaching and prayers, creating a heightened sense of religious purpose and unity. Even Elouise, although not ordained as a *Parfait* but accepted as the daughter of one, found that people would ask her for a blessing, a gesture that gave her an increasing sense of purpose.

Since her conversation with the Countess, she had thought constantly of the dilemma she faced if their resistance to the siege should fail. Should she follow her beliefs and the ultimate sacrifice that would be involved? Or should she follow the natural instincts of motherhood? These were serious matters for her to consider and she failed to arrive at a decision. To make matters worse she felt she could not discuss her feelings with Guillaume. Despite her love and affection for him she realised he was too young, too immature, to be able to help in this battle of her conscience. Besides, he had his own priorities; his duty to his father and the security of the chateau. She resolved to wait until after the baby was born then, perhaps, she would find an answer to her dilemma.

Occasionally there was a skirmish between the two sides. One night, under cover of darkness and heavy rainfall, a small party of Lacaune's men had been able to climb the hill and reach the gates of the chateau undetected. They had brought dry kindling and timber with them and their intention was to set fire to the gates. But it was almost impossible to ignite the wood; each time a spark flickered and a wisp of smoke gave them some encouragement it was quickly extinguished by the wind and rain. At daybreak the men were soon discovered by the guards on the wall and were swiftly beaten back by a flurry of arrows and hurled rocks, leaving two of their number dead on the ground.

But such futile attacks were few and far between and the siege began to resemble an impasse. Those outside the chateau felt that sooner or later the food and water of those inside would diminish and hunger and thirst would drive them to surrender. It could only be a matter of time.

The people inside the chateau felt under little threat from those outside. Water was plentiful, the rationing of provisions was unquestioned, and the frequent and undetected sorties of men over the wall kept them in touch with the outside world and even provided a supply of fresh meat from the traps that had been set. The general feeling was that if they could survive for long enough the Archbishop's men would eventually weary of waiting and consider it a lost cause, leaving them in peace. The situation seemed to have reached a state of stalemate.

CHAPTER THIRTY-EIGHT

As the tenth day of March arrived and the siege continued its slow progress, a group of Catalan mercenaries gathered in the abandoned tavern, helping themselves to a cask of wine. The men were in an ugly mood due to the lack of activity. They had been in this desolate place for more than a month with no prospect of looting the chateau and they had little respect for the noble who was supposed to be leading the siege. As the alcohol took hold of their minds and loosened their tongues a wild, crazy plan began to form. The more they discussed it the more they liked the idea; they decided they were going to attack the chateau themselves. These men from the Pyrenees, every one of them a skilled mountaineer, formed the audacious plan to climb the walls of the chateau.

Later that evening, heavily armed and with thick coils of rope around their shoulders and still drunk enough to dispel any fear, six men crept quietly up the steep slope towards the chateau. Their target was the eastern tower; the highest sheer wall but the most isolated part of the fortress. The moonless sky hid their movement from the guards above and they were soon huddled together at the foot of the tower. Looking up the wall at the round turret perched on top of the tower the idea seemed even crazier than it had in the tavern. Any fall would mean certain death as well as risk raising the alarm. Undeterred, two of the men took off their boots to allow their stockinged feet a better purchase on the stones set in the wall. With two coils of rope each and armed only with daggers, the two men were lifted up by their comrades to make sure their first grips were secure. Then, slowly, they began to climb, grasping their way gradually upward. They made use of the angle between the wall and the curve of the tower, each man finding his own route towards the top, fingers reaching out and searching for any crevice big enough to jam a hand into before pulling himself up further.

The men on the ground shivered and watched as their two comrades, arms and legs spread out at odd angles like lizards, continued to edge upwards into the darkness. The men on the wall were sweating heavily, not daring to look down. By now they were nearer to the top than the foot of the wall and still no alarm had been raised.

Luck and skill seemed to be playing equal parts in their gravity-defying ascent, as they gradually moved closer to the top. Hearts beating, but trying to hold their breath, they each put a hand over the battlement and paused to listen, every sinew in their body straining to hold their grip. One man signalled to the other that he could see two sentries guarding the tower. Silently they slithered over the wall and crouched down so that they showed no outline against the sky.

The two sentries stood no chance; they were swiftly brought down and slain, daggers slicing through their throats before they could even utter a sound. Quickly the two mercenaries dropped their ropes over the wall to the ground below and began to haul up two more of their comrades, both more heavily armed. When these two reached the tower the ropes were dropped again and more weapons and another man made it to the top. The remaining mercenary was left to make his way carefully back to the village. Once there he was able to report, with much swagger and arrogance, that the clandestine mission had been successful.

When a second pair of guards approached to take their turn at the tower they were seized and killed with equal ease, their bodies tossed over the wall to land next to those of their comrades below. It was only when the first guards failed to return to the barracks that any notion that something was wrong became apparent. This time four men were despatched to the tower to investigate. They moved in pairs along the narrow walkways on both sides of the flanking walls, approaching the tower from left and right. But the mercenaries saw them coming and, better armed now, fired bolts from their crossbows, easily picking off the leading man in each advancing pair. The two remaining guards beat a hasty retreat from the tower, one managing successfully to reach safety, the other taking a bolt in the leg, screaming and falling off the wall to break his neck on the courtyard below.

The Count convened a rapid council of war. There was no doubt the mercenaries' bold initiative had taken him by surprise. No one in living memory had ever had the courage, or the sheer stupidity, to attempt to climb the walls of the chateau. He was reluctant to commit more men to suicidal attacks on the tower. The narrowness of the walkways made it impossible for more than two men at a time to approach, and they had seen the deadly effectiveness of the mercenaries' weapons.

The Count decided that discretion would be the best policy in the short term.

He reasoned that the men on the tower could only have limited supplies of food and water; therefore they would soon weaken and possibly surrender. In effect he would lay his own siege to the enemy now occupying the eastern turret. He issued instructions that the tower should be watched day and night and that anyone needing to move about the open courtyard should do so with extreme caution, to avoid becoming another target.

The plan had its merits but it lacked the foresight to see what the besieging force would do next. Buoyed by their success at the tower the mercenaries in Lacaune's army took over command of the siege. They ordered a number of day and night time attacks on the more accessible parts of the wall to divert attention away from what was happening at the foot of the east tower. Several sorties of men scrambled up the slope to engage the chateau's defenders, drawing their firepower onto themselves, and taking many casualties in the process. Meanwhile, out of sight of the distracted defenders, the mercenaries were able to re-supply their comrades on the tower, using the ropes not only to send up vital food and water but also a weapon to escalate the attack on the chateau. A smaller version of the rock-throwing trebuchet had been constructed by the carpenters in the village and was now being sent up the wall, in parts, to be reassembled in the turret. It was a weapon of lethal potential and during the course of the following nights many buckets of small boulders were sent up on the ropes as ammunition for the launcher.

The Count and his men were aware of the continuing activity in the east tower but could do little to prevent it. Their only success had been to send out a raiding party one night to interrupt the mercenaries at the foot of the tower. They succeeded in driving the enemy back down the slopes, killing most of them in the process, but by then the threat was already in place.

The men occupying the tower took little time to assemble the trebuchet and begin practicing. Their first shots bounced harmlessly off the thick walls but served as a dangerous warning to anyone foolish enough to move about in the courtyard. The Count ordered everyone to stay inside unless it was absolutely essential, although the layout of the chateau meant that the great hall, where most people were now sheltering, was some distance from the ovens and kitchens. But when he asked for volunteers to make the journey to fetch provisions many stepped forward, willing to brave the stone missiles from above.

The mercenaries soon realised that the roofs of the chateau were weaker than the walls and altered their aim to cause as much damage as possible. Night time assaults were the worst, as heavy boulders crashed without warning through the tiles and slates of the roofs, causing death and mayhem inside. The previous unity of purpose amongst the inhabitants was put under immense strain and some chose to take their chances and huddle in corners of the courtyard, out of reach of the fearsome trebuchet, but separated from food and shelter.

The Count discussed at length with his men ways to reach the tower and attack the mercenaries. They even considered digging out enough rocks from the tower's base to cause it to collapse, but this idea was rejected on the grounds that it could create a massive breach in the chateau's walls, big enough for the enemy to pour through. They could only hope that the men in the tower would soon run out of ammunition.

But the mercenaries had other ideas. They had worked out the position of the chateau's *citerne* and began to aim a succession of boulders in that direction. They cheered when they scored a direct hit and, encouraged by their success, renewed their efforts with vigour. The next boulder caused a deep crack to appear in the wall of the *citerne*. The one after that, larger and heavier, shattered it. They stood back and gaped with genuine amazement as the water poured out across the courtyard, flooding the ground and gushing out beneath the gates. The inhabitants of the chateau could only watch in shock and horror as their precious water supply drained away.

The Count gathered everyone together in the great hall and took his place in front of the empty fireplace. By his side stood Sybille with Guillaume and Elouise. He addressed the crowd of sad faces standing before him.

'My good friends, you have all seen what has happened; now it is time for us to think about our future. If it continues to rain we will be able to collect enough water to keep us going day by day, and in the meantime we will try to repair the *citerne*. If we succeed it will still take many days of good rain to refill, but without water we will not be able to survive for long.' He paused to let this bleak statement of fact sink in before continuing.

'This evening I want you all, every person and family, to consider your options should we no longer have enough water. In my opinion we have two choices; we can decide to stay here, resist the siege and probably die slowly of thirst or hunger. Or, we can call an end to the siege and try to negotiate a settlement that will allow some of you to leave in peace.' The Count took his wife's hand in his own and kissed it. 'We all must make our choice. I ask you to think it about this evening and let me have your answers by this time tomorrow.'

Later that evening, unbeknown to the Count, the remaining knights decided to make one more attempt to dislodge the mercenaries from the tower. Creeping forward in the darkness and protected by shields they edged their way towards the furthest end of the chateau. Their approach seemed to go undetected and with a final roar they rushed into the tower, weapons drawn.

They were met by silence as their roars died away on the wind. The mercenaries had gone, their foolhardy mission accomplished. Only their ropes were left, disappearing downwards into the darkness below.

CHAPTER THIRTY-NINE

Guillaume approached Elouise in their chamber; he needed to talk to her. He couldn't hold back the feeling that she had been keeping him at a distance, but he put this down to the approaching birth of their child.

'Elouise, my love, what are you thinking about?' he asked, tentatively.

She looked up at him and smiled, aware of his nervousness and his concern for her.

'Guillaume,' she began, trying to remain calm, 'your father made it clear last night that we must all make our choice. You must understand that I am the daughter of a *Parfait*, I was brought up in the Cathar faith. If the enemies of that faith succeed in defeating the resistance of the chateau then I am prepared to accept my fate. I cannot, I will not, renounce my faith.'

'You mean you would be prepared to die?'

'Yes,' she said, a determined edge to her voice.

Guillaume found it difficult to speak and could do nothing to prevent his anger spilling out.

'And what about our unborn child? Would you seal that child's fate too? Don't you think a child deserves to have a mother?' He knew his questions were unfair and hurtful to Elouise and he had to bite his lip and clench his fists as he watched the tears start to roll down her cheeks.

'Don't you think I know that?' she cried out, her eyes pleading with him. 'Don't you see the dilemma I have given myself, to choose between my faith and our child?' Can I condemn a child to a life without a mother or should I carry the clean, pure spirit of our baby with me and let it take its place in heaven?'

They faced one another, neither of them speaking as they struggled to understand each other's feelings. Guillaume knew what his answer to her predicament would be but decided not to upset Elouise any further. Suddenly he spoke, his face alert.

'When do you think this baby of ours is going to arrive?'

Elouise, still lost in thought, hesitated for a few moments. 'I don't know exactly, but Annie says that judging by the size of my belly and the movements inside he could arrive any day now, as could Bernadette's.'

'Then I have an idea,' said Guillaume.

She looked at him, her eyes still wet with tears. 'Go on,' she said.

'I will ask my father to see if we can negotiate a few days of grace before we accept any terms of surrender; enough time at least for the babies to be born.'

Elouise could see the way his mind was working; he was hoping that once the child was born she would change her mind, and her problem would be resolved. She couldn't help admiring his determination as he kissed her and left the room.

The Count listened to his son as he sat with his advisors discussing what options they might have in their negotiations with Lacaune. He was still of the view that to offer himself, his title and his lands in return for the safety of the chateau's inhabitants would be the most honourable solution. Every man in the room pledged to stand alongside him but he rejected, with much gratitude, their offers. He was of the firm opinion that it would be best if he went alone and he would not be swayed from his decision.

Later, as people began to emerge from their prayers and deliberations and gather in the great hall, it was clear that the majority had made up their minds. For the second time the Count stood before them and spoke.

'Good people, I trust you have allowed good sense as well as your faith to guide you in your decisions. May I ask, by a show of hands, how many of you believe we can continue to resist the siege?' He looked around the room slowly; but not a single hand was raised. He cleared his throat to speak again. 'And how many of you wish me to seek a negotiation on your behalf that will allow you safe passage from the chateau.' This time several hands rose in the air but it was by no means a unanimous decision. The Count looked puzzled, not understanding their reticence. Then one of the older *Parfaits* stepped forward and bowed his head towards the Count.

'My lord, you do us an honour in asking for our opinions. Some in your position would have tried to save themselves and left these poor people at the mercy of their enemies.' He lifted his arm to indicate those who stood with him and continued, 'Those of us who are believers have spent much of yesterday and today praying and consulting together and we are all of one view. We will not recant our faith nor will we ever accept the doctrine of the Catholic Church. We will be ready to accept our fate, whatever that may be.'

The Count stepped towards the *Parfait* and put one hand upon his shoulder.

'Then, good friend, you must allow me to do the best that I can for all of us, so help me God.'

The sound of the midday bell of the chateau mingled with the bells from the village church as the gates creaked open and the Count, with his steward Pierre and Guillaume, rode out. Earlier that morning a banner had been waved from the battlements to signal that a parlay was requested. The three men carefully guided their horses down the steep path to meet the party that was now climbing towards them. Within a short while the two mounted groups were facing each other; two knights and the Bishop of Pamiers accompanied the Comte de Lacaune. The two nobles nodded acknowledgement to each other and it was Guillaume's father who spoke first.

'Sir, we are no longer able to defy your unwarranted siege, therefore I demand that you allow me to negotiate a safe passage for those innocent souls in my care.'

The Comte de Lacaune listened, impressed by his fellow noble's bold words.

'And what, Sir, do you propose?'

'That you allow all the occupants of the chateau a safe return to their homes and in return I will offer myself and my title to the King of France.'

Lacaune looked at the Count with surprise. 'But these are the same terms we proposed at the start of this siege. Terms that you rejected with your burning arrows.'

'Indeed they are, Sir, nothing has changed my mind.'

The Comte de Lacaune looked across at the Bishop then back to the Count. He couldn't hide the sadness in his face, 'Then the matter is out of my hands.'

Guillaume's father turned his attention towards the Bishop, fixing him with a stern look. 'And what does the man of the church have to say?' The Bishop stiffened under the glare and tightened his grip on the saddle, unaccustomed to being on horseback. He cleared his throat to speak.

'This matter is not about nobles and titles and land,' he said, with disdain, 'it is about heresy and those who defend it. I am empowered by my Archbishop to state the following conditions. All those souls who are ready to recant and accept the sacraments of the Holy Roman Church will be allowed safe passage. All others will be considered to be heretics and must accept their fate.'

'And what fate would that be?' asked the Count.

'To be purified by the flames,' replied the Bishop.

The Count turned towards Pierre and Guillaume to see how they had reacted to the Bishop's bleak words; both men were unflinching and showed no reaction. At that moment the Count could not have been prouder of his son. He returned to address his fellow noble, remembering the earlier conversation with Guillaume.

'Then I request that you allow us ten days of grace; that those who wish to leave may leave and those who decide to stay may prepare themselves for the fate that awaits them.'

It was an unusual request but the Comte de Lacaune could not help but admire his words and felt honour bound to accept. 'In the circumstances I see no reason why we should not allow you this period of grace. But ten days only and then your gates must be opened to us.'

The two nobles bowed their heads to each other in agreement; it signalled the end of the rendezvous and both groups turned and headed back in the direction they had come from.

'Ten days,' the Bishop mulled over to himself, 'at least that will be enough time for the Archbishop to get here and witness for himself the final solution to his problem'.

The news of the terms of surrender and the period of grace was met with a mood of grim determination by the occupants of the chateau. The Count made it clear that everyone should listen to their heads and not just their hearts when making a decision whether to leave or stay. By the end of the second day it was clear that of the nearly two hundred souls in the chateau less than forty were preparing to leave. Most of those choosing to go were ordinary villagers, people who had come to the chateau for its protection, rather than stay in the deserted village. Two of the knights who had been loyal to the Count, together with their young squires, also decided to leave. They were not *croyants* and preferred to offer their services to another noble. The others who had chosen to leave had come to the sad conclusion that they lacked certainty in the true strength of their faith. They were going to return the salvation of their souls to the custody of the Catholic Church.

Many of those abandoning the chateau were friends or relatives of those who were choosing to stay and the farewells were long and tearful, especially so when it involved members of the same family. But everyone had worthy reasons for staying or leaving and there was neither guilt nor recrimination. When the big gates opened again to let out those who had chosen to depart it was a solemn procession that exited from the chateau. There were no signs of relief amongst them nor expressions of congratulations from the besieging troops. Rather they descended and were met in silence, uncertain of their future outside the protection of the Comte de Quillan.

Within the chateau an atmosphere of intense religious fervour prevailed amongst the remaining occupants. The *Parfaits* were kept busy holding prayer meetings throughout the days and nights, preparing the *croyants* to face their fate. Elouise found it truly uplifting to see how each person accepted that they would soon be leaving their earthly body, allowing their spirit to be reborn on its journey to heaven. It would only require the final blessing of the *consolamentum* to set every individual spirit free. In these circumstances hunger was soon forgotten, to be replaced by a thirst for knowledge about their destiny.

CHAPTER FORTY

Elouise and Bernadette gave birth on the same day; to Bernadette a boy in the morning and to Elouise, after long hours of labour, a baby girl in the afternoon. Both babies were wrapped tightly in swaddling sheets and rested in makeshift cribs next to their exhausted mothers. Guillaume hurried to tell his parents the news that the babies had been born.

He found his mother and father sitting closely together in their chamber, holding hands. There had never been any possibility that they would be separated from each other. Sybille had made her own decision on the very day the chateau had been lost and her husband, despite his attempts to offer himself to save others, knew that he could never leave his wife. They felt closer to each other now than they had ever been, calm and happy.

'So, my boy,' said his father gently, 'now you're a father too. How does it feel?' Guillaume looked at his parents, pleasure and despair in equal measures on his face.

'I don't know whether to smile or cry. She's so beautiful, just like her mother. How can it come to this that her life will be so short?' He slumped to his knees, unable to bear the pain. Sybille stroked her son's hair, just as she had when he'd been a little boy. 'You know, maybe it was meant to be this way. Your baby already has a new spirit, untouched by this earthly hell. If she submits now then her spirit will always be pure; she will probably reach heaven before we do. Have you thought of that?' In truth Guillaume had been through so many emotions since his argument with Elouise that he had trouble accepting his mother's words, but he smiled at her anyway to show that he appreciated her concern.

'How is Elouise?' asked his mother.

'She's tired, but happy she had a girl.'

'Blanche,' said Sybille softly, remembering her conversation with Elouise.

'And Bernadette, is she well too?'

'Yes mother, they're both fine.'

It was Michel who came up with a plan to save the two babies. He knew Elouise better than anyone and knew the dilemma she had been facing about her faith and the life of her child.

'Do you really think it will work?' asked Elouise, concern and worry etched on her face. Michel sat next to her on the bed, as she nursed the hungry Blanche.

'Of course it will, Lou-Lou, it couldn't be simpler. You just leave it to me.'

He leant forward to kiss her on her forehead then stood up to leave 'I'll go and talk to Bernadette.'

Elouise continued to feed Blanche after Michel had left. She looked down at her baby's face and recognised her father's chin and Guillaume's nose. If anyone else had been in the room they would have told her that the baby had her mother's eyes too. Elouise watched as Blanche sucked on her nipple. She bent her head to rub her cheek gently across the baby's soft hair, taking in the smells of her new born skin. Her mind raced with the thoughts of the decision she had to take. Before the birth her reasoning had seemed quite clear; she was a Cathar, the daughter of a *Parfait*, and she would accept, indeed embrace, her destiny. But now, in hardly a moment, the bond of motherhood had been formed and she was torn between her faith and her feelings. Could she really go to the flames knowing that she was leaving behind a child without a mother, just like her own life? Could she really separate herself from this innocent soul, rejecting all her natural instincts to be a good mother? As her tears began to flow, dropping gently from her cheek to her baby's face, she wished with all her heart that her father could be here to guide her.

That evening, as they took it in turns to cuddle their baby, Elouise explained Michel's plan to Guillaume. 'Michel is going to take the babies with Bernadette and escape over the wall at night. They'll hide in the woods until daybreak then make their way to safety, somewhere far from here. Bernadette is a strong, healthy young girl and she'll have enough milk to feed both babies. The more I think about it the more I'm convinced it's the right thing to do.'

Guillaume couldn't help fretting about the idea; he began pacing up and down.

'But what about the danger? It's all very well fit young men going over the wall but how will Bernadette cope? How will they manage with two babies?'

'I trust Michel and I believe Bernadette will be able to do it. She's a very capable young woman, her natural instinct as a mother will help her.'

'And if they should fall and die then they will only have saved themselves from the flames,' thought Elouise, but decided to keep that notion to herself.

Elouise waited whilst she watched Guillaume struggle to accept the idea before speaking again.

'Guillaume, there is just one part of Michel's plan I want to change. I know you love me and I know you say you want us to be together to the very end, but I want you to escape too, with Blanche.'

Guillaume looked at her, not wanting to hear her words.

'How can you say that? What about the vows we made?

Don't you remember we promised to love each other until death?' his eyes filled with tears of anger and frustration, 'I couldn't live without you, Elouise'

There was silence between them for long moments before Elouise spoke again.

'And what about Blanche?' she said softly,' don't you think she deserves a life with her father?'

'Well then, why don't you come too?' he argued, 'Then she'd have a mother *and* a father.'

Elouise sighed. 'You know I can't do that.'

'Because of your faith!' taunted Guillaume 'You'd choose to die rather than live with your child!'

Elouise said nothing, waiting for his anger to subside.

'Guillaume,' she began gently, 'a year ago none of this was happening. I was content to be with my father and Michel, wandering the hillsides. There was none of this campaign of persecution against our beliefs. I hadn't expected to meet you, I wasn't thinking about falling in love; I certainly didn't expect to have a child... I didn't know I was going to lose my father.' She paused to see if he was listening, then continued. 'But all of these things have happened. I don't understand why there cannot be harmony between two faiths. But I do know that even though I may choose to die for my beliefs, my instincts will not allow me to wish that on our daughter if there is a chance for her to escape. That's why, because I love you both, I want you to go with her.' Guillaume looked at her then turned his face away.

'I can't do it, I won't leave you. If you die then I die too.' was all he could say. The stubborn look on his face told Elouise it was pointless to try and change his mind. As she placed Blanche over her shoulder and gently patted her she couldn't help feeling sorry for Guillaume, realising, perhaps for the first time, that he would never really understand her.

It was the last night of the ten days of grace but very few of the chateau's inhabitants were asleep. Prayers were said, loved ones were farewelled; an incredible fusion of joy and expectation prevailed as people prepared their minds for the ordeal ahead.

Elouise, Guillaume and Michel stood together, the baby cradled in its mother's arms. Elouise was weeping as she said her silent goodbyes to her child. Slowly she bent forward and placed a long kiss on her baby's brow then passed the sleeping child to Guillaume. Her tears continued to flow as she held out her arms to embrace Michel and the two of them clung tightly to each other.

'Farewell, my best friend' she said, sobbing into his neck, 'take good care of Blanche for me. Tell her one day that she had a mother who loved her very much.' Michel pulled back and for the first time in his life kissed Elouise gently on the lips.

'Don't worry, Lou-Lou, I will.' He looked at her for a long moment, as if making up his mind about something. 'Adieu, little sister. Be strong.'

He turned to take Blanche from Guillaume.

'Wait,' said Elouise. She unfastened her necklace, the one that had belonged to her mother and given to her by Jean. 'Give this to her, Michel, on her sixteenth birthday, just as my father gave it to me.' Michel took the necklace and held it tightly in his hand.

'It's time to go,' he said firmly, and began to make for the door.

Elouise looked across at Guillaume. 'Go with them, please, and make sure they get over the wall safely.' He looked into her eyes and could see that she was distressed to the point of collapsing. He wanted to hold her and comfort her but she signalled him to leave.

As she watched Guillaume's back disappear into the night Elouise finally succumbed to all the feelings she had held inside her; she fell sobbing to the floor, clutching her stomach with the pain of separation from Blanche.

Outside, shivering in the cold night air, Guillaume caught up with Michel. As they began to climb the steps to reach the battlement on the west tower Michel suddenly stopped and gripped Guillaume by the arm.

'Guillaume, we must swap places,' he said urgently.

'What do you mean?

'You should take Blanche and go over the wall with Bernadette and her baby.'

'I can't. I can't leave Elouise, she needs me.'

Michel relaxed his grip and placed his hand gently on Guillaume's shoulder.

'Yes you can, my friend. Elouise knows better than anyone that a girl needs a father and you will be a wonderful father to Blanche. It's what Elouise would want, believe me. I've known her since she was five years old.'

'But what about Elouise? I can't leave her on her own.'

'I'll stay with her,' said Michel calmly.

'But that means…'

'No more buts…come on, please, you must go quickly. Here, take this.' Michel pushed the necklace into Guillaume's hand. 'Take it, please.' Guillaume looked at the necklace and realised that the decision had been made for him. He knew he would have to go even though it meant never seeing Elouise again.

When they reached the battlement Bernadette was already waiting, her baby strapped tightly to her back. Her father and brother were both there to help; they didn't seem surprised when Michel told them about the change in plan. Quickly they bound Blanche to her father then attached ropes firmly to Guillaume and Bernadette. Guillaume stepped onto the battlement and braced his legs against the wall. The men took up the strain of the rope and very slowly began to lower him. Bernadette followed, her eyes shut tightly as she gripped the rope with both hands, mouthing a silent prayer. Mercifully the two babies stayed asleep throughout the manoeuvre and gradually the ropes were lowered towards the ground. Guillaume used his feet to keep himself away from the wall, letting go with one hand to prevent Bernadette from spinning around. Soon the men on the wall could no longer see them in the darkness but continued lowering until they felt the ropes slacken, the signal that the pair had at last reached the steep ground at the foot of the tower.

When he was sure that Guillaume and Bernadette had not been detected Michel made his way back to Elouise. He found her in darkness, still slumped on the ground. She sensed him enter the room.

'Guillaume, is that you? Are they safe?' her voice was hoarse from crying.

Michel paused before speaking.

'No Lou-Lou, it's me...and yes, they are safe.'

Elouise looked up suddenly at the sound of her friend's voice.

'Michel, what happened? Where's Guillaume?'

Michel looked down at her and smiled.

'I persuaded him that a daughter needs a father; that's what you wanted isn't it?'

Elouise stood up and threw her arms around her friend.

'Oh, Michel, you are such a wonderful person. I can't believe you have given up your chance to escape.'

'Then you probably don't know how much I have loved you and your father. You are all I have.'

Elouise could say nothing but hold her friend tightly.

'Come' she said at last, 'let's sit down and I will pray for us, then we will talk until the morning comes.' They sat and prayed together, and talked through every memory they had ever shared since Elouise had been a little girl.

The day was dry and bright as the gates opened and the Comte de Quillan and his wife, for the first time in three months, led out the occupants of the chateau. Despite the chill of a spring morning everyone was barefoot and dressed in the best white garments they had been able to find.

Outside the gates of the village the Archbishop of Albi watched as the procession made its way down the steep path. The soldiers had been expecting to have to enter the chateau and drag out the heretics in chains, but now they could only stand in silent bewilderment as they watched the approaching white column.

'What's that sound?' the Archbishop asked with irritation, turning to one of the inquisitors who had arrived to observe.

'They're singing, my lord Archbishop,' the man replied, 'it's the Pater Noster, the only prayer which Christ taught and the only one the Cathars recognise.'

The Archbishop sighed heavily and looked across at the activity to his left.

There, on the flattest part of land flanking the village wall, a strange wooden structure had been erected. Stout palisades enclosed a large platform. The space underneath the platform had been packed tightly with dry timbers soaked in pitch and oil and anything else that would burn quickly. Two soldiers stood at each corner of the structure, unlit torches in their hands.

As the procession drew nearer a few of the remaining troops began to goad and jeer but they provoked no response from the men, women and children filing past. The recent inhabitants of the chateau remained in a state of emotional intensity, singing even louder as if in a joyful trance. Clasping the hand of his wife, with Elouise and Michel, still strumming his lute in the crowd close behind, the Count led the procession up the crude steps and onto the platform until they were all gathered closely together, each person holding onto the next, still singing at the top of their voices.

The Archbishop made no attempt to speak to his victims, but simply nodded a signal to the soldiers at each corner. Within moments the torches had been lit and, in full flame, were thrust deeply into the dry timbers. It didn't take long before the entire structure was ablaze and the figures trapped within were soon hidden by the thick smoke that rose and swirled in the stiff breeze. The roar from the fire quickly overpowered the singing voices and, mercifully, disguised the screams that followed. With eyes streaming Elouise watched as Michel's lute burst into flames and she held him tightly as they shared their last moments alive together.

The few onlookers could bear to watch no longer, driven back by the intensity of the flames and the sickly stench of burning flesh. All except one. The priest, Villac, stood and watched with gloating satisfaction as the flames soared into the morning sky. But the soldiers who had built the pyre had done their job well. Suddenly an explosion of pitch and resin sent a fireball bursting sideways from the platform. Villac, stumbling on his lame leg, was engulfed by a river of fire and was soon alight and screaming on the ground, as the flames claimed their last victim.

The Archbishop, taking one last look at the blazing slaughter, crossed himself before turning away.

'Let that be an end to it,' he said, to no one in particular.

On a hillside some distance from the chateau Guillaume and Bernadette stopped and looked back through a clearing in the trees. They couldn't see the village but they could see the thick column of black smoke that rose above the trees, smothering the blue sky and hiding the empty chateau from view. They both sobbed and shed tears as they thought about the final moments of the loved ones they had left behind. Very tenderly, Guillaume took Bernadette by the shoulder and turned her away from the awful scene.

'Come on, Bernadette, we need to keep moving if we are to reach my sister at Mirapoix before nightfall.'

The two lone parents held their babies tightly and continued to walk along the wooded path. Soon they were hidden again by the thick green oaks of the forest.

AUTHOR'S NOTES

Whilst my story is fiction it has been based on fact.

The Cathar religion flourished in the Languedoc and by the beginning of the 13th century there were many thousands of believers. In an attempt to eliminate the threat to the established Church (and to conquer new land) the Pope and the King of France agreed to support a new crusade. Many towns and villages were destroyed and thousands of people died before the crusade was over.

During the winter of 1243 the chateau at Montsegur was besieged. When the siege was broken a truce was requested and, most unusually, granted. The rumours that surround this truce are well documented. Some say that the Cathars were the guardians of the Holy Grail and needed to hide it; others believe they had accumulated great wealth and wished to protect their treasure.

I chose to imagine that the 'treasure' they wished to save was the daughter of Elouise.

In March 1244 the 400 occupants of the chateau were burnt. If you visit the remains of the chateau today you will find a plaque to mark the spot where they perished. Within a hundred years the Cathars had faded into folklore only to be rediscovered in recent years and utilised as a tourist attraction throughout the Languedoc today.

If you Google 'Cathar' today you will find hundreds of factual books and articles written about the Cathar movement and its place in history.

Some of the books that I have found both interesting and useful are:

The Albigensian Crusade – Jonathan Sumption
The Cathars – Malcolm Lambert
La Vie Quotidenne des Cathars du Languedoc au X111 Siecle – Rene Nelli
The World of the Troubadors – Linda M Paterson
Cathars – Yves Rouquette
Montaillou – Emmanuel Le Roy Ladurie
The Perfect Heresy – Stephen O'Shea
The Yellow Cross – Rene Weis
A Brief History of Fortified Castles in France – Fragile Editions
Clothing in the Middle Ages – Crabtree

Verse on page 121 translated by Laura Stokes from an original *Fin Amour*.

Verse on page 169, author's own.

THANKS

This book could not have been completed without the help and encouragement of a large number of people. Firstly, thank you to the staff of the Centre d'Etude de Cathares in Carcassonne, an excellent source of information. My heartfelt thanks go to Pam and Brian Glanville for their interest and friendly advice over many cups of tea in their kitchen; to my daughters, Amber and Laura, and my friends Dib, Laura and Liz for reading the first draft and giving me positive vibes at a time when I was nervous of showing it to anyone; to my golfing pals who never failed to ask 'how's the book going?'; to Jeannie and Pam for their encouragement and to Esther for listening; to Miriam Hastings for her professional help and valuable insights into characters and storytelling; to Haydn Middleton, who I found via the Writers' Workshop, for his keen editing eye and sympathetic suggestions; to my good friend in France, Monique, for correcting my English; to Jeremy Thompson and everyone at Matador for their professional approach to the business of publishing, their genuine enthusiasm and always friendly advice – I would recommend them to any writer; and lastly, but without doubt by no means least, I would like to give enormous thanks to my wonderful partner Bridget for her encouragement and belief and for introducing me to the story of the Cathars in the first place.

Thank you everyone.